ARCHIE COMIC PU~~~~~

S0-BNX-458

chairman and co-publisher
MICHAEL I. SILBERKLEIT

president and co-publisher
RICHARD H. GOLDWATER

vp/managing editor
VICTOR GORELICK

vp/director of circulation
FRED MAUSSER

editor
MIKE PELLERITO

art director
JOE PEP

covers
PATRICK SPAZIANTE

www.archiecomics.com
www.sega.com

SONIC THE HEDGEHOG ARCHIVES,
Volume 2. Second Printing May 2008.
Printed in Canada. Published by
Archie Comic Publications, Inc., 325 Fayette
Avenue, Mamaroneck, NY 10543-2318.
Richard H. Goldwater, President and Co-Publisher.
Michael I. Silberkleit, Chairman and Co-Publisher.
Sega is registered in the U.S. Patent and Trademark
Office. SEGA, Sonic The Hedgehog, and all related
characters and indicia are either registered trademarks
or trademarks of SEGA CORPORATION © 1991-2008.
SEGA CORPORATION and SONICTEAM, LTD./SEGA
CORPORATION © 2001-2008. All Rights Reserved. The product
is manufactured under license from Sega of America, Inc., 650
Townsend St., Ste. 650, San Francisco, CA 94103 www.sega.com.
Any similarities between characters, names, persons, and/or institutions
in this book and any living, dead or fictional characters, names, persons,
and/or institutions are not intended and if they exist, are purely coincidental.
Nothing may be reprinted in whole or part without written permission from
Archie Comic Publications, Inc.
ISBN-13: 978-1-879794-21-4   ISBN-10: 1-879794-21-7

TABLE OF CONTENTS

"Sorceress in Distress" (issue #7):
Sally goes to the Great Forest in search of a suitable wooden staff to complete her Halloween Sorceress costume. When Robotnik comes upon her, he believes Sally to be a real sorceress and kidnaps her with the intention of marrying her!

"Bots All Folks!" (issue #8):
Jealous that one of his lackeys is secretly a fan of Sonic, Robotnik unleashes his fury with new ruthless robots to attack the blue blur!

"A Little Music Goes a Long Way" (issue #8):
All Sonic and his friends want to do is make beautiful music, but a certain robotic meanie has other ideas—namely shrinking the mirthful music makers!

(SPECIAL BONUS):
Sonic The Hedgehog-Who's Who
You've read the stories now learn more about some of your favorite Sonic characters.

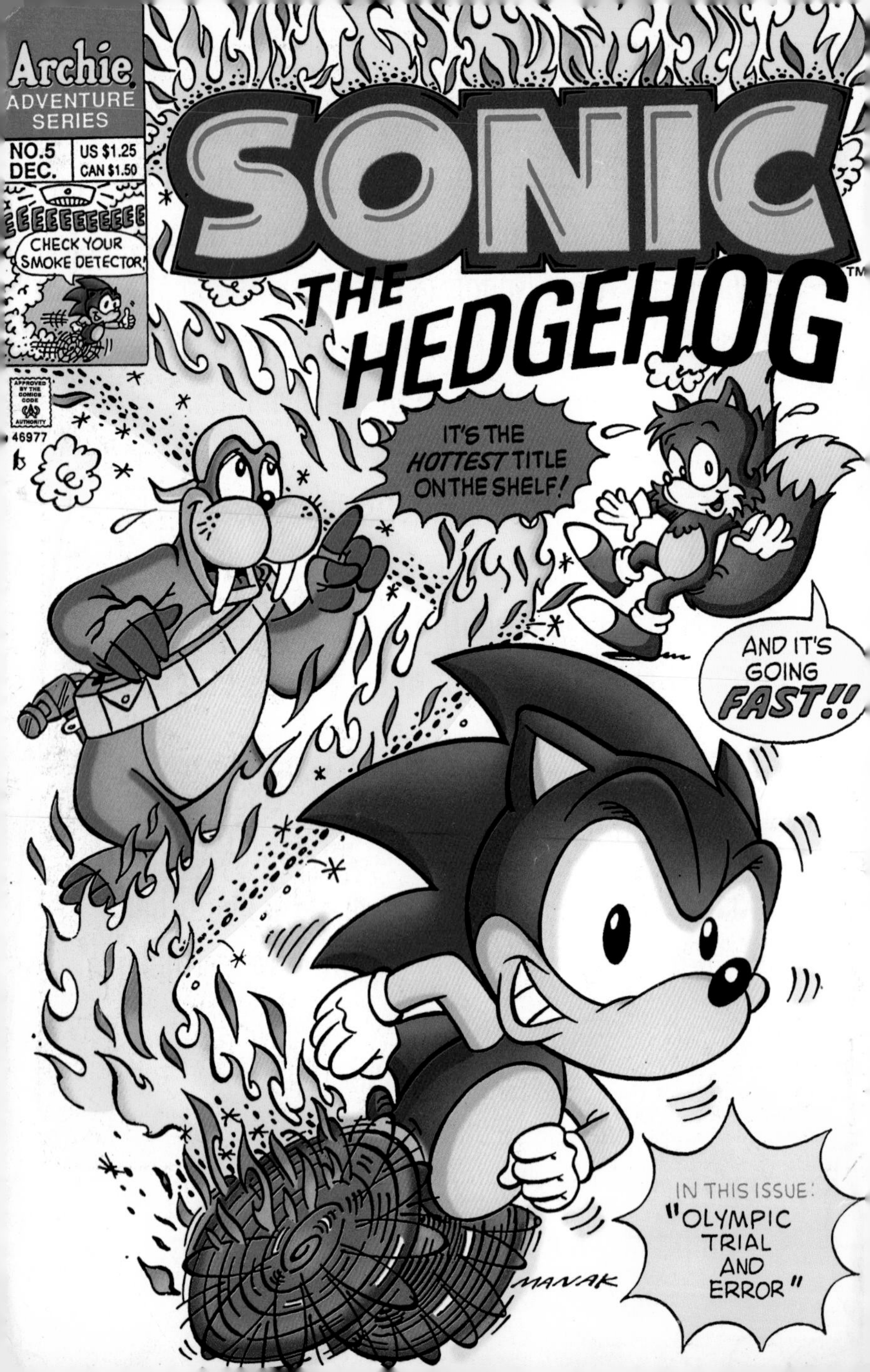

Archie ADVENTURE SERIES
NO.5 DEC.
US $1.25 CAN $1.50
EEEEEEEEEEEE
CHECK YOUR SMOKE DETECTOR!
APPROVED BY THE COMICS CODE AUTHORITY
46977
SONIC THE HEDGEHOG™
IT'S THE HOTTEST TITLE ON THE SHELF!
AND IT'S GOING FAST!!
IN THIS ISSUE: "OLYMPIC TRIAL AND ERROR"
MANAK

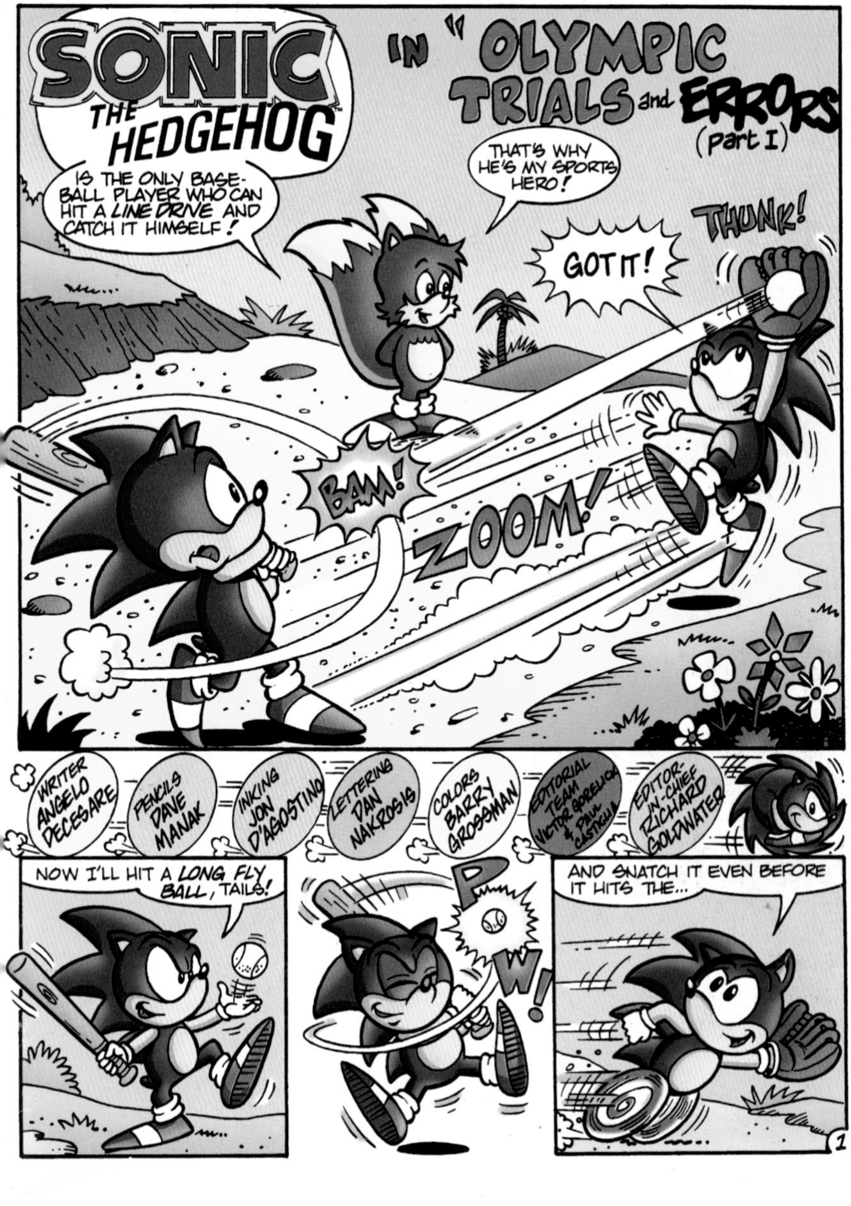
SONIC THE HEDGEHOG
IN "OLYMPIC TRIALS and ERRORS (part I)
IS THE ONLY BASE-BALL PLAYER WHO CAN HIT A LINE DRIVE AND CATCH IT HIMSELF!
THAT'S WHY HE'S MY SPORTS HERO!
THUNK!
GOT IT!
BAM!
ZOOM!
WRITER ANGELO DECESARE
PENCILS DAVE MANAK
INKING JON D'AGOSTINO
LETTERING DAN NAKROSIS
COLORS BARRY GROSSMAN
EDITORIAL TEAM VICTOR GORELICK & PAUL CASTIGLIA
EDITOR-IN-CHIEF RICHARD GOLDWATER
NOW I'LL HIT A LONG FLY BALL, TAILS!
POW!
AND SNATCH IT EVEN BEFORE IT HITS THE...

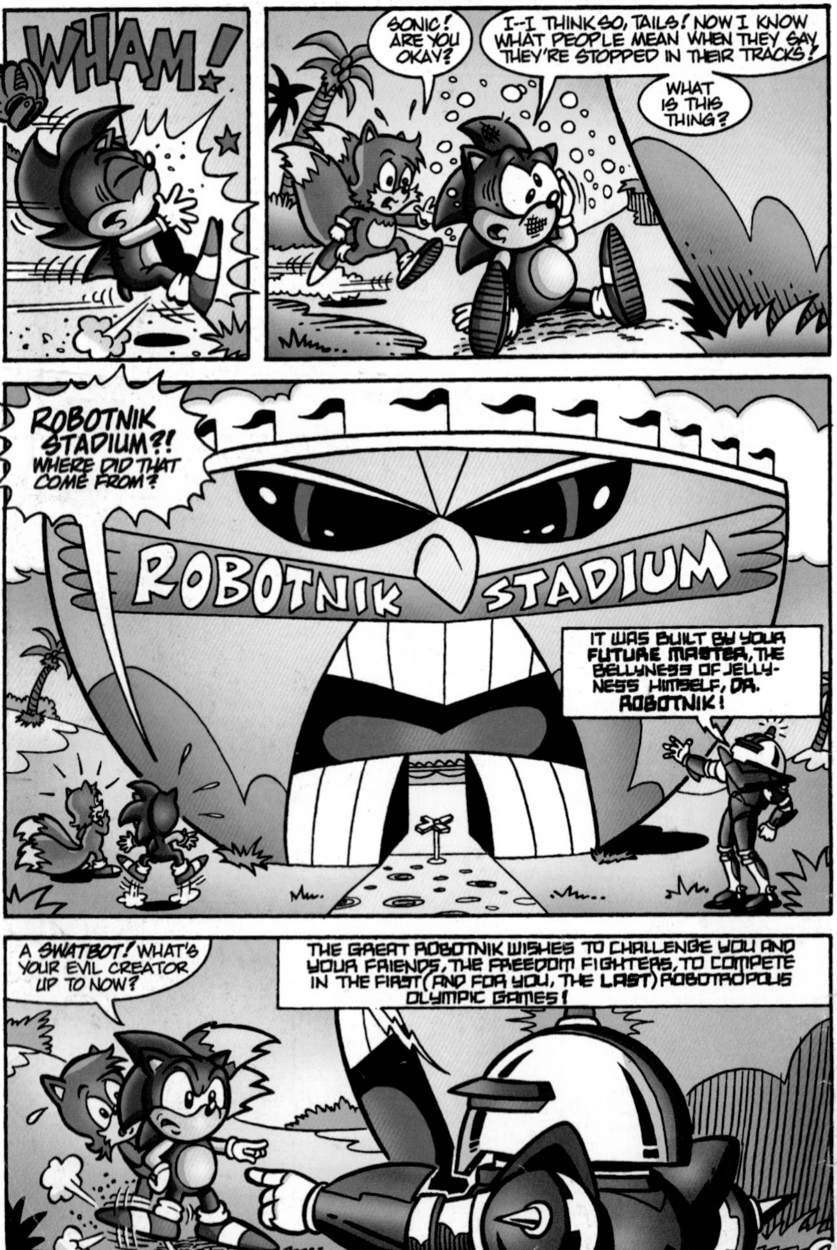
WHAM!
SONIC! ARE YOU OKAY?
I--I THINK SO, TAILS! NOW I KNOW WHAT PEOPLE MEAN WHEN THEY SAY THEY'RE STOPPED IN THEIR TRACKS!
WHAT IS THIS THING?
ROBOTNIK STADIUM?! WHERE DID THAT COME FROM?
ROBOTNIK STADIUM
IT WAS BUILT BY YOUR FUTURE MASTER, THE BELLYNESS OF JELLY-NESS HIMSELF, DR. ROBOTNIK!
A SWATBOT! WHAT'S YOUR EVIL CREATOR UP TO NOW?
THE GREAT ROBOTNIK WISHES TO CHALLENGE YOU AND YOUR FRIENDS, THE FREEDOM FIGHTERS, TO COMPETE IN THE FIRST (AND FOR YOU, THE LAST) ROBOTROPOLIS OLYMPIC GAMES!

IF YOUR TEAM CAN WIN **ONE** OUT OF **FOUR** EVENTS, MY MASTER PROMISES TO RETURN PLANET MOBIUS TO **NORMAL**...

...BUT IF YOU FAIL TO WIN AN EVENT, THEN YOU MUST ALLOW YOURSELVES TO BE TURNED INTO **ROBOTS**!

AND NOW, A PERSONAL MESSAGE FROM ROBOTNIK TO SONIC THE HEDGEHOG...

...**YOU CAN'T BEAT US!**--NYAH-NYAH-NYAH-NYAH!

OOOOH! I HATE THAT!

TELL ROBOTNIK THAT THE FREEDOM FIGHTERS ACCEPT HIS CHALLENGE! IN FACT, I KNOW EXACTLY WHAT MY FRIENDS WILL SAY!

BACK AT KNOTHOLE FOREST...

NO WAY SONIC!

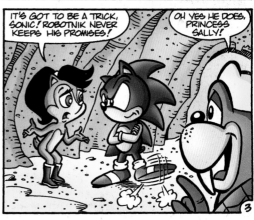

IT'S GOT TO BE A TRICK, SONIC! ROBOTNIK NEVER KEEPS HIS PROMISES!

OH YES HE DOES, PRINCESS SALLY!

3

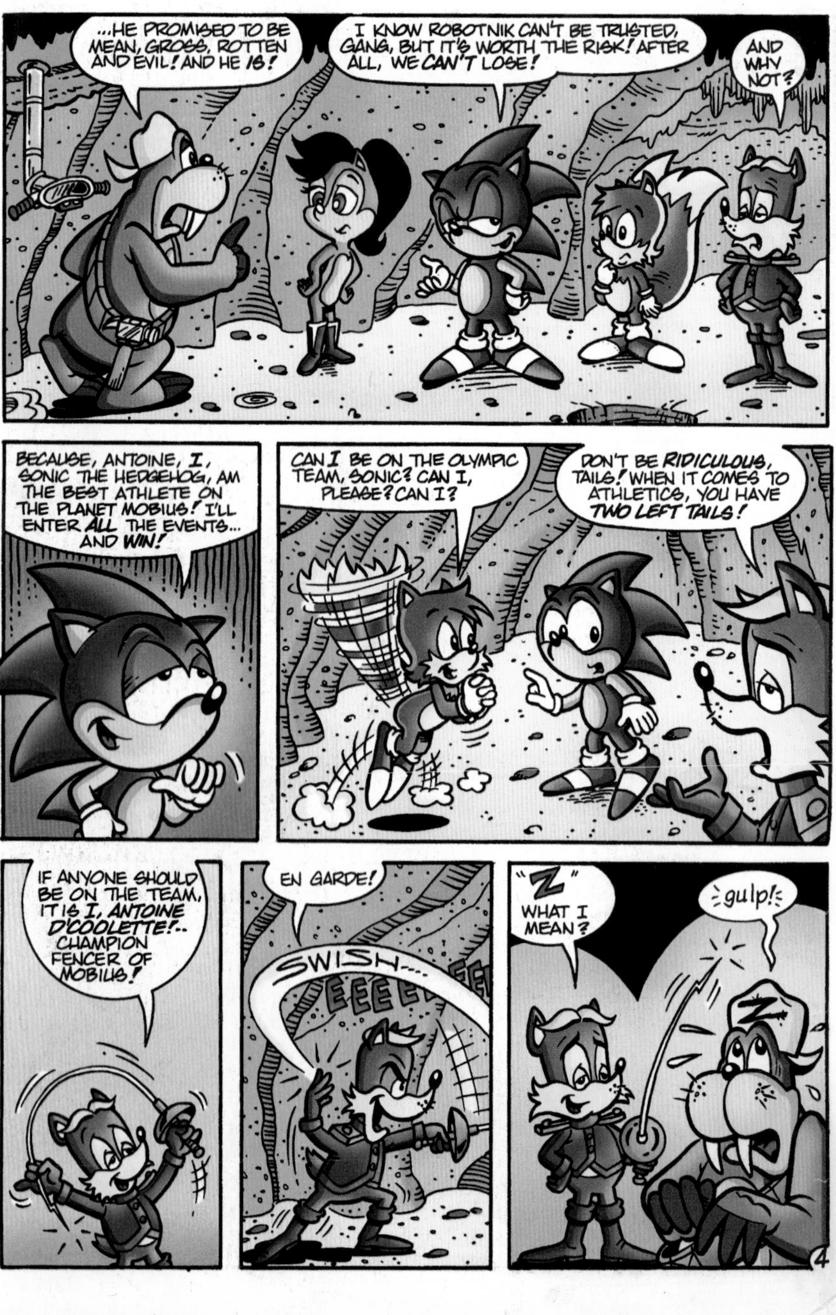
...HE PROMISED TO BE MEAN, GROSS, ROTTEN AND EVIL! AND HE IS!
I KNOW ROBOTNIK CAN'T BE TRUSTED, GANG, BUT IT'S WORTH THE RISK! AFTER ALL, WE CAN'T LOSE!
AND WHY NOT?
BECAUSE, ANTOINE, I, SONIC THE HEDGEHOG, AM THE BEST ATHLETE ON THE PLANET MOBIUS! I'LL ENTER ALL THE EVENTS... AND WIN!
CAN I BE ON THE OLYMPIC TEAM, SONIC? CAN I, PLEASE? CAN I?
DON'T BE RIDICULOUS, TAILS! WHEN IT COMES TO ATHLETICS, YOU HAVE TWO LEFT TAILS!
IF ANYONE SHOULD BE ON THE TEAM, IT IS I, ANTOINE D'COOLETTE!.. CHAMPION FENCER OF MOBIUS!
EN GARDE!
SWISH---
EEEEE
"Z" WHAT I MEAN?
gulp!

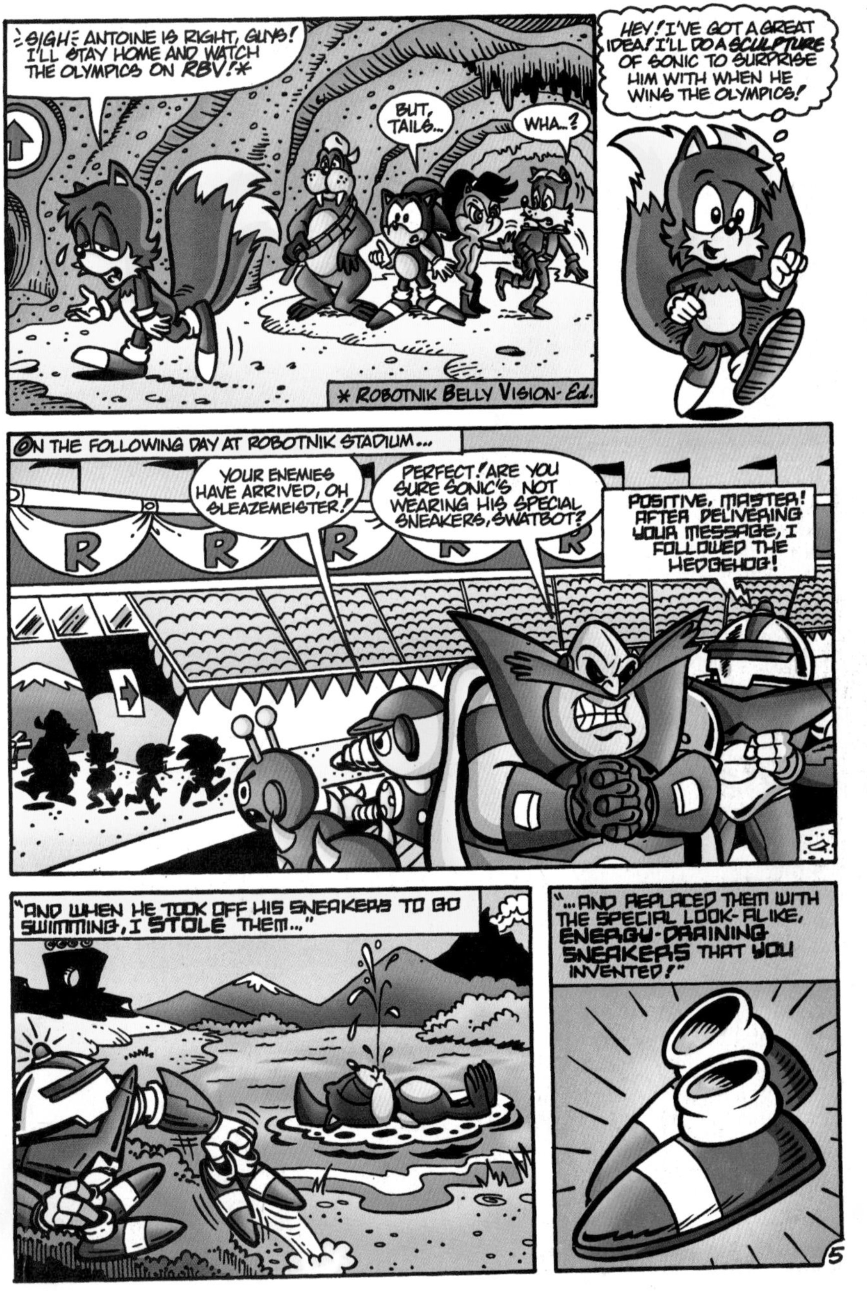

:SIGH: ANTOINE IS RIGHT, GUYS! I'LL STAY HOME AND WATCH THE OLYMPICS ON RBV!*
BUT, TAILS...
WHA...?
* ROBOTNIK BELLY VISION- Ed.
HEY! I'VE GOT A GREAT IDEA! I'LL DO A SCULPTURE OF SONIC TO SURPRISE HIM WITH WHEN HE WINS THE OLYMPICS!
ON THE FOLLOWING DAY AT ROBOTNIK STADIUM...
YOUR ENEMIES HAVE ARRIVED, OH SLEAZEMEISTER!
PERFECT! ARE YOU SURE SONIC'S NOT WEARING HIS SPECIAL SNEAKERS, SWATBOT?
POSITIVE, MASTER! AFTER DELIVERING YOUR MESSAGE, I FOLLOWED THE HEDGEHOG!
"AND WHEN HE TOOK OFF HIS SNEAKERS TO GO SWIMMING, I STOLE THEM..."
"...AND REPLACED THEM WITH THE SPECIAL LOOK-ALIKE, ENERGY-DRAINING SNEAKERS THAT YOU INVENTED!"

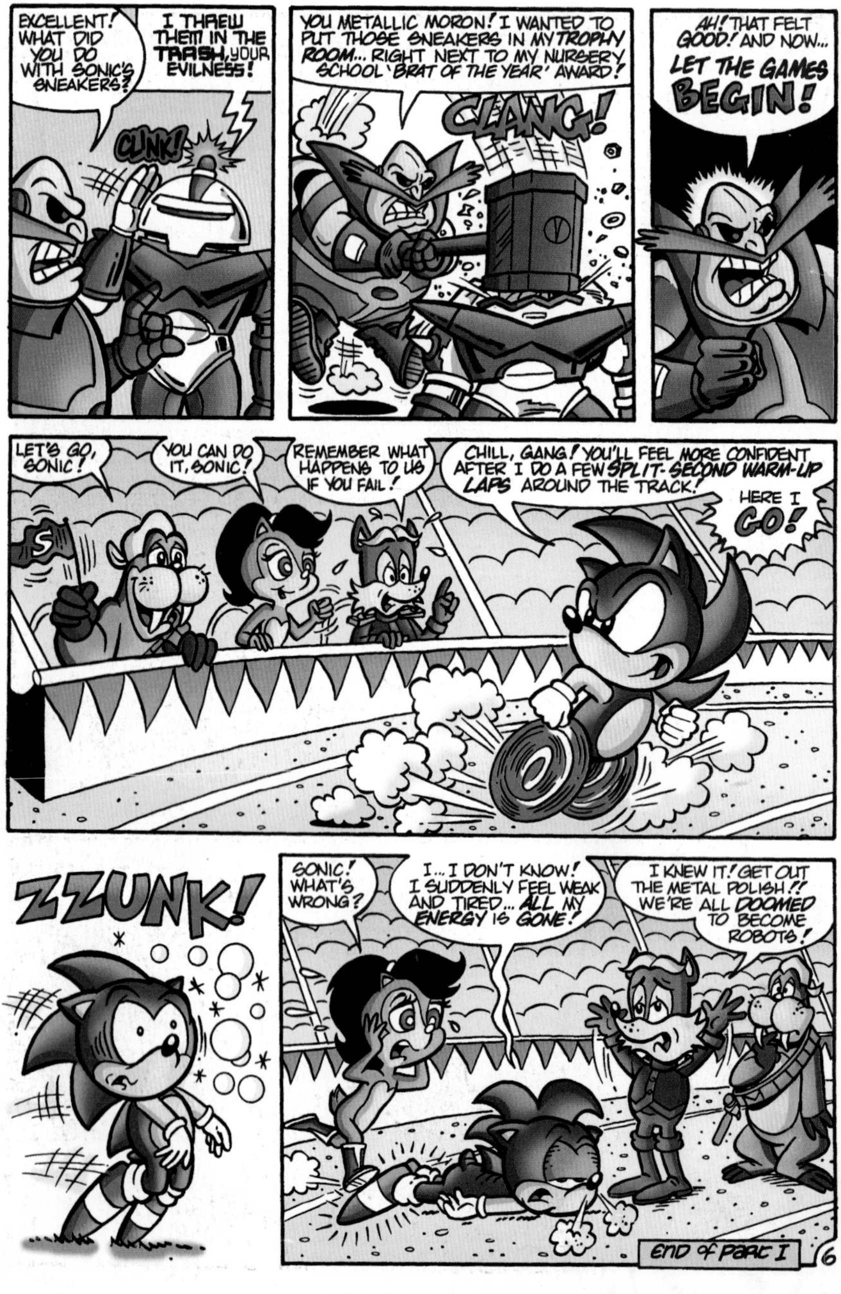
EXCELLENT! WHAT DID YOU DO WITH SONIC'S SNEAKERS?
I THREW THEM IN THE TRASH, YOUR EVILNESS!
CLINK!
YOU METALLIC MORON! I WANTED TO PUT THOSE SNEAKERS IN MY TROPHY ROOM... RIGHT NEXT TO MY NURSERY SCHOOL 'BRAT OF THE YEAR' AWARD!
CLANG!
AH! THAT FELT GOOD! AND NOW... LET THE GAMES BEGIN!
LET'S GO, SONIC!
YOU CAN DO IT, SONIC!
REMEMBER WHAT HAPPENS TO US IF YOU FAIL!
CHILL, GANG! YOU'LL FEEL MORE CONFIDENT AFTER I DO A FEW SPLIT-SECOND WARM-UP LAPS AROUND THE TRACK!
HERE I GO!
ZZUNK!
SONIC! WHAT'S WRONG?
I... I DON'T KNOW! I SUDDENLY FEEL WEAK AND TIRED... ALL MY ENERGY IS GONE!
I KNEW IT! GET OUT THE METAL POLISH!! WE'RE ALL DOOMED TO BECOME ROBOTS!
END OF PART I

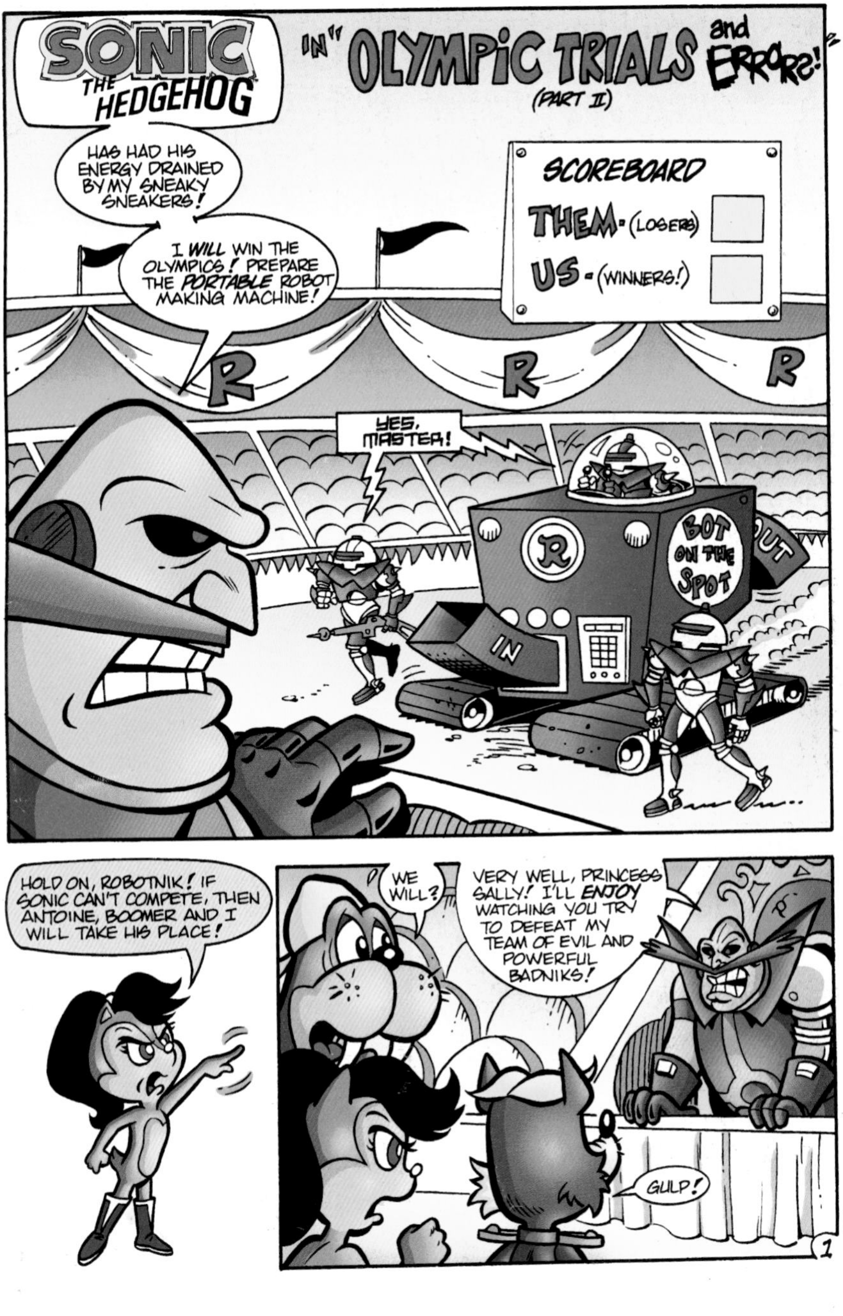
SONIC THE HEDGEHOG
IN "OLYMPIC TRIALS and ERRORS!"
(PART II)
HAS HAD HIS ENERGY DRAINED BY MY SNEAKY SNEAKERS!
I WILL WIN THE OLYMPICS! PREPARE THE PORTABLE ROBOT MAKING MACHINE!
SCOREBOARD
THEM - (LOSERS)
US - (WINNERS!)
R
YES, MASTER!
BOT ON THE SPOT
OUT
IN
HOLD ON, ROBOTNIK! IF SONIC CAN'T COMPETE, THEN ANTOINE, BOOMER AND I WILL TAKE HIS PLACE!
WE WILL?
VERY WELL, PRINCESS SALLY! I'LL ENJOY WATCHING YOU TRY TO DEFEAT MY TEAM OF EVIL AND POWERFUL BADNIKS!
GULP!

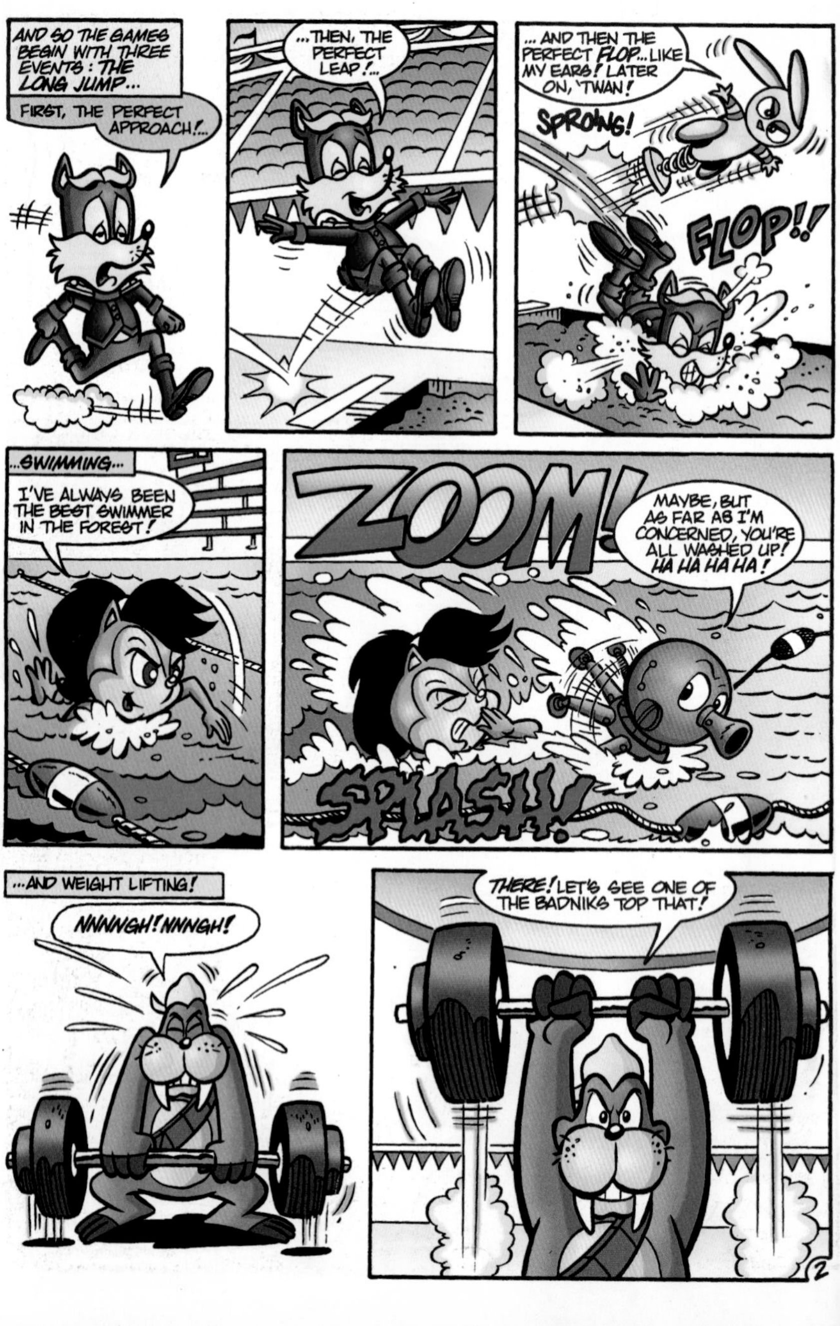
AND SO THE GAMES BEGIN WITH THREE EVENTS : THE LONG JUMP...
FIRST, THE PERFECT APPROACH!...
...THEN, THE PERFECT LEAP!...
... AND THEN THE PERFECT FLOP... LIKE MY EARS! LATER ON, 'TWAN!
SPROING!
FLOP!!
...SWIMMING...
I'VE ALWAYS BEEN THE BEST SWIMMER IN THE FOREST!
ZOOM!
MAYBE, BUT AS FAR AS I'M CONCERNED, YOU'RE ALL WASHED UP! HA HA HA HA!
SPLASH!
...AND WEIGHT LIFTING!
NNNNGH! NNNGH!
THERE! LET'S SEE ONE OF THE BADNIKS TOP THAT!
2

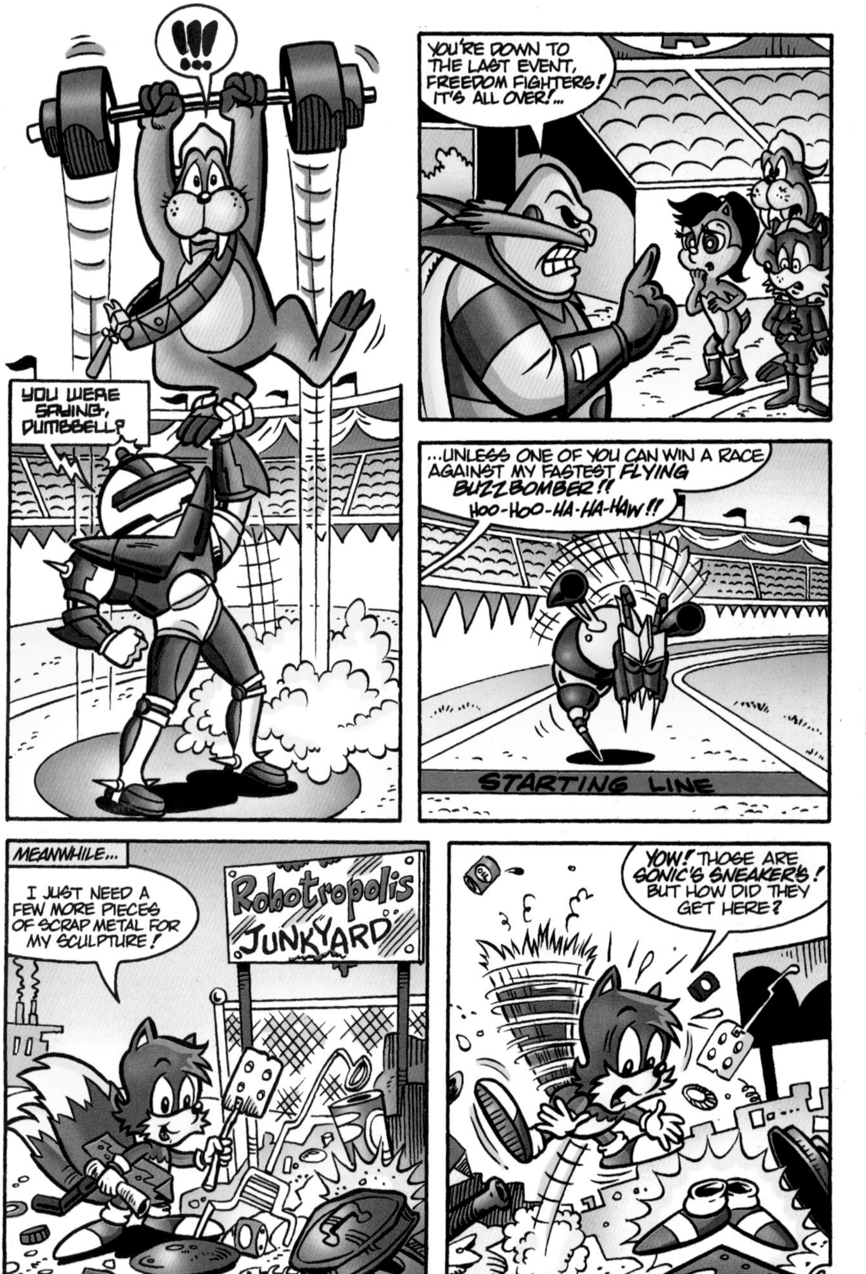
!!!
YOU WERE SAYING, DUMBBELL?
YOU'RE DOWN TO THE LAST EVENT, FREEDOM FIGHTERS! IT'S ALL OVER!...
...UNLESS ONE OF YOU CAN WIN A RACE AGAINST MY FASTEST FLYING BUZZBOMBER!!
HOO-HOO-HA-HA-HAW!!
STARTING LINE
MEANWHILE...
I JUST NEED A FEW MORE PIECES OF SCRAP METAL FOR MY SCULPTURE!
Robotropolis JUNKYARD
YOW! THOSE ARE SONIC'S SNEAKERS! BUT HOW DID THEY GET HERE?

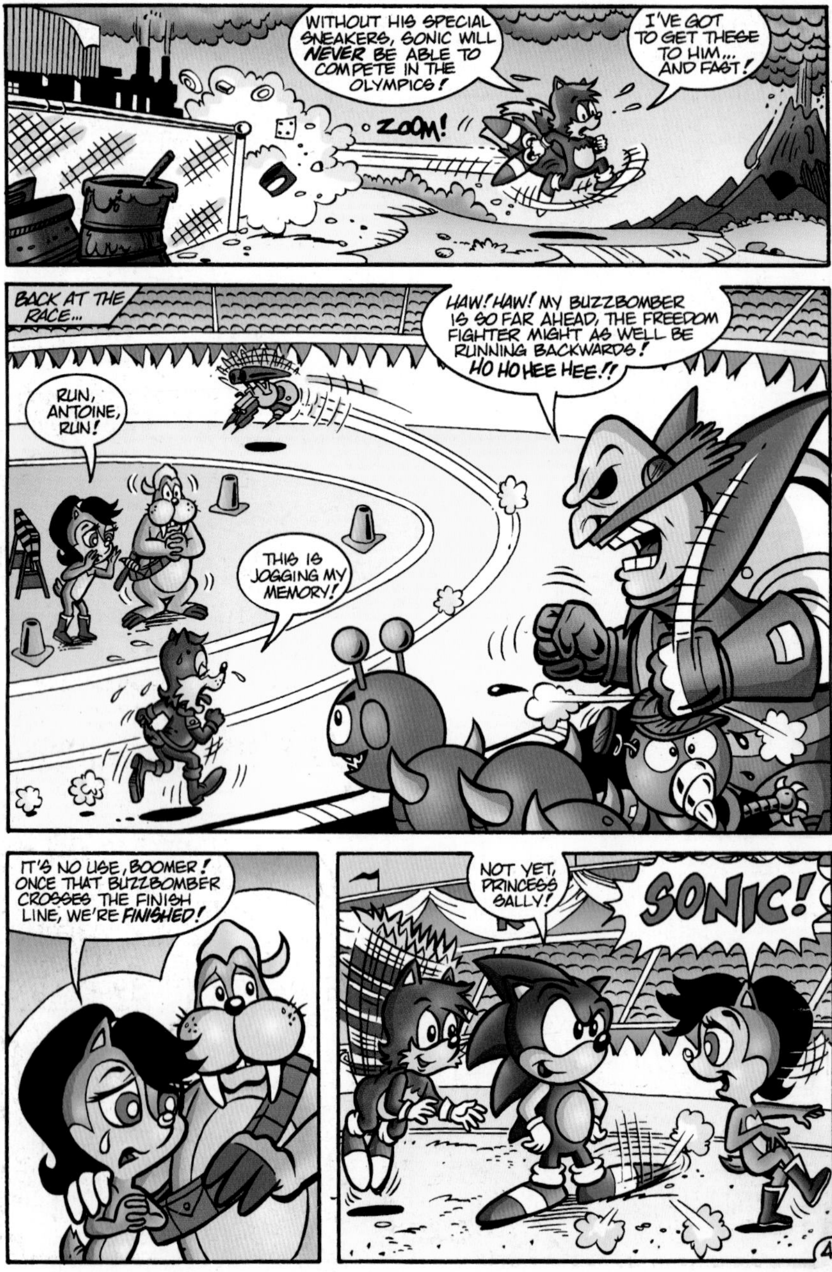
WITHOUT HIS SPECIAL SNEAKERS, SONIC WILL NEVER BE ABLE TO COMPETE IN THE OLYMPICS!
I'VE GOT TO GET THESE TO HIM... AND FAST!
ZOOM!
BACK AT THE RACE...
HAW! HAW! MY BUZZBOMBER IS SO FAR AHEAD, THE FREEDOM FIGHTER MIGHT AS WELL BE RUNNING BACKWARDS! HO HO HEE HEE!!
RUN, ANTOINE, RUN!
THIS IS JOGGING MY MEMORY!
IT'S NO USE, BOOMER! ONCE THAT BUZZBOMBER CROSSES THE FINISH LINE, WE'RE FINISHED!
NOT YET, PRINCESS SALLY!
SONIC!
4

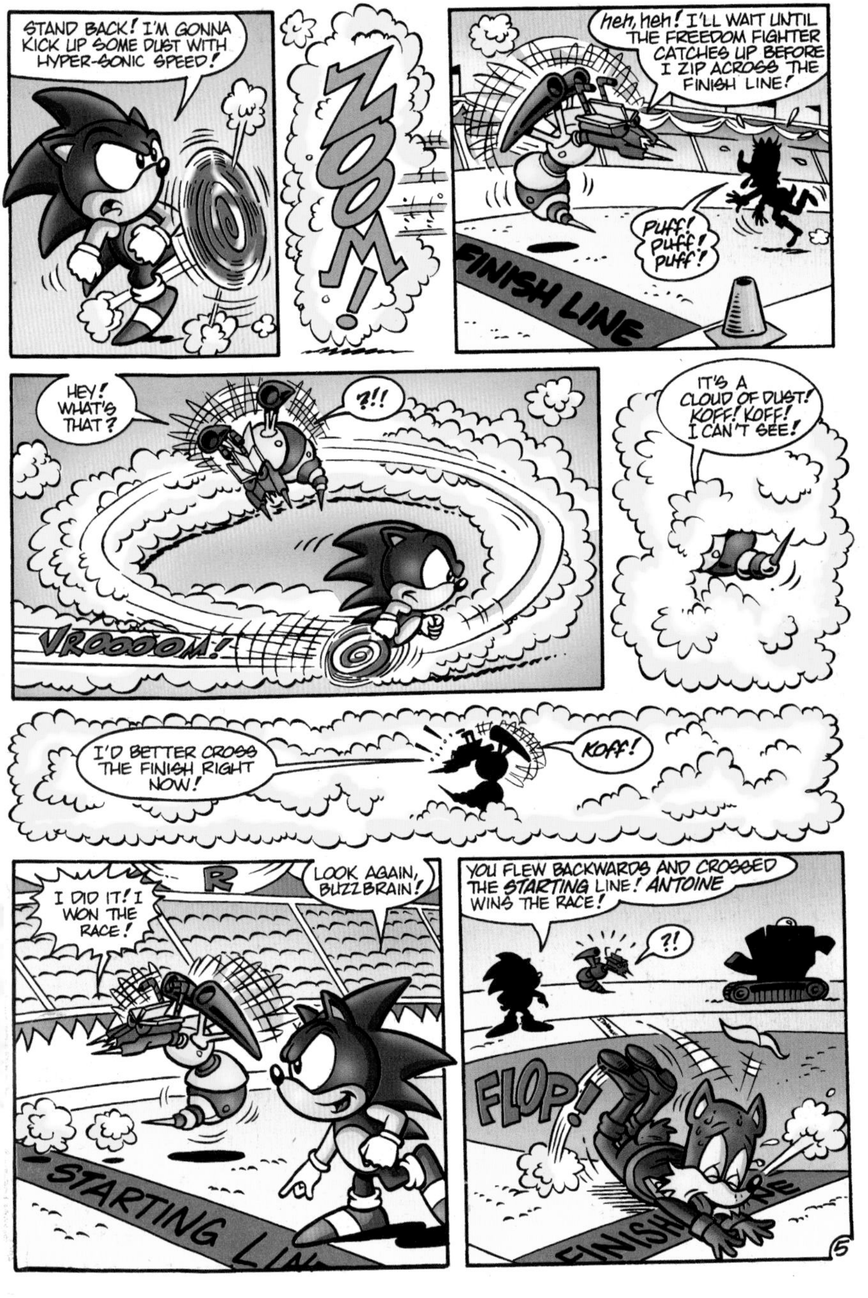
STAND BACK! I'M GONNA KICK UP SOME DUST WITH HYPER-SONIC SPEED!
ZOOM!
heh, heh! I'LL WAIT UNTIL THE FREEDOM FIGHTER CATCHES UP BEFORE I ZIP ACROSS THE FINISH LINE!
Puff! puff! puff!
FINISH LINE
HEY! WHAT'S THAT?
?!!
VROOOOOM!
IT'S A CLOUD OF DUST! KOFF! KOFF! I CAN'T SEE!
I'D BETTER CROSS THE FINISH RIGHT NOW!
KOFF!
I DID IT! I WON THE RACE!
LOOK AGAIN, BUZZBRAIN!
STARTING LIN
YOU FLEW BACKWARDS AND CROSSED THE STARTING LINE! ANTOINE WINS THE RACE!
?!
FLOP!
FINISH

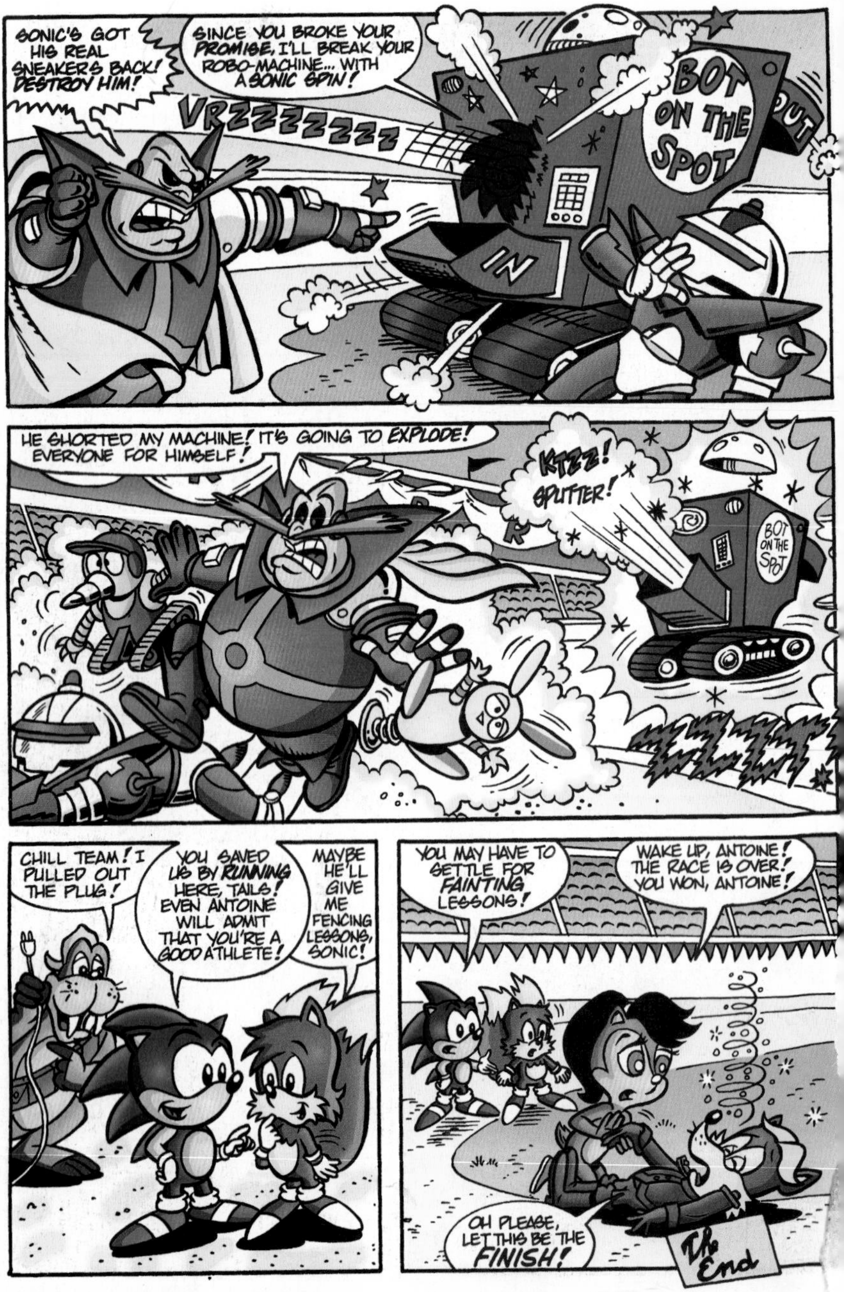
SONIC'S GOT HIS REAL SNEAKERS BACK! DESTROY HIM!
SINCE YOU BROKE YOUR PROMISE, I'LL BREAK YOUR ROBO-MACHINE... WITH A SONIC SPIN!
VRZZZZZZZZ
BOT ON THE SPOT
OUT
IN
HE SHORTED MY MACHINE! IT'S GOING TO EXPLODE! EVERYONE FOR HIMSELF!
KTZZ! SPUTTER!
BOT ON THE SPOT
CHILL TEAM! I PULLED OUT THE PLUG!
YOU SAVED US BY RUNNING HERE, TAILS! EVEN ANTOINE WILL ADMIT THAT YOU'RE A GOOD ATHLETE!
MAYBE HE'LL GIVE ME FENCING LESSONS, SONIC!
YOU MAY HAVE TO SETTLE FOR FAINTING LESSONS!
WAKE UP, ANTOINE! THE RACE IS OVER! YOU WON, ANTOINE!
OH PLEASE, LET THIS BE THE FINISH!
The End

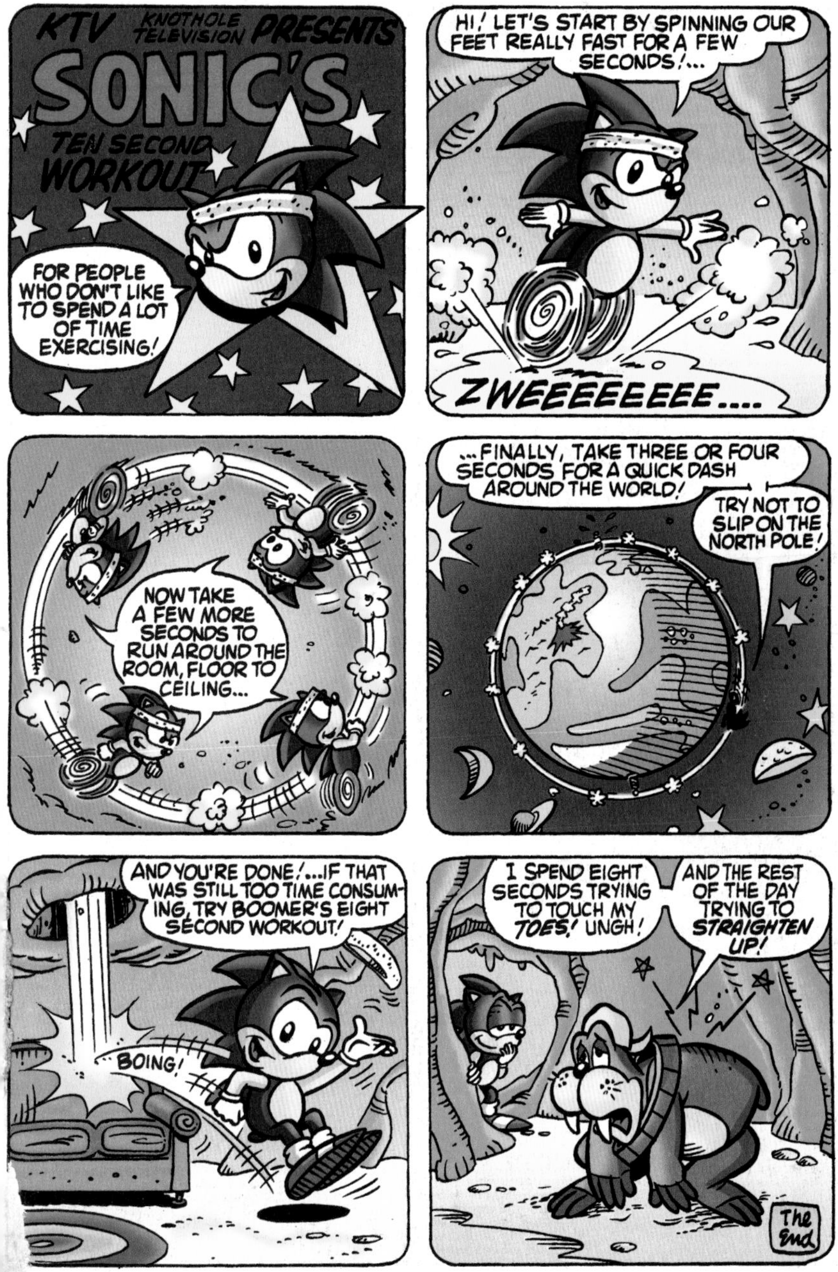
KTV KNOTHOLE TELEVISION PRESENTS
SONIC'S TEN SECOND WORKOUT
FOR PEOPLE WHO DON'T LIKE TO SPEND A LOT OF TIME EXERCISING!
HI! LET'S START BY SPINNING OUR FEET REALLY FAST FOR A FEW SECONDS!...
ZWEEEEEEEEE....
NOW TAKE A FEW MORE SECONDS TO RUN AROUND THE ROOM, FLOOR TO CEILING...
...FINALLY, TAKE THREE OR FOUR SECONDS FOR A QUICK DASH AROUND THE WORLD!
TRY NOT TO SLIP ON THE NORTH POLE!
AND YOU'RE DONE!...IF THAT WAS STILL TOO TIME CONSUMING, TRY BOOMER'S EIGHT SECOND WORKOUT!
BOING!
I SPEND EIGHT SECONDS TRYING TO TOUCH MY TOES! UNGH!
AND THE REST OF THE DAY TRYING TO STRAIGHTEN UP!
The end

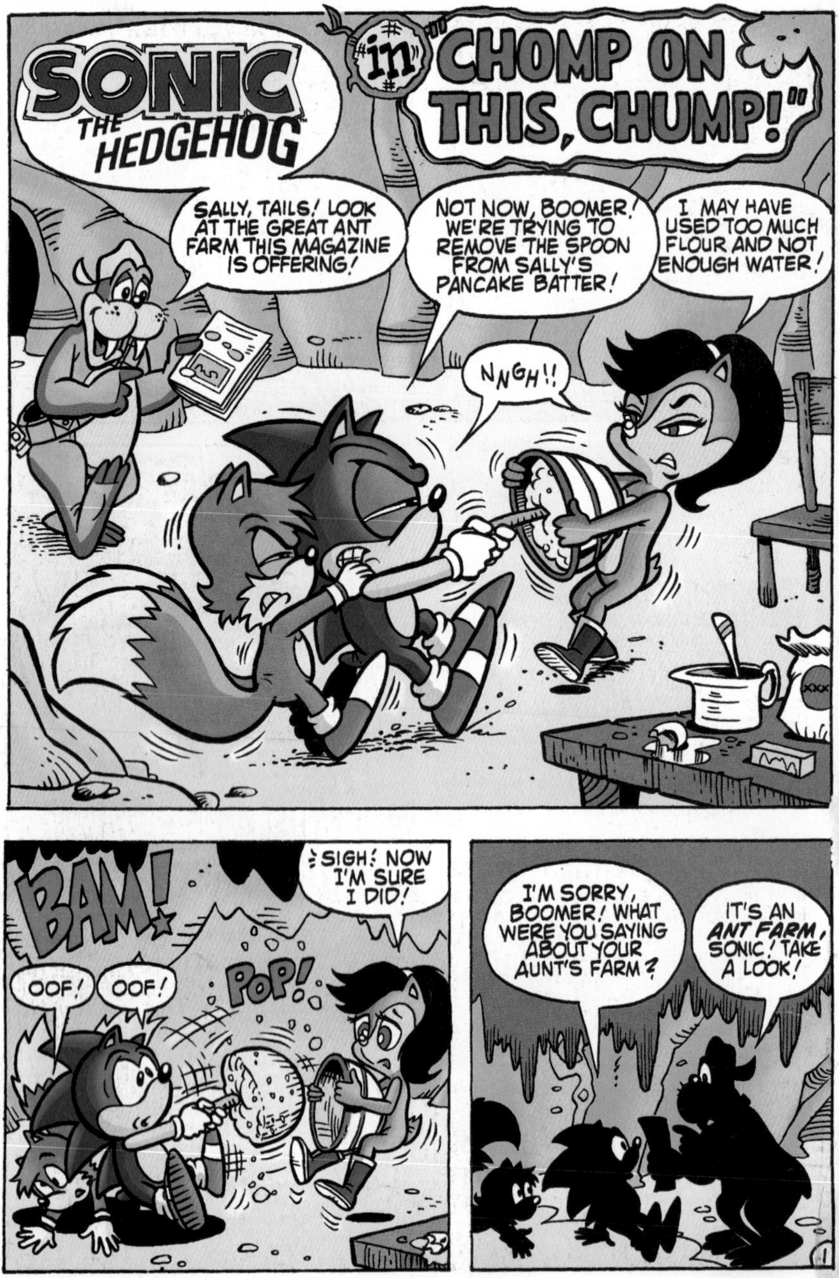
SONIC THE HEDGEHOG
in
"CHOMP ON THIS, CHUMP!"
SALLY, TAILS! LOOK AT THE GREAT ANT FARM THIS MAGAZINE IS OFFERING!
NOT NOW, BOOMER! WE'RE TRYING TO REMOVE THE SPOON FROM SALLY'S PANCAKE BATTER!
I MAY HAVE USED TOO MUCH FLOUR AND NOT ENOUGH WATER!
NNGH!!
BAM!
SIGH! NOW I'M SURE I DID!
OOF!
OOF!
POP!
I'M SORRY, BOOMER! WHAT WERE YOU SAYING ABOUT YOUR AUNT'S FARM?
IT'S AN ANT FARM, SONIC! TAKE A LOOK!
1

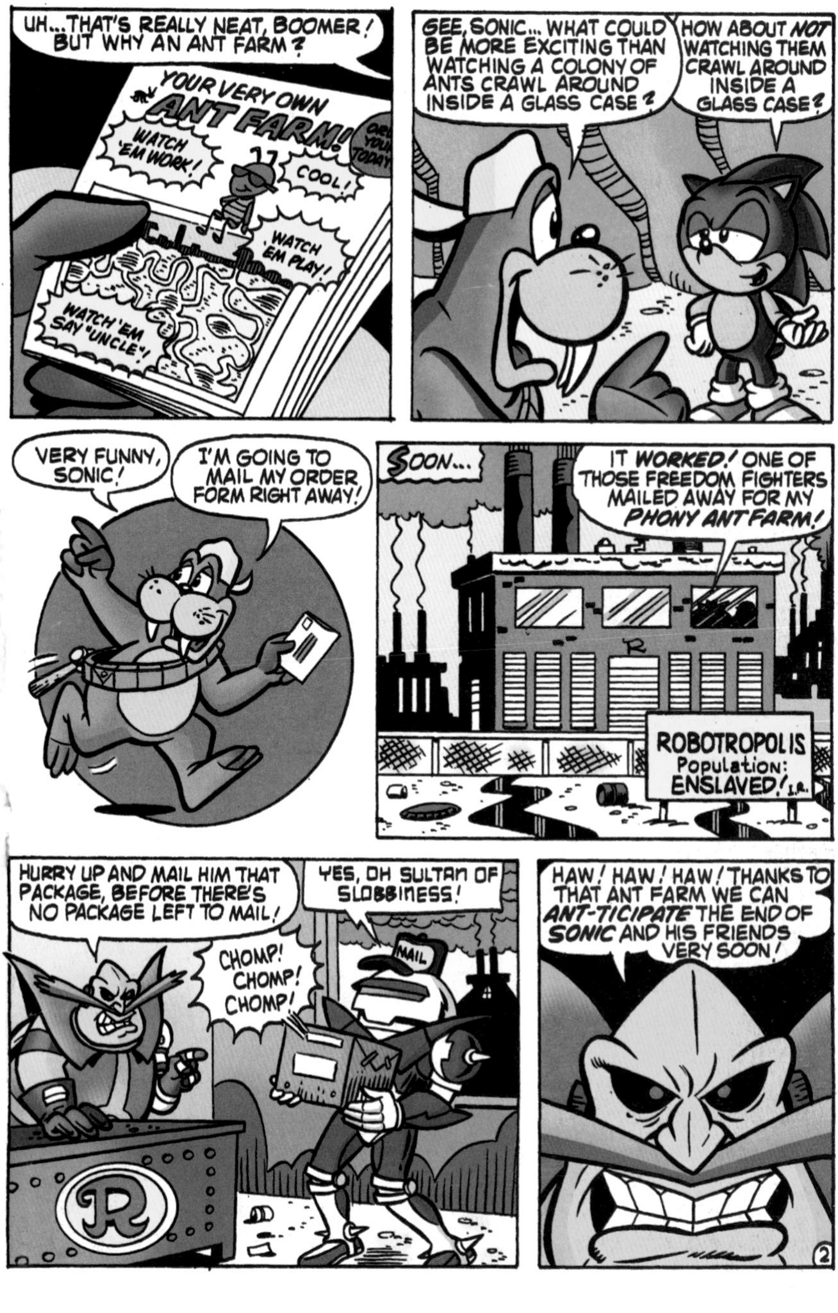
UH...THAT'S REALLY NEAT, BOOMER! BUT WHY AN ANT FARM?
YOUR VERY OWN ANT FARM!
WATCH 'EM WORK!
COOL!
WATCH 'EM PLAY!
WATCH 'EM SAY "UNCLE"!
GEE, SONIC... WHAT COULD BE MORE EXCITING THAN WATCHING A COLONY OF ANTS CRAWL AROUND INSIDE A GLASS CASE?
HOW ABOUT NOT WATCHING THEM CRAWL AROUND INSIDE A GLASS CASE?
VERY FUNNY, SONIC!
I'M GOING TO MAIL MY ORDER FORM RIGHT AWAY!
SOON...
IT WORKED! ONE OF THOSE FREEDOM FIGHTERS MAILED AWAY FOR MY PHONY ANT FARM!
ROBOTROPOLIS
Population:
ENSLAVED!
HURRY UP AND MAIL HIM THAT PACKAGE, BEFORE THERE'S NO PACKAGE LEFT TO MAIL!
YES, OH SULTAN OF SLOBBINESS!
CHOMP! CHOMP! CHOMP!
MAIL
HAW! HAW! HAW! THANKS TO THAT ANT FARM WE CAN ANT-TICIPATE THE END OF SONIC AND HIS FRIENDS VERY SOON!

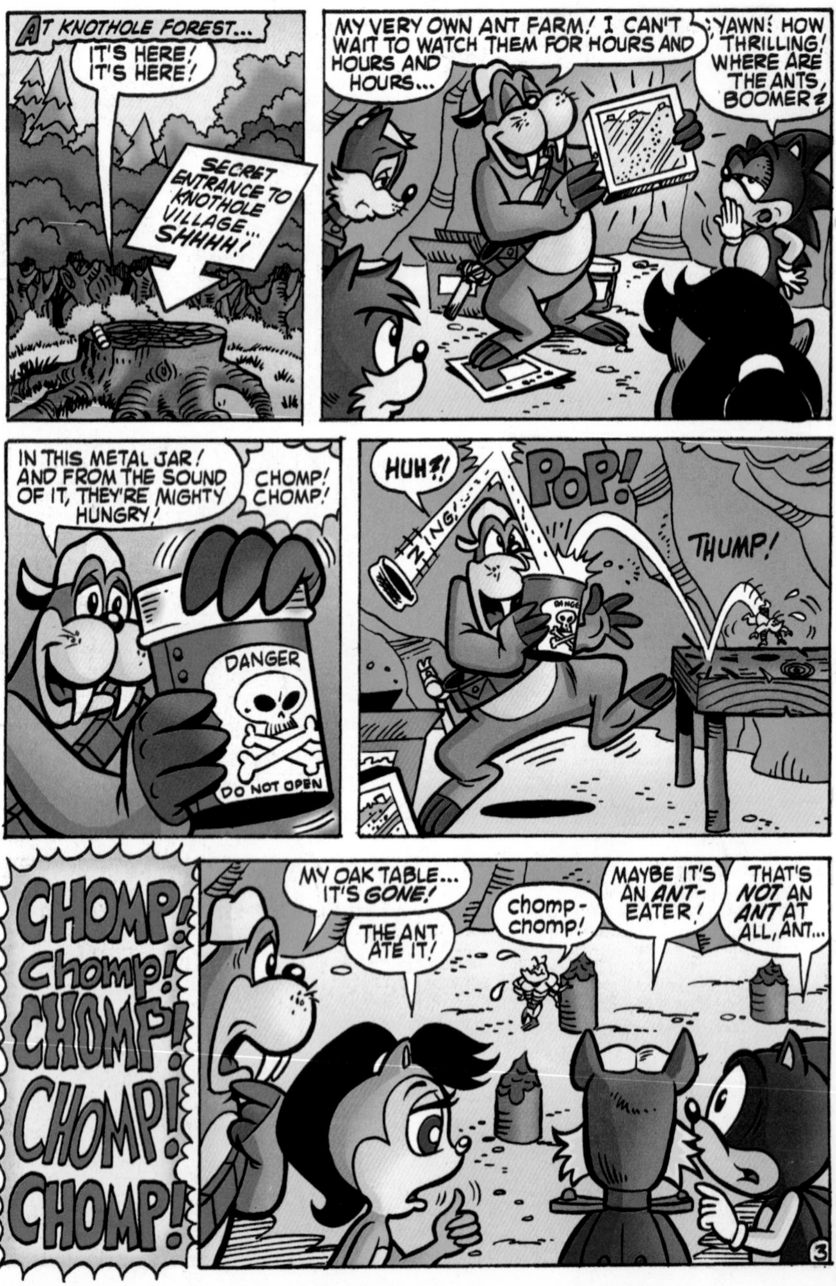
AT KNOTHOLE FOREST...
IT'S HERE! IT'S HERE!
SECRET ENTRANCE TO KNOTHOLE VILLAGE... SHHHH!
MY VERY OWN ANT FARM! I CAN'T WAIT TO WATCH THEM FOR HOURS AND HOURS AND HOURS...
:YAWN: HOW THRILLING! WHERE ARE THE ANTS, BOOMER?
IN THIS METAL JAR! AND FROM THE SOUND OF IT, THEY'RE MIGHTY HUNGRY!
CHOMP! CHOMP!
DANGER
DO NOT OPEN
HUH?!
POP!
ZING!
THUMP!
CHOMP! Chomp! CHOMP! CHOMP! CHOMP!
MY OAK TABLE... IT'S GONE!
THE ANT ATE IT!
chomp-chomp!
MAYBE IT'S AN ANT-EATER!
THAT'S NOT AN ANT AT ALL, ANT...

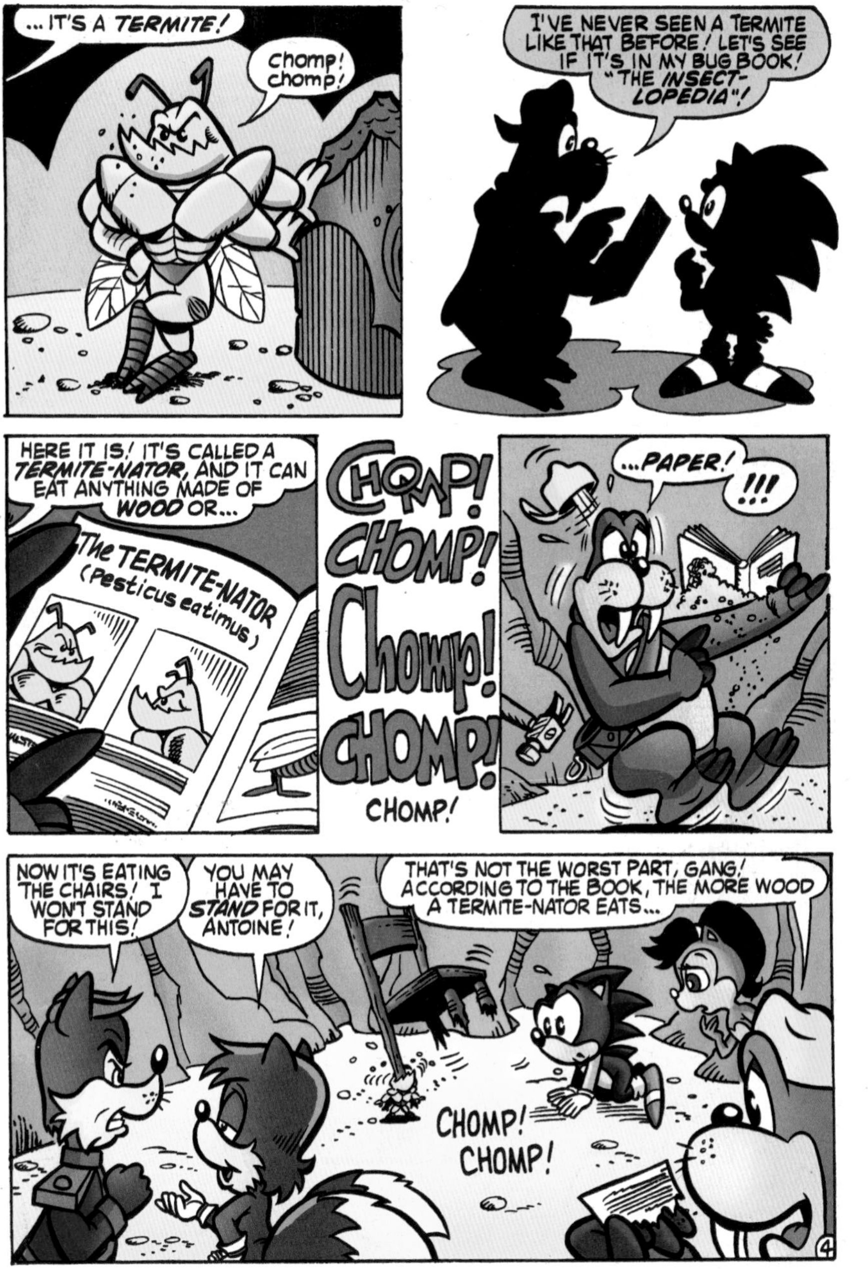

... IT'S A TERMITE!
Chomp! chomp!
I'VE NEVER SEEN A TERMITE LIKE THAT BEFORE! LET'S SEE IF IT'S IN MY BUG BOOK! "THE INSECT-LOPEDIA"!
HERE IT IS! IT'S CALLED A TERMITE-NATOR, AND IT CAN EAT ANYTHING MADE OF WOOD OR...
The TERMITE-NATOR (Pesticus eatimus)
CHOMP! CHOMP! Chomp! CHOMP! CHOMP!
...PAPER!
!!!
NOW IT'S EATING THE CHAIRS! I WON'T STAND FOR THIS!
YOU MAY HAVE TO STAND FOR IT, ANTOINE!
THAT'S NOT THE WORST PART, GANG! ACCORDING TO THE BOOK, THE MORE WOOD A TERMITE-NATOR EATS...
CHOMP! CHOMP!
4

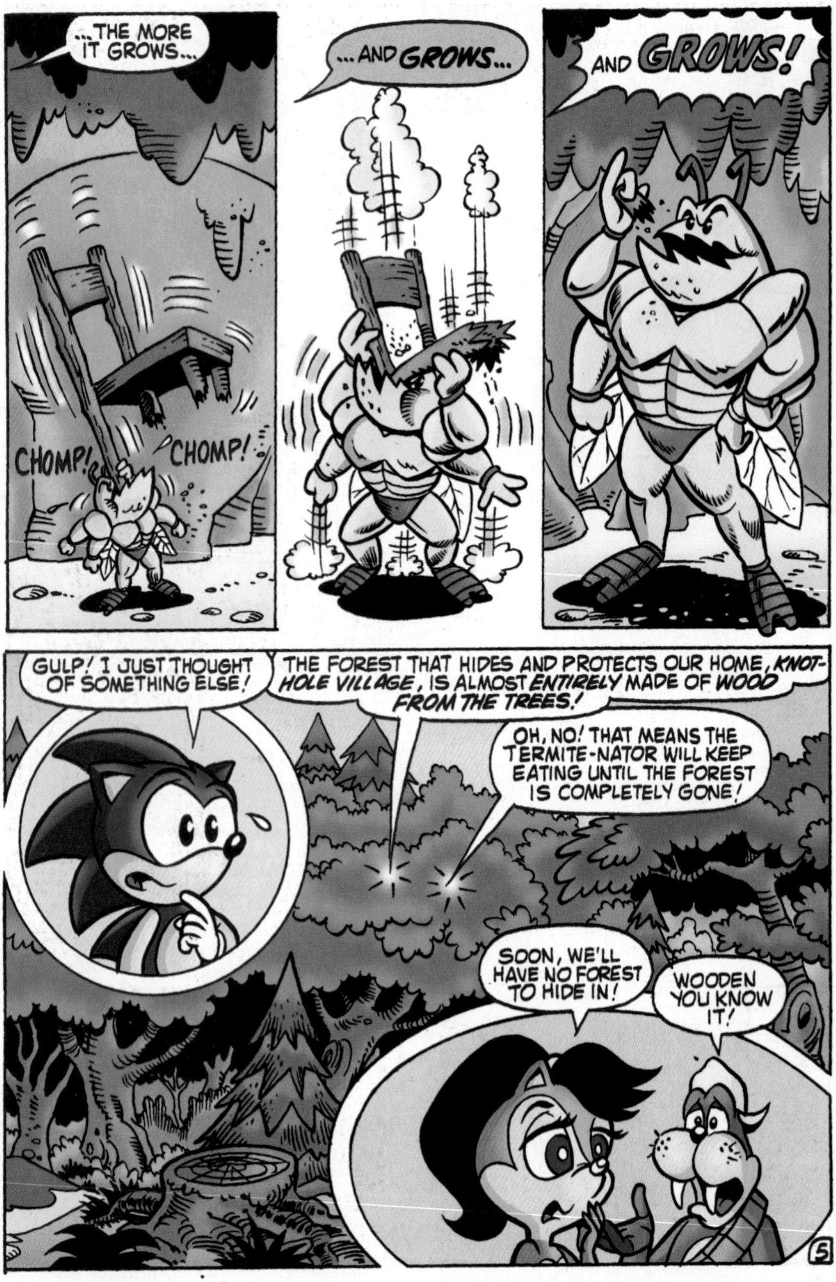
...THE MORE IT GROWS...
CHOMP! CHOMP!
...AND GROWS...
AND GROWS!
GULP! I JUST THOUGHT OF SOMETHING ELSE!
THE FOREST THAT HIDES AND PROTECTS OUR HOME, KNOT-HOLE VILLAGE, IS ALMOST ENTIRELY MADE OF WOOD FROM THE TREES!
OH, NO! THAT MEANS THE TERMITE-NATOR WILL KEEP EATING UNTIL THE FOREST IS COMPLETELY GONE!
SOON, WE'LL HAVE NO FOREST TO HIDE IN!
WOODEN YOU KNOW IT!

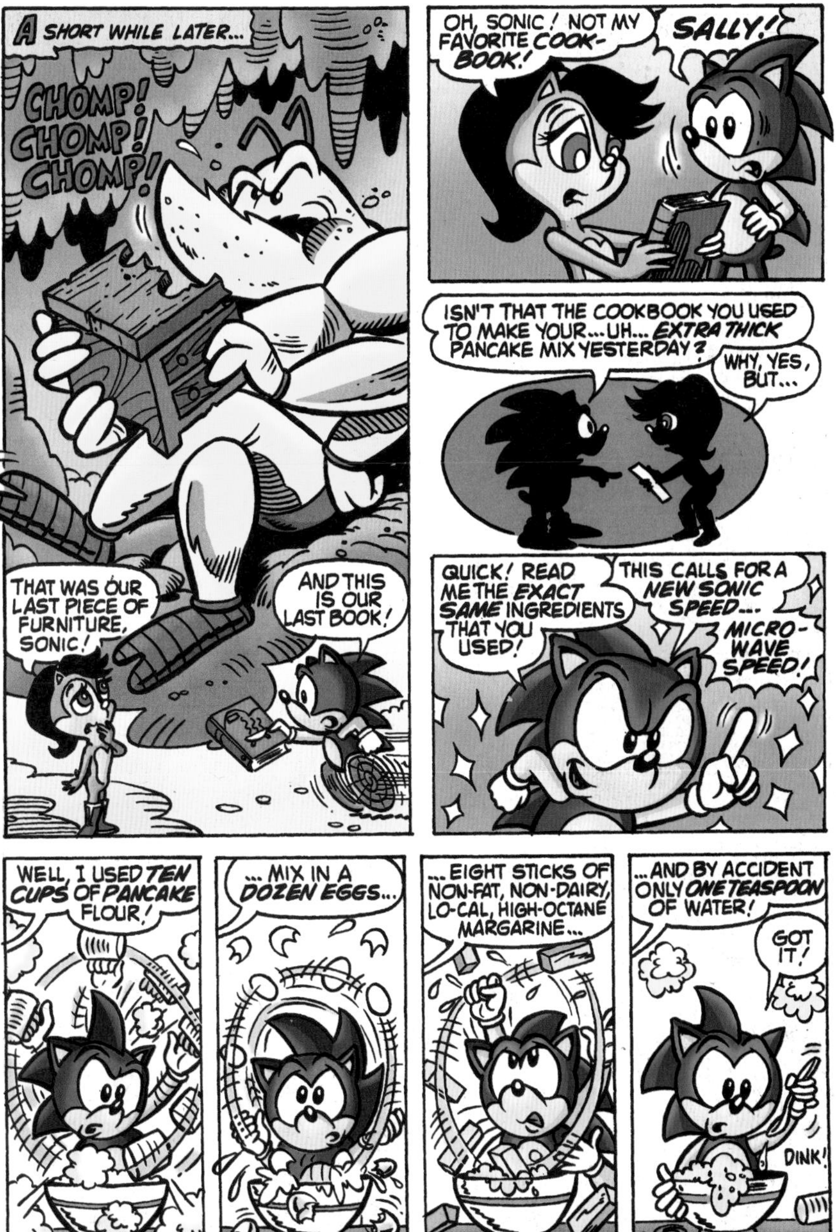
A SHORT WHILE LATER...
CHOMP! CHOMP! CHOMP!
THAT WAS OUR LAST PIECE OF FURNITURE, SONIC!
AND THIS IS OUR LAST BOOK!
OH, SONIC! NOT MY FAVORITE COOK-BOOK!
SALLY!
ISN'T THAT THE COOKBOOK YOU USED TO MAKE YOUR...UH... EXTRA THICK PANCAKE MIX YESTERDAY?
WHY, YES, BUT...
QUICK! READ ME THE EXACT SAME INGREDIENTS THAT YOU USED!
THIS CALLS FOR A NEW SONIC SPEED... MICRO-WAVE SPEED!
WELL, I USED TEN CUPS OF PANCAKE FLOUR!
... MIX IN A DOZEN EGGS...
... EIGHT STICKS OF NON-FAT, NON-DAIRY, LO-CAL, HIGH-OCTANE MARGARINE...
... AND BY ACCIDENT ONLY ONE TEASPOON OF WATER!
GOT IT!
DINK!
6

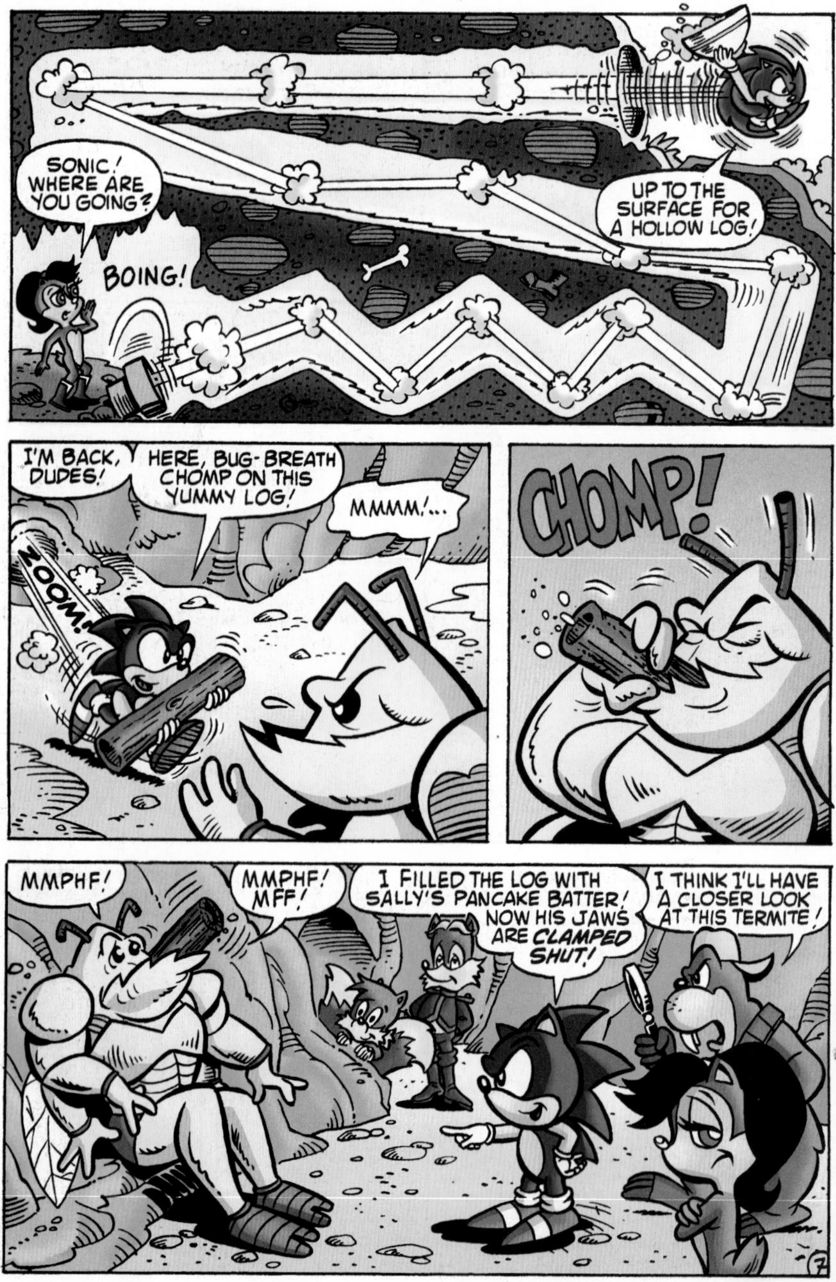
SONIC! WHERE ARE YOU GOING?
UP TO THE SURFACE FOR A HOLLOW LOG!
BOING!
I'M BACK, DUDES!
HERE, BUG-BREATH CHOMP ON THIS YUMMY LOG!
ZOOM!
MMMM!...
CHOMP!
MMPHF!
MMPHF! MFF!
I FILLED THE LOG WITH SALLY'S PANCAKE BATTER! NOW HIS JAWS ARE CLAMPED SHUT!
I THINK I'LL HAVE A CLOSER LOOK AT THIS TERMITE!
7

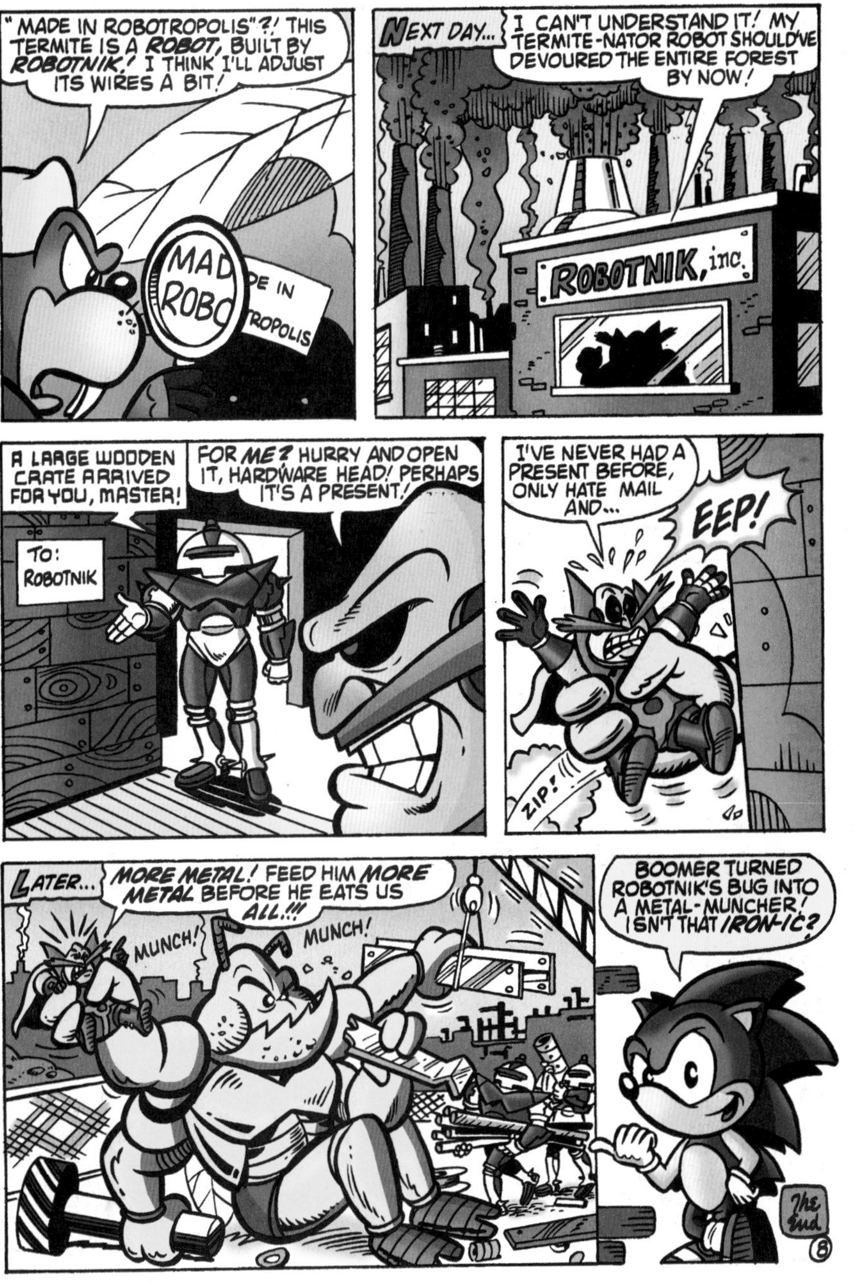
"MADE IN ROBOTROPOLIS"?! THIS TERMITE IS A ROBOT, BUILT BY ROBOTNIK! I THINK I'LL ADJUST ITS WIRES A BIT!
MAD ROBO
DE IN TROPOLIS
NEXT DAY...
I CAN'T UNDERSTAND IT! MY TERMITE-NATOR ROBOT SHOULD'VE DEVOURED THE ENTIRE FOREST BY NOW!
ROBOTNIK, inc.
A LARGE WOODEN CRATE ARRIVED FOR YOU, MASTER!
TO: ROBOTNIK
FOR ME? HURRY AND OPEN IT, HARDWARE HEAD! PERHAPS IT'S A PRESENT!
I'VE NEVER HAD A PRESENT BEFORE, ONLY HATE MAIL AND...
EEP!
ZIP!
LATER...
MORE METAL! FEED HIM MORE METAL BEFORE HE EATS US ALL!!!
MUNCH!
MUNCH!
BOOMER TURNED ROBOTNIK'S BUG INTO A METAL-MUNCHER! ISN'T THAT IRON-IC?
The End
8

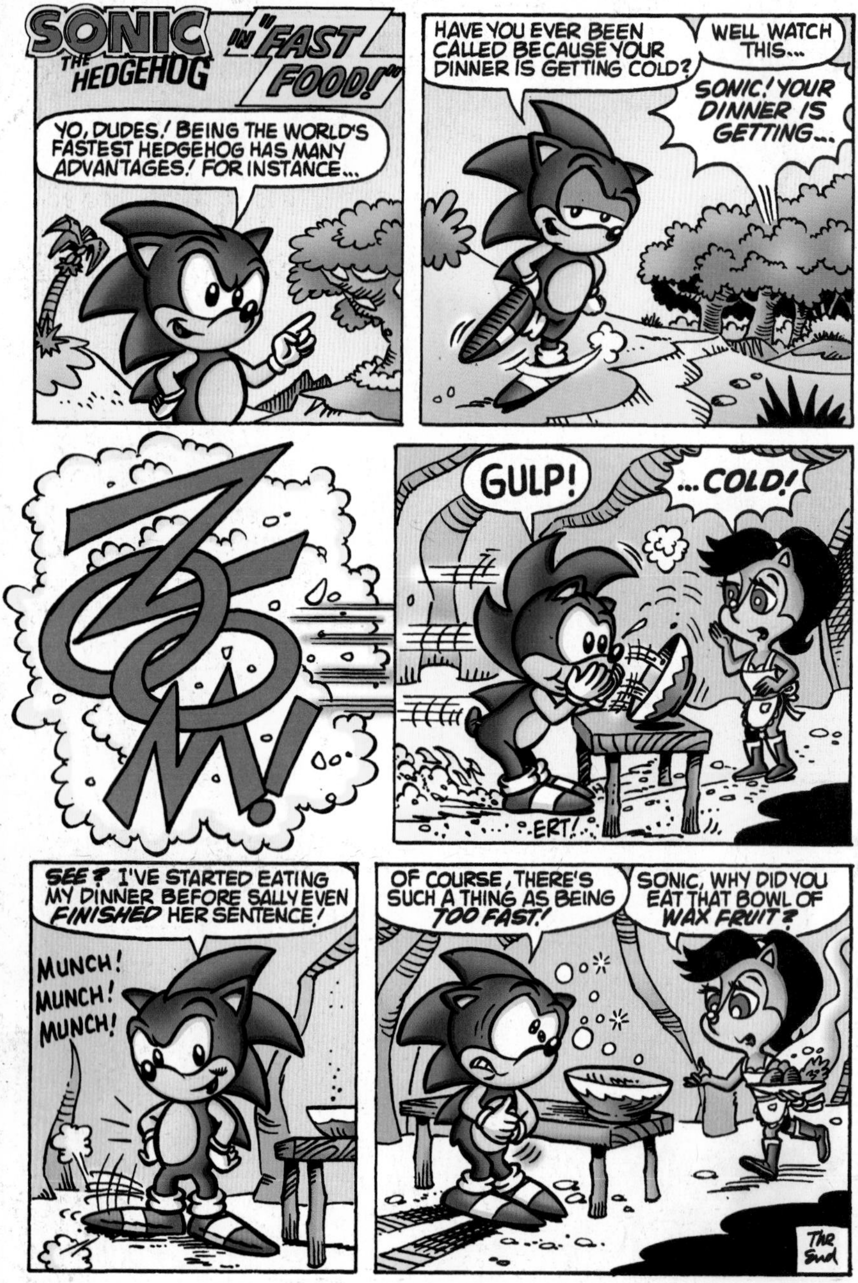

SONIC THE HEDGEHOG
IN "FAST FOOD!"
YO, DUDES! BEING THE WORLD'S FASTEST HEDGEHOG HAS MANY ADVANTAGES! FOR INSTANCE...
HAVE YOU EVER BEEN CALLED BECAUSE YOUR DINNER IS GETTING COLD?
WELL WATCH THIS...
SONIC! YOUR DINNER IS GETTING...
ZOOM!
GULP!
...COLD!
ERT!
SEE? I'VE STARTED EATING MY DINNER BEFORE SALLY EVEN FINISHED HER SENTENCE!
MUNCH! MUNCH! MUNCH!
OF COURSE, THERE'S SUCH A THING AS BEING TOO FAST!
SONIC, WHY DID YOU EAT THAT BOWL OF WAX FRUIT?
THE END

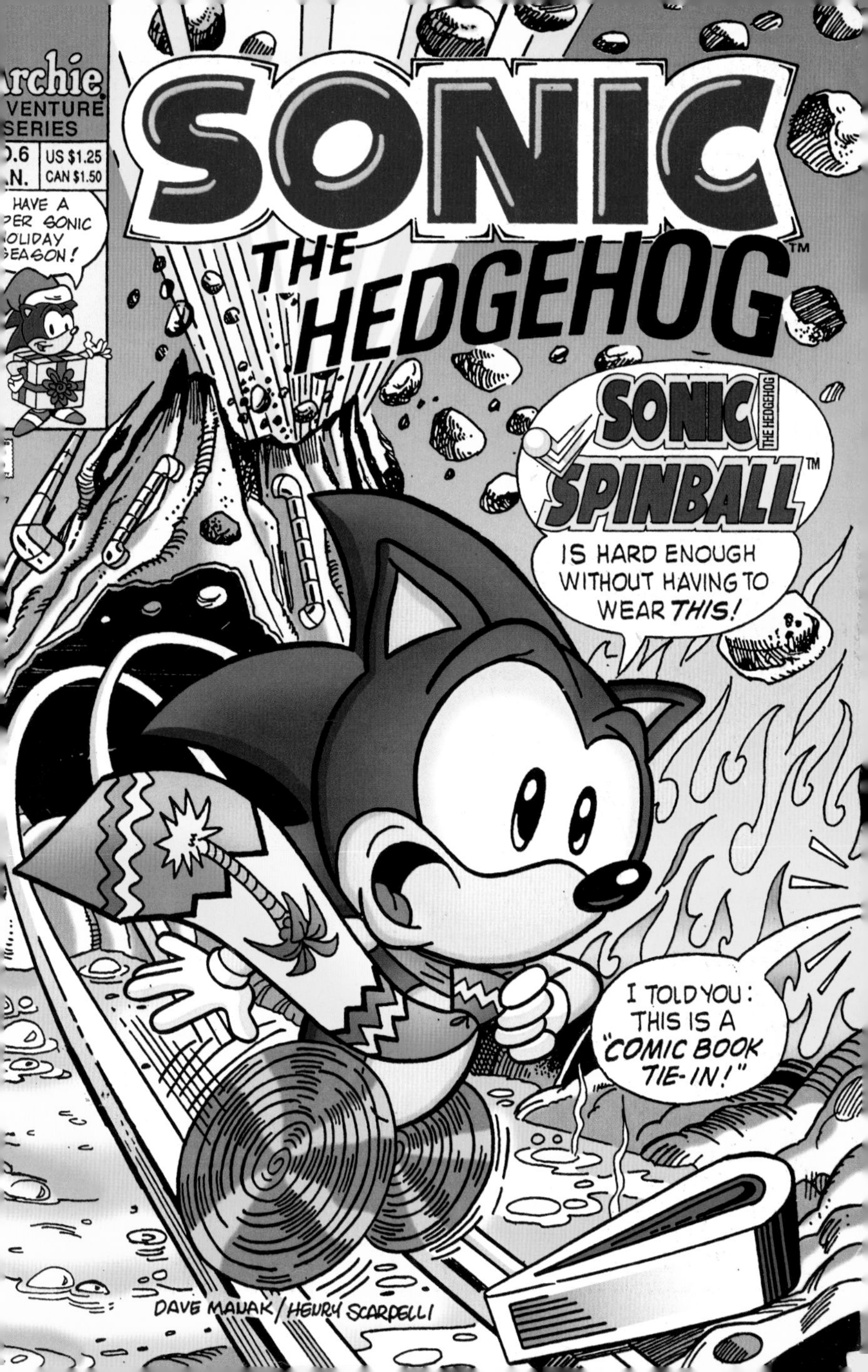
Archie
ADVENTURE SERIES
NO.6
JAN.
US $1.25
CAN $1.50
HAVE A SUPER SONIC HOLIDAY SEASON!
SONIC THE HEDGEHOG™
SONIC THE HEDGEHOG SPINBALL™
IS HARD ENOUGH WITHOUT HAVING TO WEAR THIS!
I TOLD YOU: THIS IS A "COMIC BOOK TIE-IN!"
DAVE MANAK / HENRY SCARPELLI

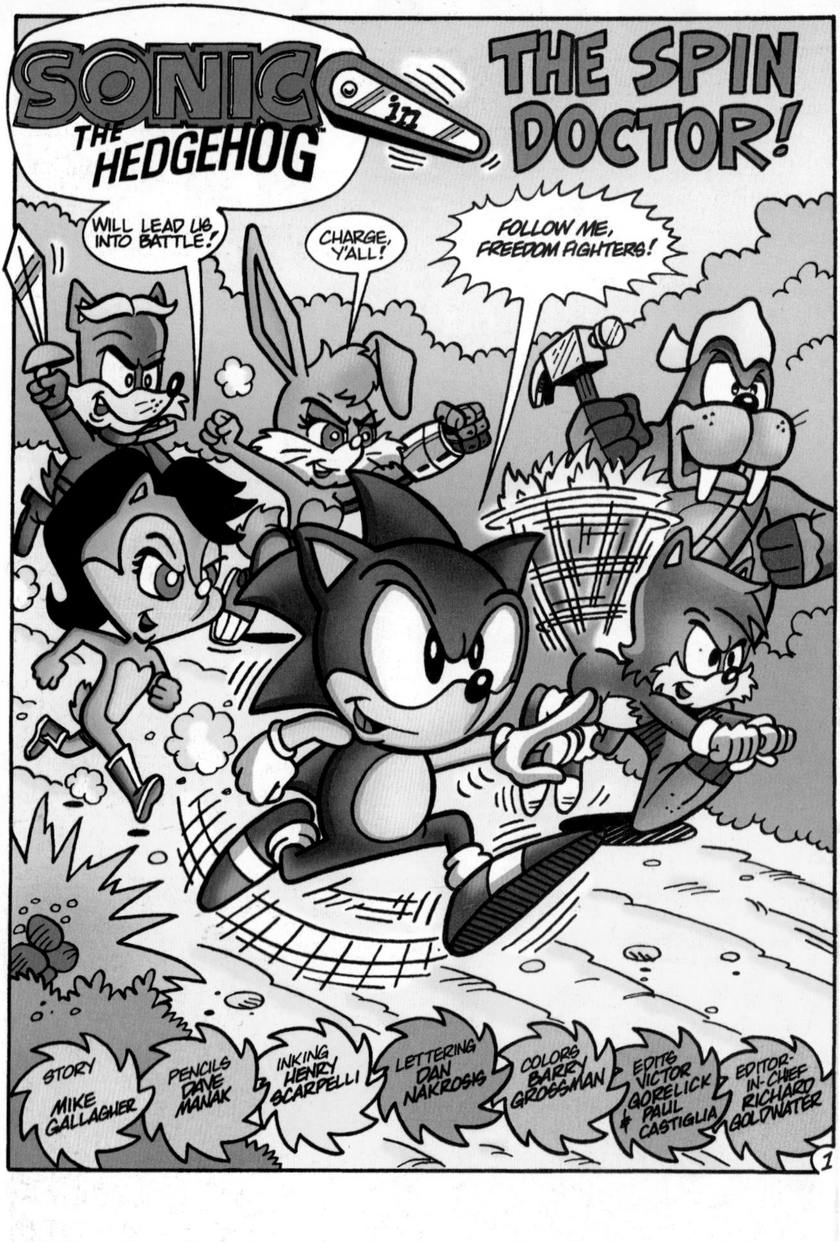
SONIC THE HEDGEHOG
in
THE SPIN DOCTOR!
WILL LEAD US INTO BATTLE!
CHARGE, Y'ALL!
FOLLOW ME, FREEDOM FIGHTERS!
STORY MIKE GALLAGHER
PENCILS DAVE MANAK
INKING HENRY SCARPELLI
LETTERING DAN NAKROSIS
COLORS BARRY GROSSMAN
EDITS VICTOR GORELICK & PAUL CASTIGLIA
EDITOR-IN-CHIEF RICHARD GOLDWATER
1

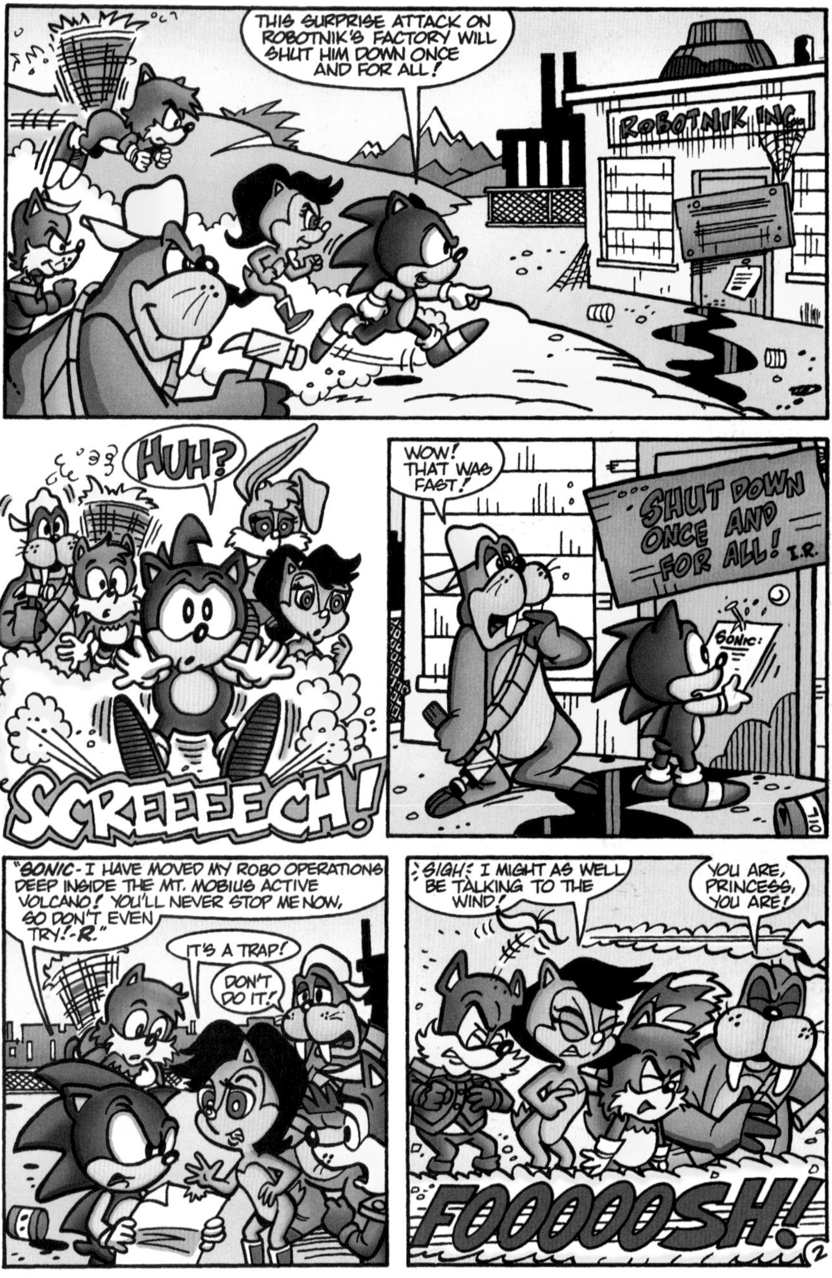
THIS SURPRISE ATTACK ON ROBOTNIK'S FACTORY WILL SHUT HIM DOWN ONCE AND FOR ALL!
ROBOTNIK INC.
HUH?
SCREEEECH!
WOW! THAT WAS FAST!
SHUT DOWN ONCE AND FOR ALL! I.R.
SONIC:
"SONIC- I HAVE MOVED MY ROBO OPERATIONS DEEP INSIDE THE MT. MOBIUS ACTIVE VOLCANO! YOU'LL NEVER STOP ME NOW, SO DON'T EVEN TRY!-R."
IT'S A TRAP!
DON'T DO IT!
SIGH: I MIGHT AS WELL BE TALKING TO THE WIND!
YOU ARE, PRINCESS, YOU ARE!
FOOOOOSH!

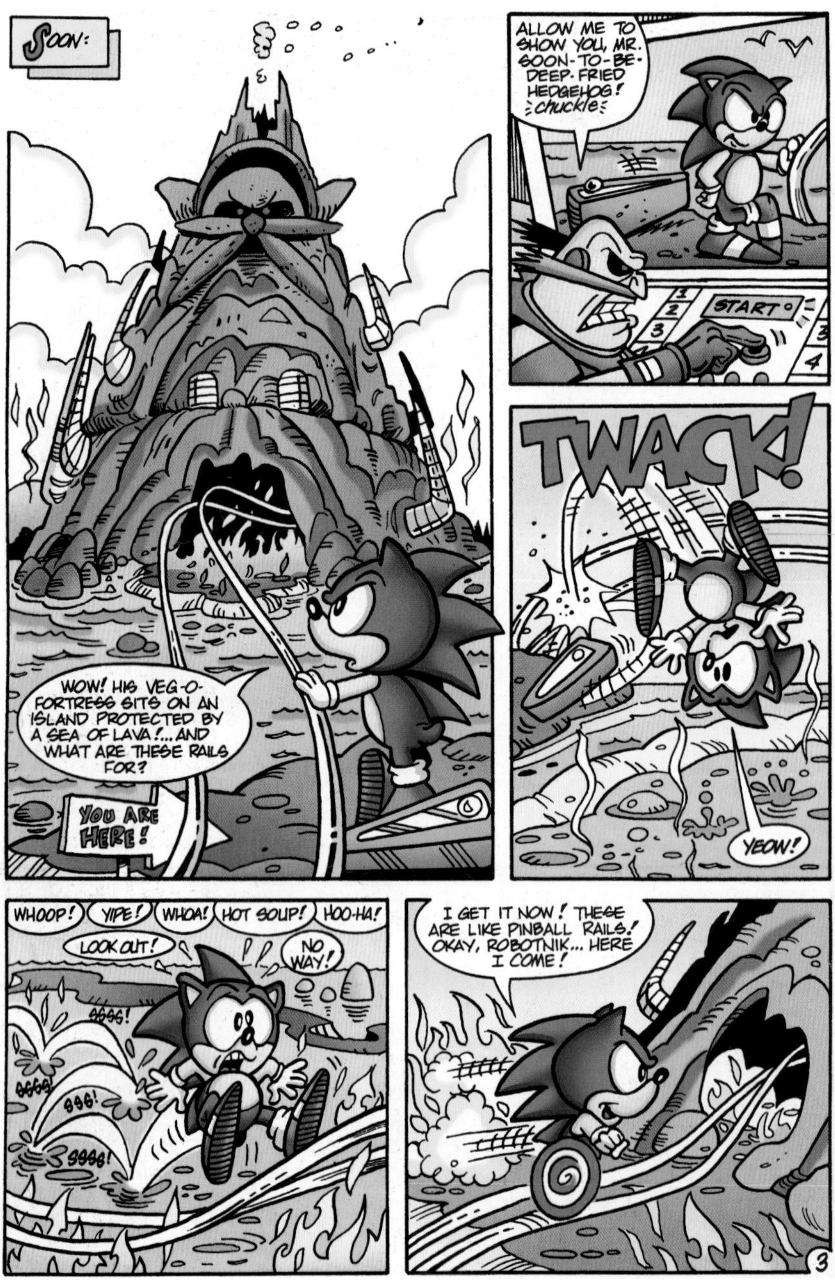

SOON:
WOW! HIS VEG-O-FORTRESS SITS ON AN ISLAND PROTECTED BY A SEA OF LAVA!... AND WHAT ARE THESE RAILS FOR?
YOU ARE HERE!
ALLOW ME TO SHOW YOU, MR. SOON-TO-BE-DEEP-FRIED HEDGEHOG! chuckle
START
1
2
3
3
4
TWACK!
YEOW!
WHOOP!
YIPE!
WHOA!
HOT SOUP!
HOO-HA!
LOOK OUT!
NO WAY!
SSSS!
SSSS!
SSS!
SSSS!
I GET IT NOW! THESE ARE LIKE PINBALL RAILS! OKAY, ROBOTNIK... HERE I COME!

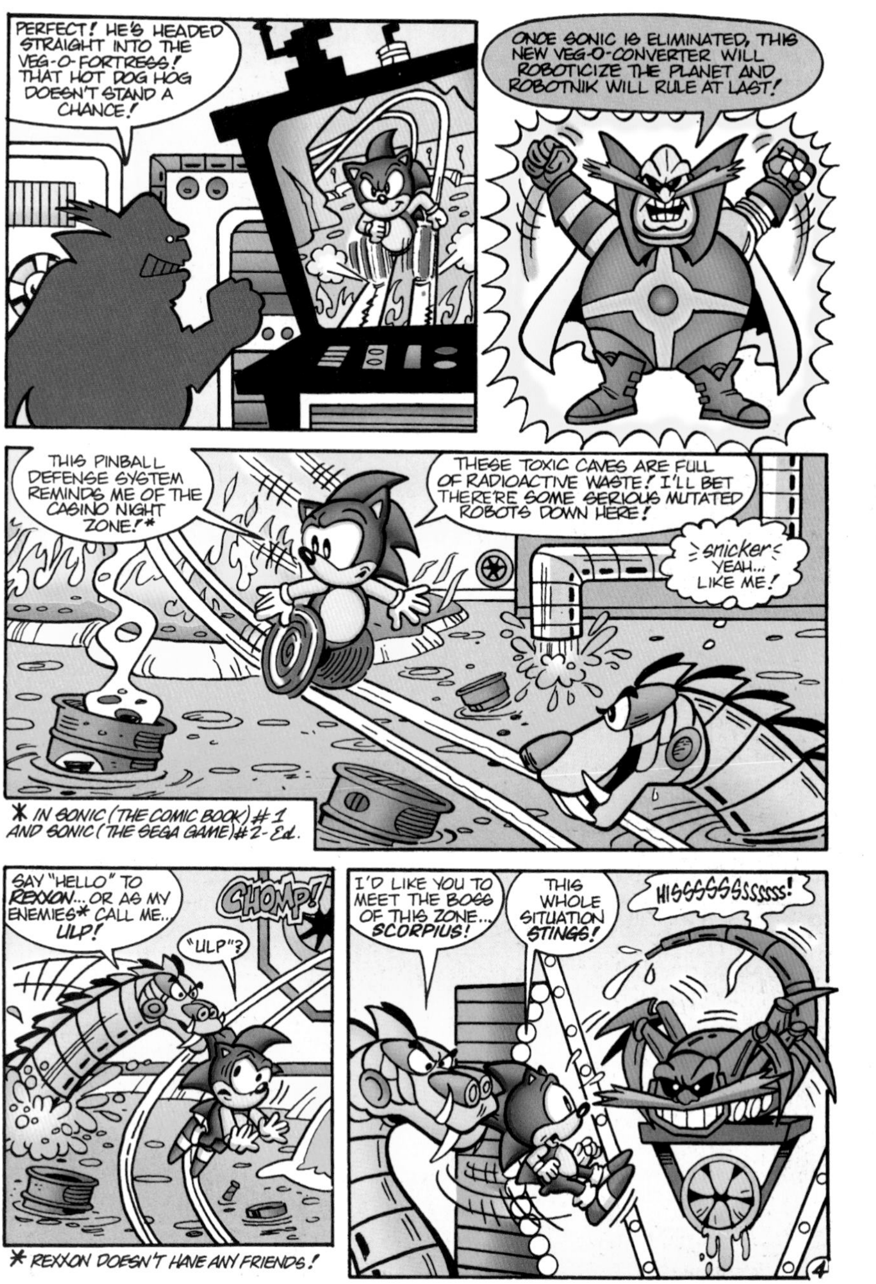
PERFECT! HE'S HEADED STRAIGHT INTO THE VEG-O-FORTRESS! THAT HOT DOG HOG DOESN'T STAND A CHANCE!
ONCE SONIC IS ELIMINATED, THIS NEW VEG-O-CONVERTER WILL ROBOTICIZE THE PLANET AND ROBOTNIK WILL RULE AT LAST!
THIS PINBALL DEFENSE SYSTEM REMINDS ME OF THE CASINO NIGHT ZONE!*
THESE TOXIC CAVES ARE FULL OF RADIOACTIVE WASTE! I'LL BET THERE'RE SOME SERIOUS MUTATED ROBOTS DOWN HERE!
snicker YEAH... LIKE ME!
* IN SONIC (THE COMIC BOOK) #1 AND SONIC (THE SEGA GAME) #2 - Ed.
SAY "HELLO" TO REXXON... OR AS MY ENEMIES* CALL ME... ULP!
CHOMP!
"ULP"?
* REXXON DOESN'T HAVE ANY FRIENDS!
I'D LIKE YOU TO MEET THE BOSS OF THIS ZONE... SCORPIUS!
THIS WHOLE SITUATION STINGS!
HISSSSSSssssss!

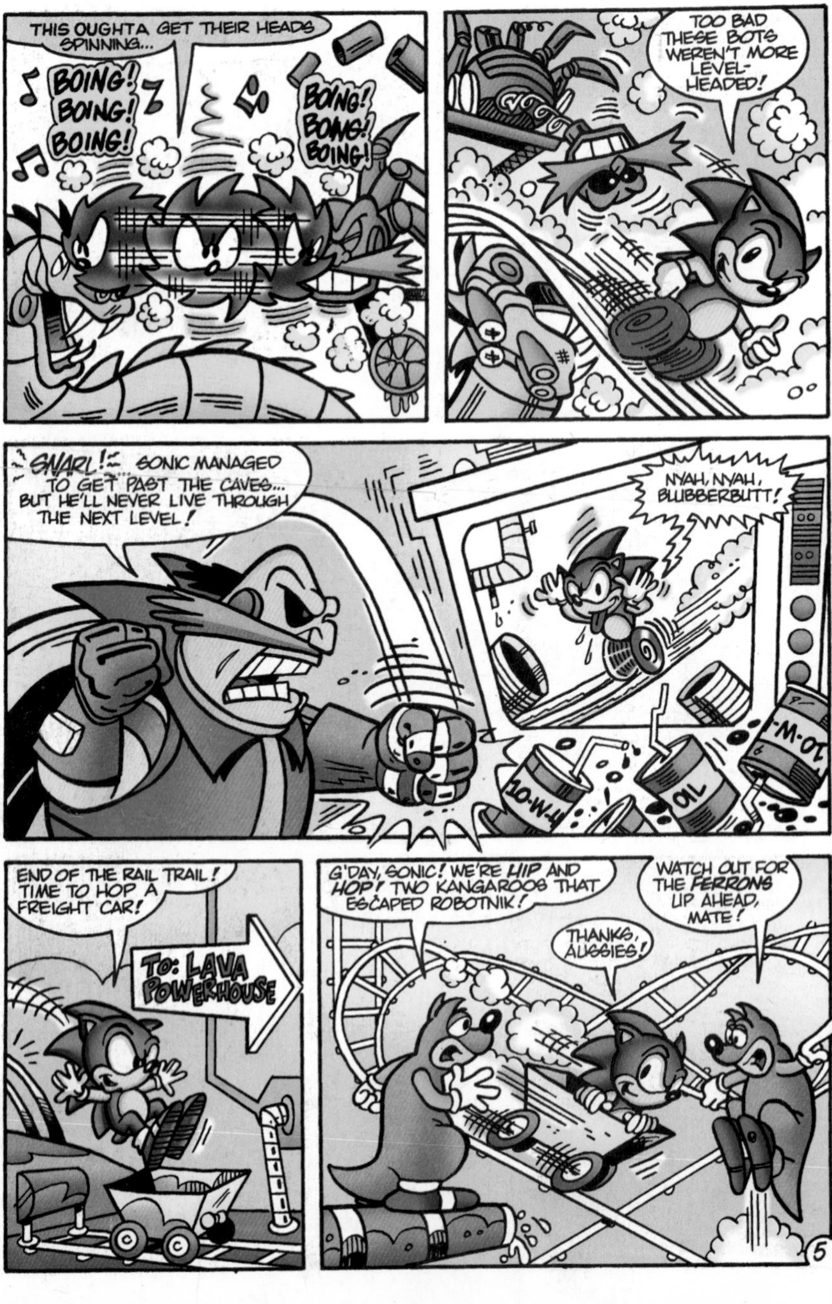
THIS OUGHTA GET THEIR HEADS SPINNING...
BOING! BOING! BOING!
BOING! BOING! BOING!
TOO BAD THESE BOTS WEREN'T MORE LEVEL-HEADED!
SNARL! SONIC MANAGED TO GET PAST THE CAVES... BUT HE'LL NEVER LIVE THROUGH THE NEXT LEVEL!
NYAH, NYAH, BLUBBERBUTT!
10-W-4
OIL
10-W-
END OF THE RAIL TRAIL! TIME TO HOP A FREIGHT CAR!
TO: LAVA POWERHOUSE
G'DAY, SONIC! WE'RE HIP AND HOP! TWO KANGAROOS THAT ESCAPED ROBOTNIK!
WATCH OUT FOR THE FERRONS UP AHEAD, MATE!
THANKS, AUSSIES!

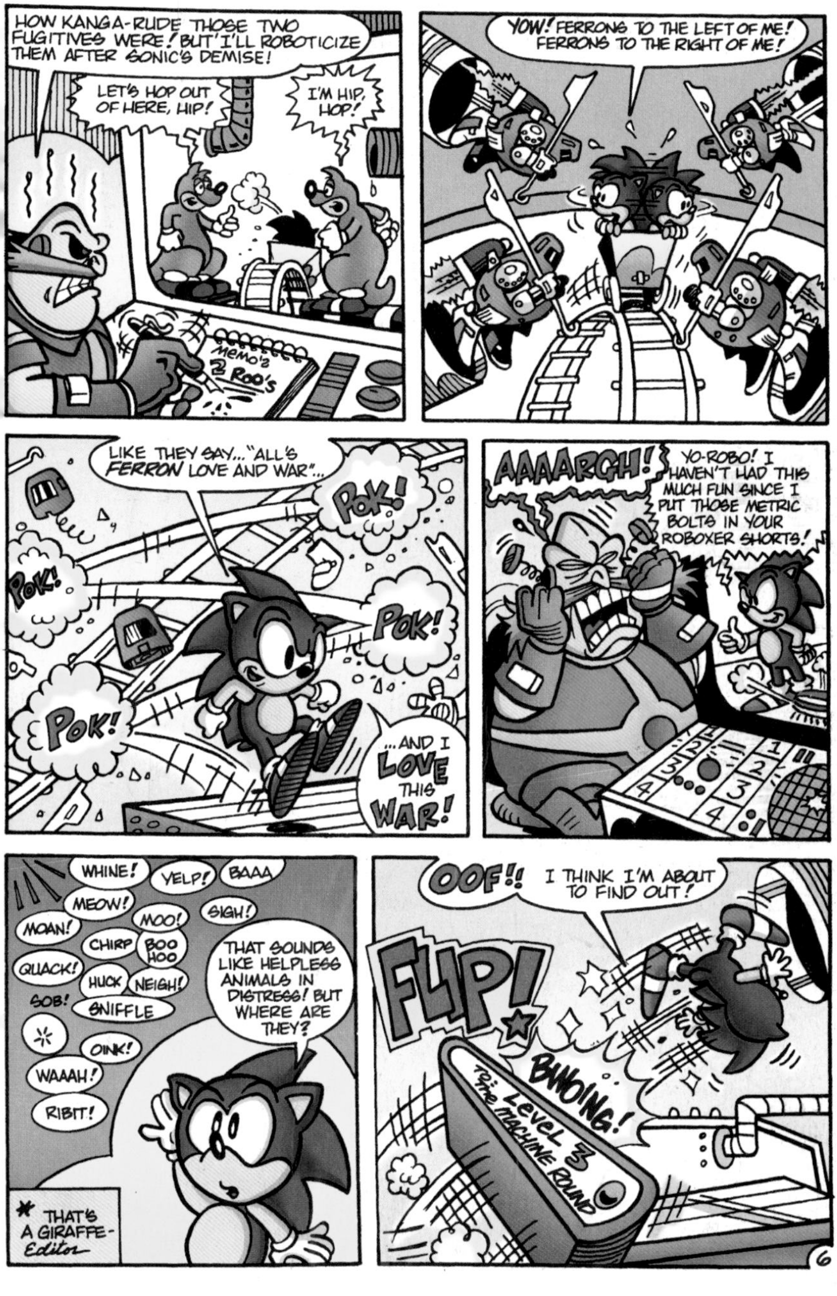
HOW KANGA-RUDE THOSE TWO FUGITIVES WERE! BUT I'LL ROBOTICIZE THEM AFTER SONIC'S DEMISE!
LET'S HOP OUT OF HERE, HIP!
I'M HIP, HOP!
MEMO'S 2 ROO'S
YOW! FERRONS TO THE LEFT OF ME! FERRONS TO THE RIGHT OF ME!
LIKE THEY SAY... "ALL'S FERRON LOVE AND WAR"...
POK!
POK!
POK!
POK!
...AND I LOVE THIS WAR!
AAAARGH!
YO-ROBO! I HAVEN'T HAD THIS MUCH FUN SINCE I PUT THOSE METRIC BOLTS IN YOUR ROBOXER SHORTS!
WHINE!
YELP!
BAAA
MEOW!
SIGH!
MOAN!
MOO!
CHIRP
BOO HOO
QUACK!
HUCK
NEIGH!
SOB!
SNIFFLE
*
OINK!
WAAAH!
RIBIT!
THAT SOUNDS LIKE HELPLESS ANIMALS IN DISTRESS! BUT WHERE ARE THEY?
* THAT'S A GIRAFFE - Editor
OOF!!
I THINK I'M ABOUT TO FIND OUT!
FLIP!
BWOING!
LEVEL 3 TO THE MACHINE ROUND

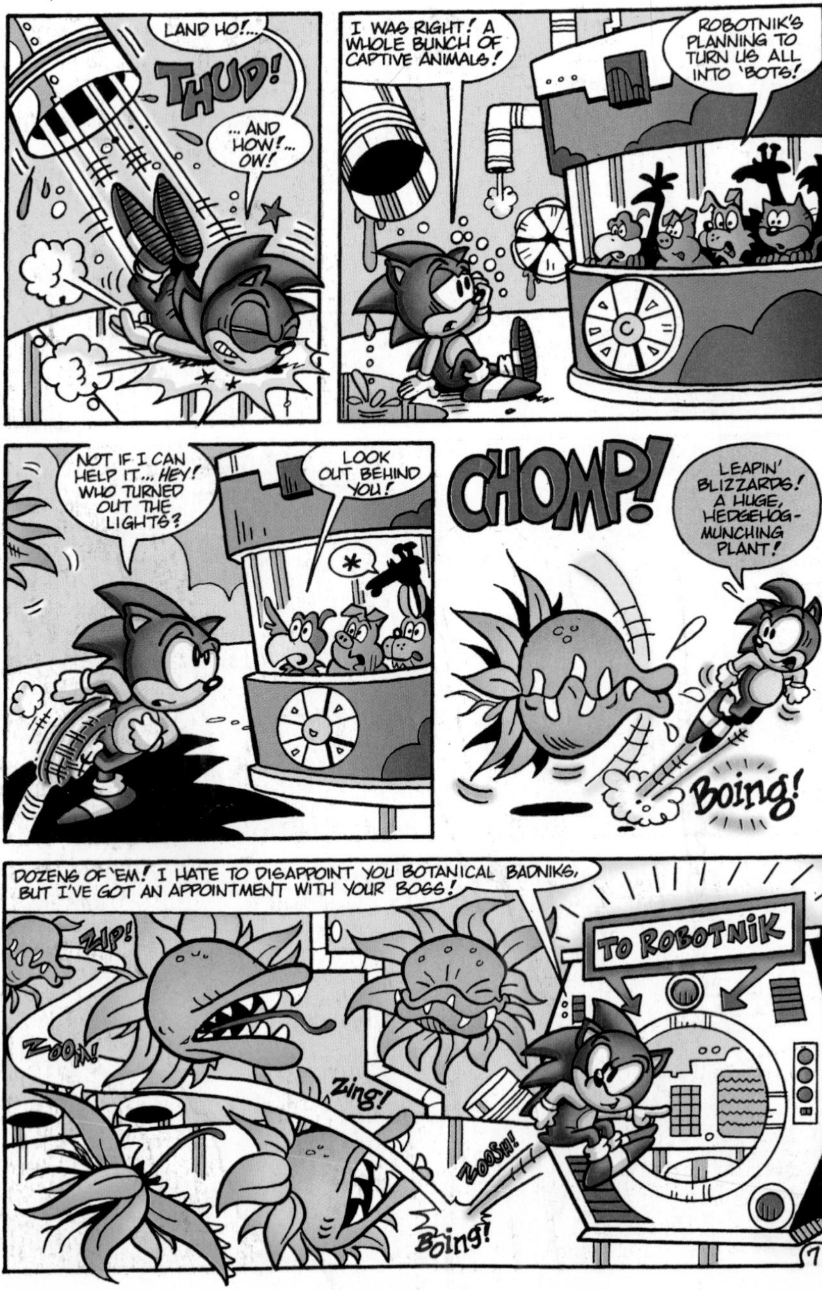
LAND HO!...
THUD!
...AND HOW!... OW!
I WAS RIGHT! A WHOLE BUNCH OF CAPTIVE ANIMALS!
ROBOTNIK'S PLANNING TO TURN US ALL INTO 'BOTS!
NOT IF I CAN HELP IT... HEY! WHO TURNED OUT THE LIGHTS?
LOOK OUT BEHIND YOU!
*
CHOMP!
LEAPIN' BLIZZARDS! A HUGE, HEDGEHOG-MUNCHING PLANT!
Boing!
DOZENS OF 'EM! I HATE TO DISAPPOINT YOU BOTANICAL BADNIKS, BUT I'VE GOT AN APPOINTMENT WITH YOUR BOSS!
ZIP!
TO ROBOTNIK
ZOOM!
Zing!
ZOOSH!
Boing!

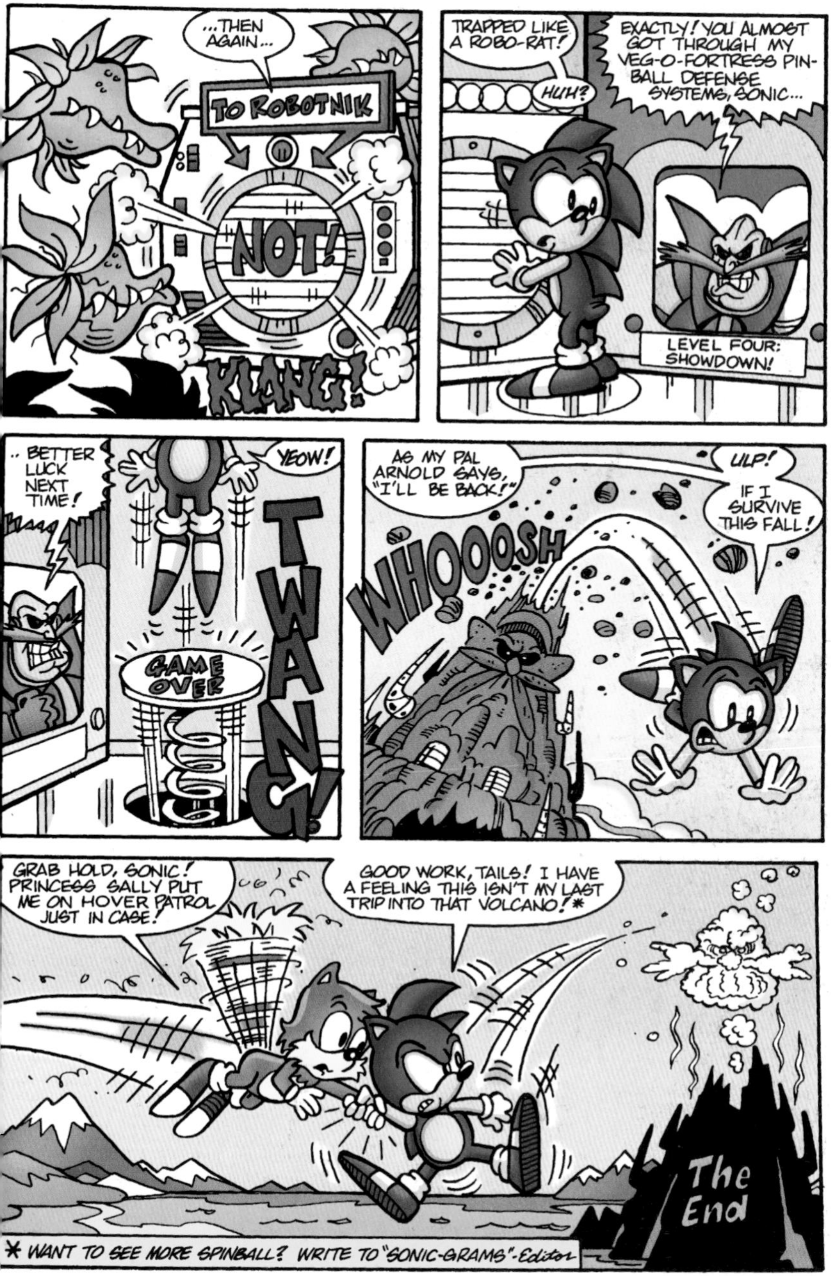
...THEN AGAIN...
TO ROBOTNIK
NOT!
KLANG!
TRAPPED LIKE A ROBO-RAT!
HUH?
EXACTLY! YOU ALMOST GOT THROUGH MY VEG-O-FORTRESS PIN-BALL DEFENSE SYSTEMS, SONIC...
LEVEL FOUR: SHOWDOWN!
.. BETTER LUCK NEXT TIME!
YEOW!
GAME OVER
TWANG!
AS MY PAL ARNOLD SAYS, "I'LL BE BACK!"
ULP!
IF I SURVIVE THIS FALL!
WHOOOSH
GRAB HOLD, SONIC! PRINCESS SALLY PUT ME ON HOVER PATROL JUST IN CASE!
GOOD WORK, TAILS! I HAVE A FEELING THIS ISN'T MY LAST TRIP INTO THAT VOLCANO!*
The End
* WANT TO SEE MORE SPINBALL? WRITE TO "SONIC-GRAMS" - Editor

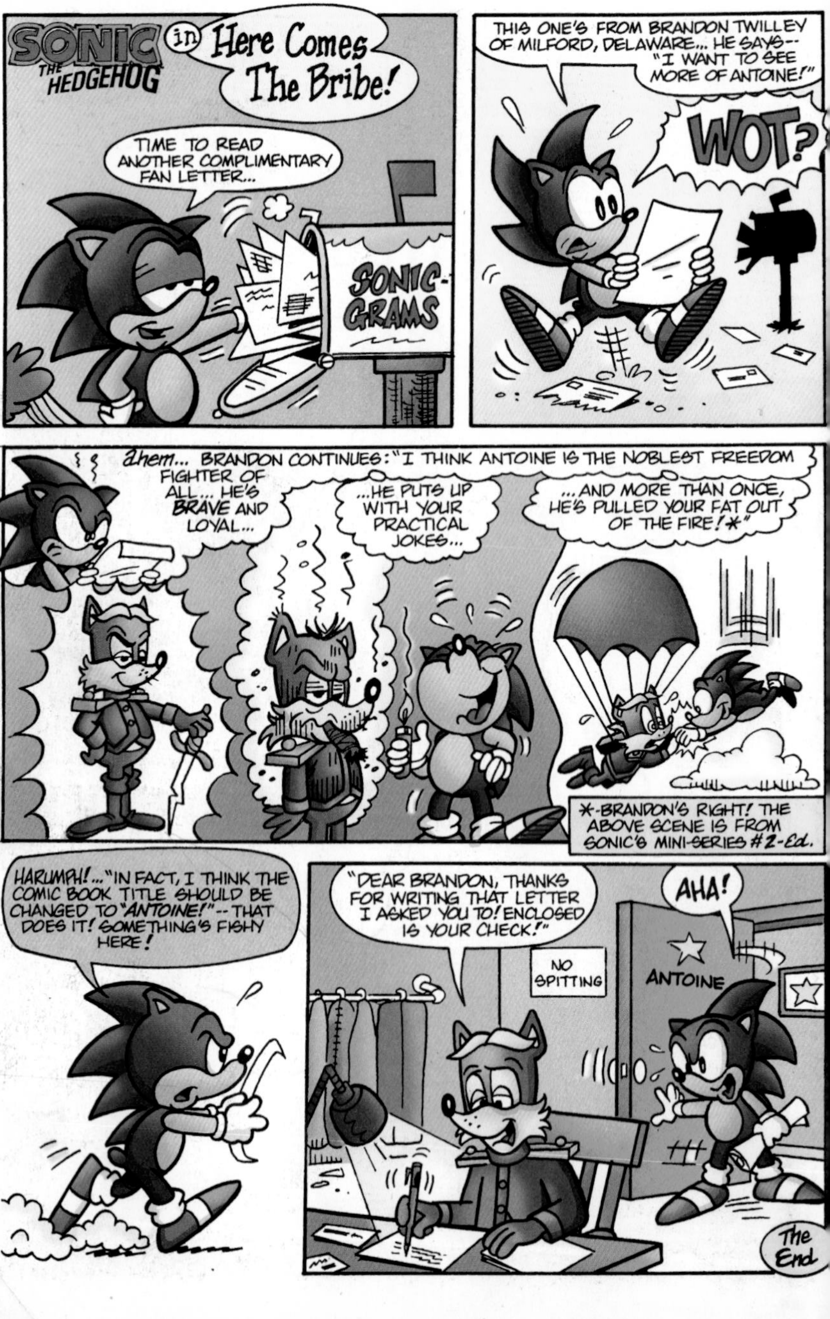

SONIC THE HEDGEHOG
in
Here Comes The Bribe!
TIME TO READ ANOTHER COMPLIMENTARY FAN LETTER...
SONIC-GRAMS
THIS ONE'S FROM BRANDON TWILLEY OF MILFORD, DELAWARE... HE SAYS-- "I WANT TO SEE MORE OF ANTOINE!"
WOT?
ahem... BRANDON CONTINUES: "I THINK ANTOINE IS THE NOBLEST FREEDOM FIGHTER OF ALL... HE'S BRAVE AND LOYAL...
...HE PUTS UP WITH YOUR PRACTICAL JOKES...
...AND MORE THAN ONCE, HE'S PULLED YOUR FAT OUT OF THE FIRE!*"
*-BRANDON'S RIGHT! THE ABOVE SCENE IS FROM SONIC'S MINI-SERIES #2-Ed.
HARUMPH!..."IN FACT, I THINK THE COMIC BOOK TITLE SHOULD BE CHANGED TO "ANTOINE!"--THAT DOES IT! SOMETHING'S FISHY HERE!
"DEAR BRANDON, THANKS FOR WRITING THAT LETTER I ASKED YOU TO! ENCLOSED IS YOUR CHECK!"
AHA!
NO SPITTING
ANTOINE
The End

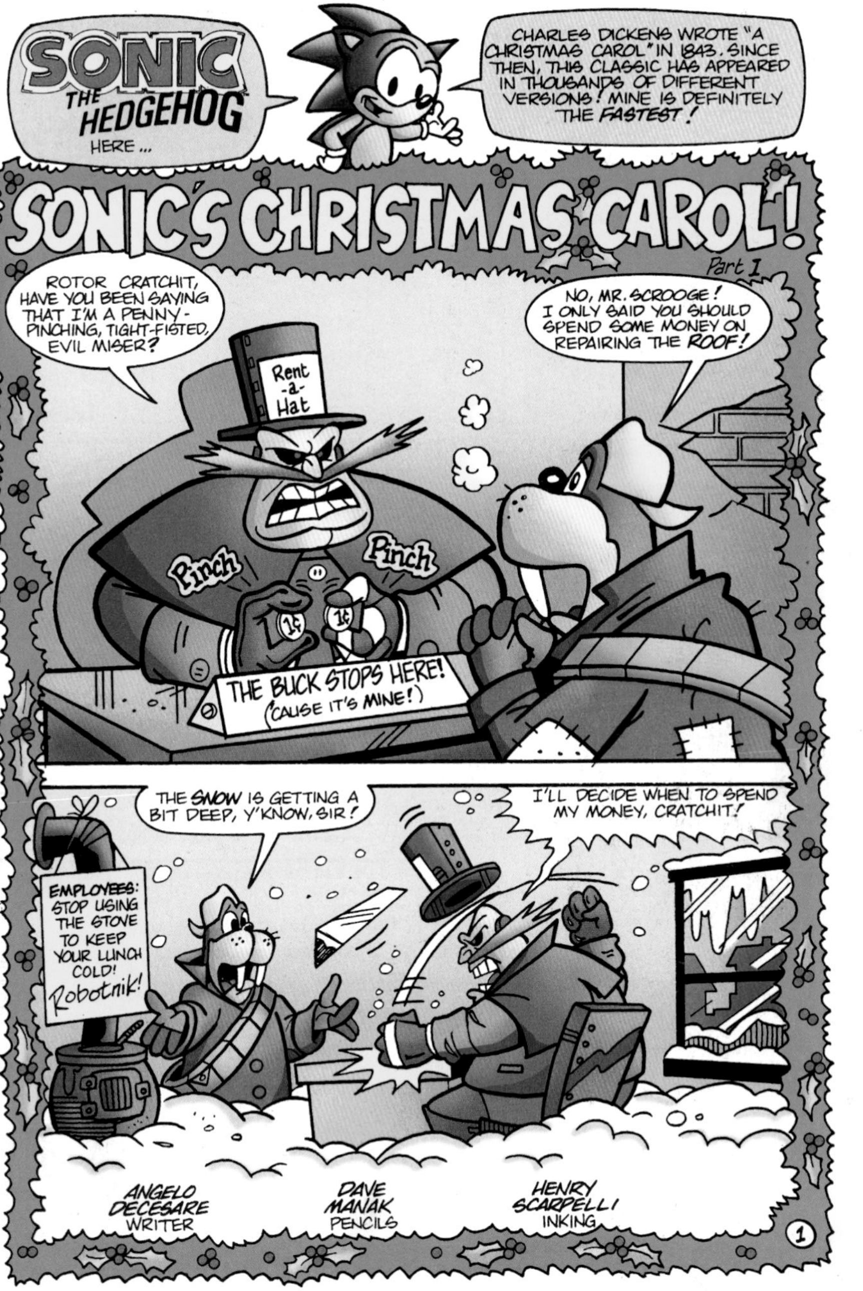

SONIC THE HEDGEHOG HERE...
CHARLES DICKENS WROTE "A CHRISTMAS CAROL" IN 1843. SINCE THEN, THIS CLASSIC HAS APPEARED IN THOUSANDS OF DIFFERENT VERSIONS! MINE IS DEFINITELY THE FASTEST!
SONIC'S CHRISTMAS CAROL!
Part 1
ROTOR CRATCHIT, HAVE YOU BEEN SAYING THAT I'M A PENNY-PINCHING, TIGHT-FISTED, EVIL MISER?
NO, MR. SCROOGE! I ONLY SAID YOU SHOULD SPEND SOME MONEY ON REPAIRING THE ROOF!
Rent -a- Hat
Pinch
Pinch
1¢
1¢
THE BUCK STOPS HERE! ('CAUSE IT'S MINE!)
THE SNOW IS GETTING A BIT DEEP, Y'KNOW, SIR!
I'LL DECIDE WHEN TO SPEND MY MONEY, CRATCHIT!
EMPLOYEES: STOP USING THE STOVE TO KEEP YOUR LUNCH COLD! Robotnik!
ANGELO DECESARE WRITER
DAVE MANAK PENCILS
HENRY SCARPELLI INKING
1

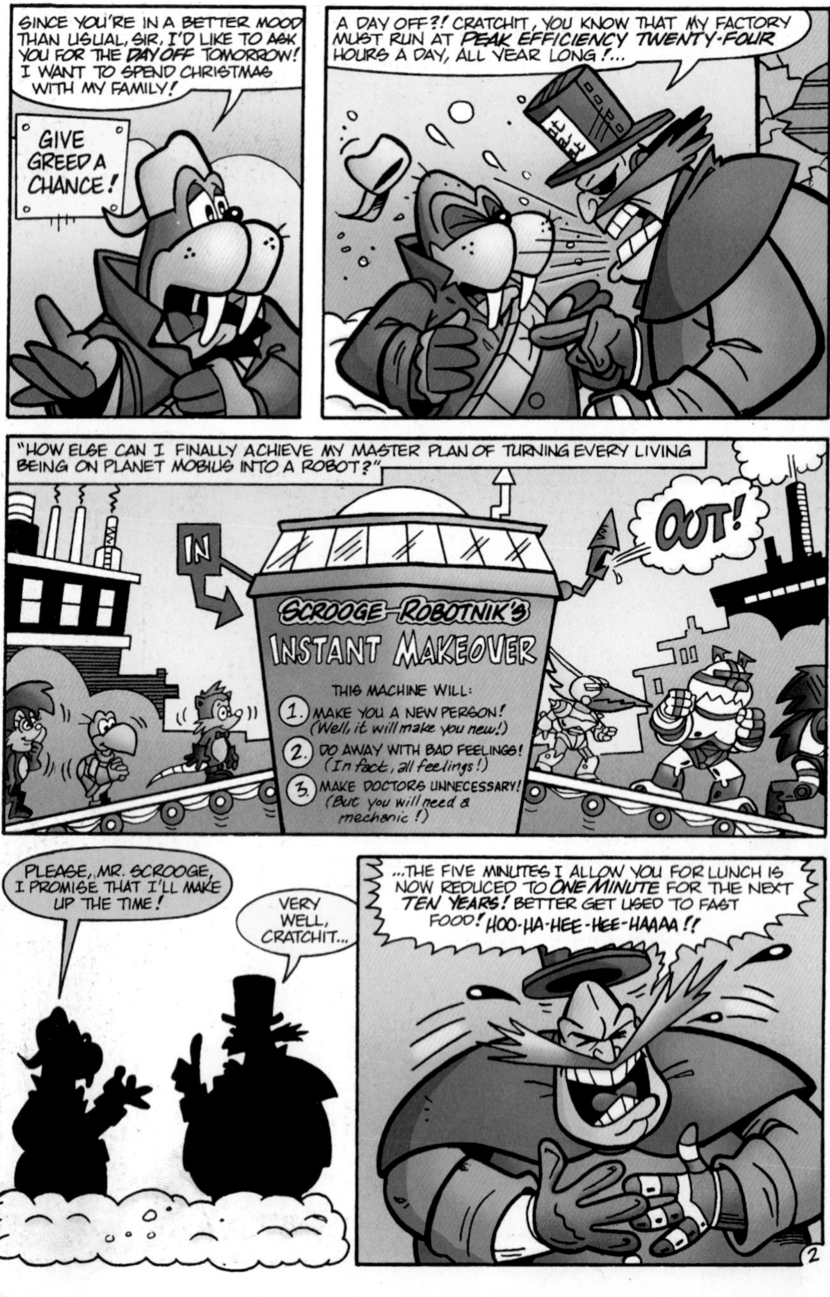
SINCE YOU'RE IN A BETTER MOOD THAN USUAL, SIR, I'D LIKE TO ASK YOU FOR THE DAY OFF TOMORROW! I WANT TO SPEND CHRISTMAS WITH MY FAMILY!
GIVE GREED A CHANCE!
A DAY OFF?! CRATCHIT, YOU KNOW THAT MY FACTORY MUST RUN AT PEAK EFFICIENCY TWENTY-FOUR HOURS A DAY, ALL YEAR LONG!...
"HOW ELSE CAN I FINALLY ACHIEVE MY MASTER PLAN OF TURNING EVERY LIVING BEING ON PLANET MOBIUS INTO A ROBOT?"
IN
OUT!
SCROOGE-ROBOTNIK'S
INSTANT MAKEOVER
THIS MACHINE WILL:
1. MAKE YOU A NEW PERSON! (Well, it will make you new!)
2. DO AWAY WITH BAD FEELINGS! (In fact, all feelings!)
3. MAKE DOCTORS UNNECESSARY! (But you will need a mechanic!)
PLEASE, MR. SCROOGE, I PROMISE THAT I'LL MAKE UP THE TIME!
VERY WELL, CRATCHIT...
...THE FIVE MINUTES I ALLOW YOU FOR LUNCH IS NOW REDUCED TO ONE MINUTE FOR THE NEXT TEN YEARS! BETTER GET USED TO FAST FOOD! HOO-HA-HEE-HEE-HAAAA!!

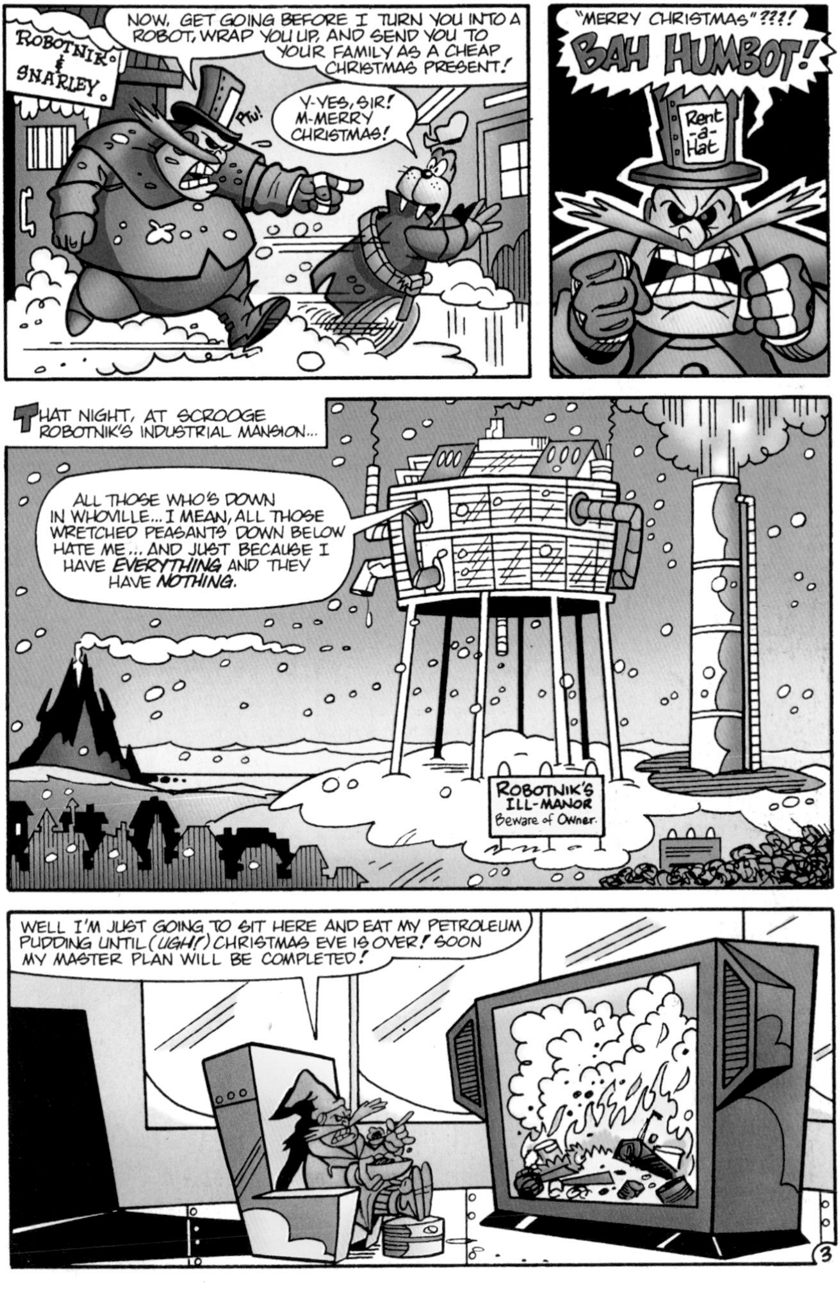
ROBOTNIK & SNARLEY
NOW, GET GOING BEFORE I TURN YOU INTO A ROBOT, WRAP YOU UP, AND SEND YOU TO YOUR FAMILY AS A CHEAP CHRISTMAS PRESENT!
PTU!
Y-YES, SIR! M-MERRY CHRISTMAS!
"MERRY CHRISTMAS"???!
BAH HUMBOT!
Rent -a- Hat
THAT NIGHT, AT SCROOGE ROBOTNIK'S INDUSTRIAL MANSION...
ALL THOSE WHO'S DOWN IN WHOVILLE... I MEAN, ALL THOSE WRETCHED PEASANTS DOWN BELOW HATE ME... AND JUST BECAUSE I HAVE EVERYTHING AND THEY HAVE NOTHING.
ROBOTNIK'S ILL-MANOR Beware of Owner.
WELL I'M JUST GOING TO SIT HERE AND EAT MY PETROLEUM PUDDING UNTIL (UGH!) CHRISTMAS EVE IS OVER! SOON MY MASTER PLAN WILL BE COMPLETED!

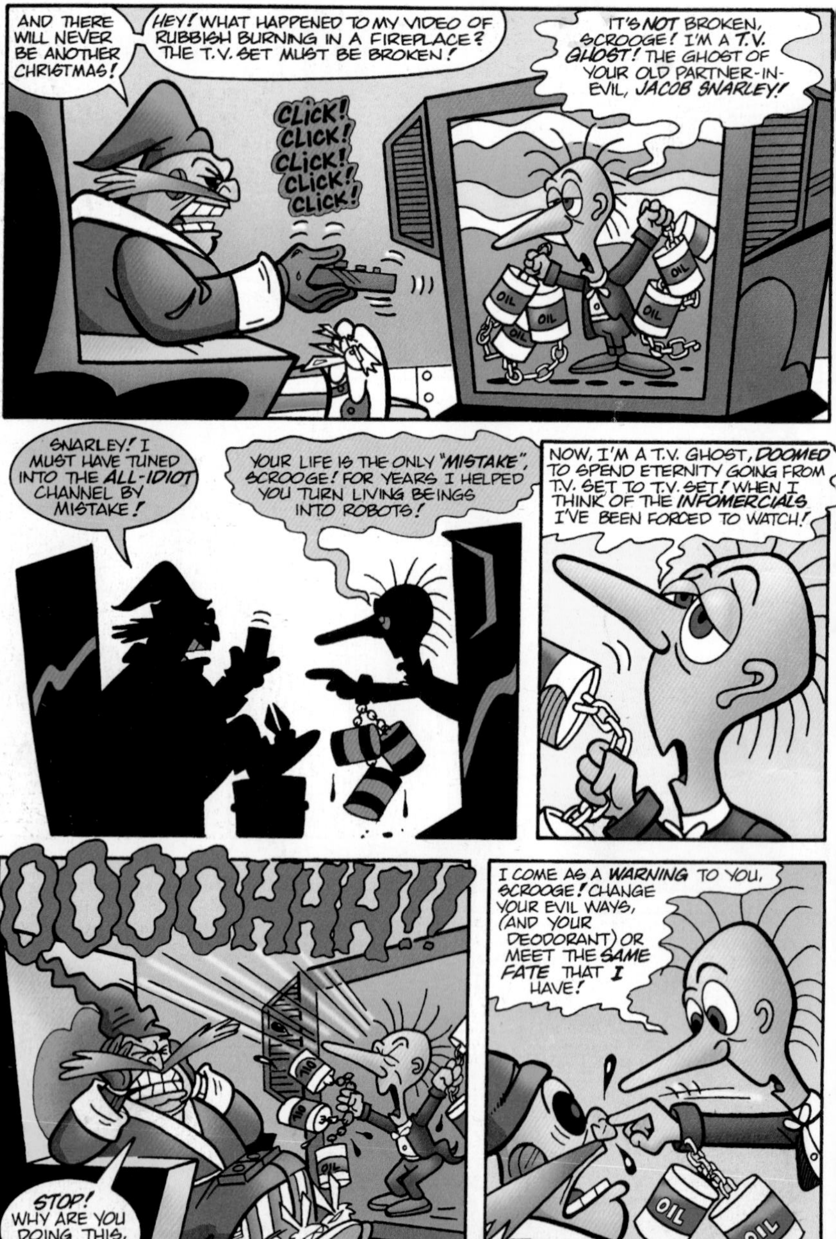
AND THERE WILL NEVER BE ANOTHER CHRISTMAS!
HEY! WHAT HAPPENED TO MY VIDEO OF RUBBISH BURNING IN A FIREPLACE? THE T.V. SET MUST BE BROKEN!
CLICK! CLICK! CLICK! CLICK! CLICK!
IT'S NOT BROKEN, SCROOGE! I'M A T.V. GHOST! THE GHOST OF YOUR OLD PARTNER-IN-EVIL, JACOB SNARLEY!
OIL
SNARLEY! I MUST HAVE TUNED INTO THE ALL-IDIOT CHANNEL BY MISTAKE!
YOUR LIFE IS THE ONLY "MISTAKE", SCROOGE! FOR YEARS I HELPED YOU TURN LIVING BEINGS INTO ROBOTS!
NOW, I'M A T.V. GHOST, DOOMED TO SPEND ETERNITY GOING FROM T.V. SET TO T.V. SET! WHEN I THINK OF THE INFOMERCIALS I'VE BEEN FORCED TO WATCH!
OOOOHHH!!
STOP! WHY ARE YOU DOING THIS, SNARLEY?
I COME AS A WARNING TO YOU, SCROOGE! CHANGE YOUR EVIL WAYS, (AND YOUR DEODORANT) OR MEET THE SAME FATE THAT I HAVE!
OIL
OIL

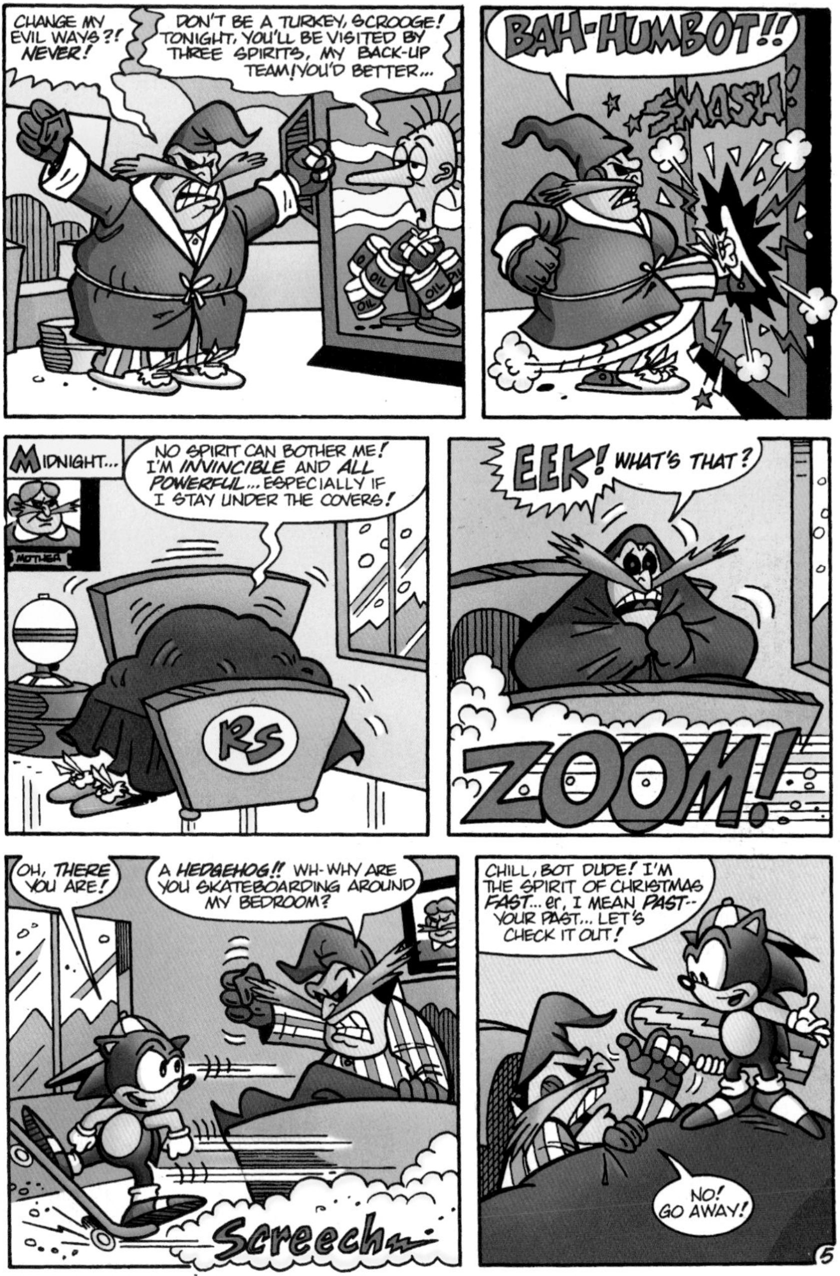
CHANGE MY EVIL WAYS?! NEVER!
DON'T BE A TURKEY, SCROOGE! TONIGHT, YOU'LL BE VISITED BY THREE SPIRITS, MY BACK-UP TEAM! YOU'D BETTER...
OIL
BAH-HUMBOT!!
SMASH!
MIDNIGHT...
NO SPIRIT CAN BOTHER ME! I'M INVINCIBLE AND ALL POWERFUL... ESPECIALLY IF I STAY UNDER THE COVERS!
MOTHER
RS
EEK! WHAT'S THAT?
ZOOM!
OH, THERE YOU ARE!
A HEDGEHOG!! WH-WHY ARE YOU SKATEBOARDING AROUND MY BEDROOM?
Screech
CHILL, BOT DUDE! I'M THE SPIRIT OF CHRISTMAS FAST... er, I MEAN PAST-- YOUR PAST... LET'S CHECK IT OUT!
NO! GO AWAY!

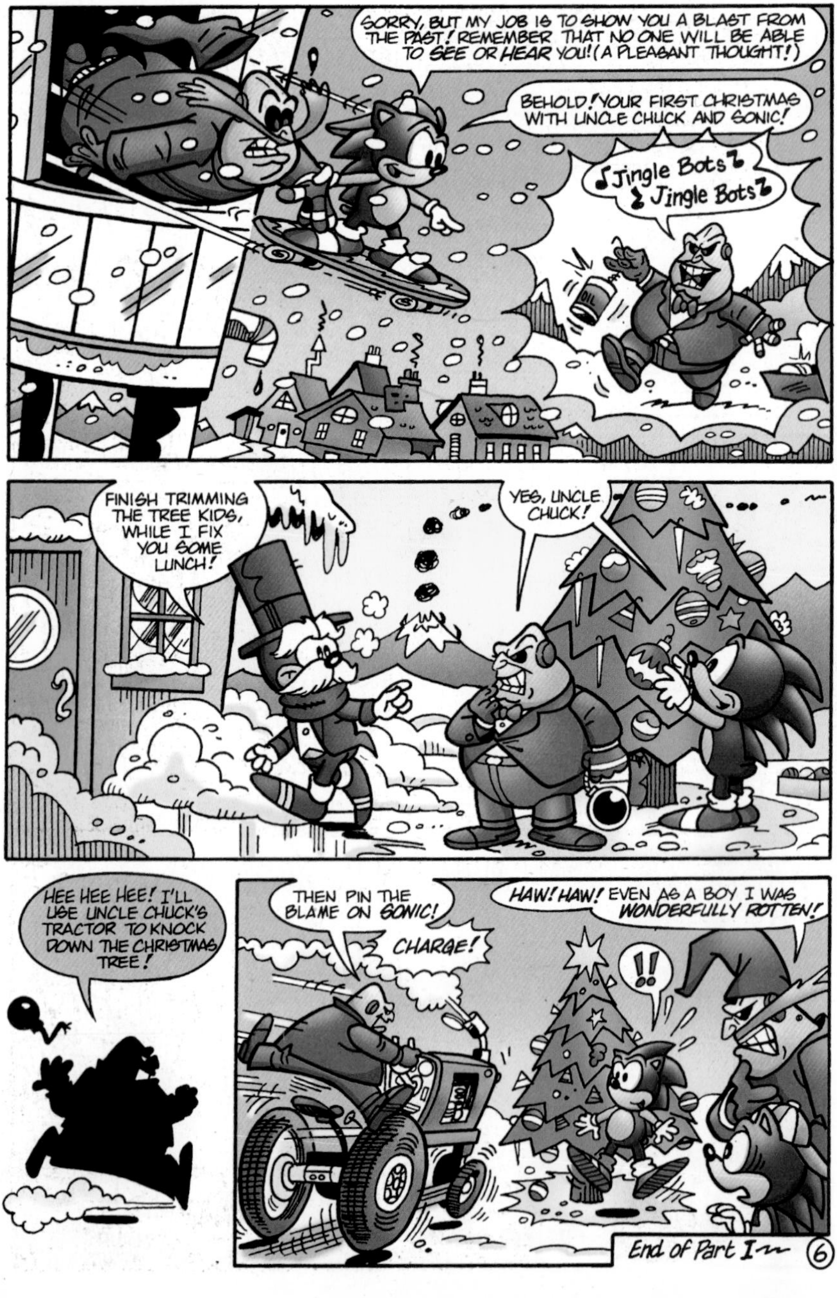
SORRY, BUT MY JOB IS TO SHOW YOU A BLAST FROM THE PAST! REMEMBER THAT NO ONE WILL BE ABLE TO SEE OR HEAR YOU! (A PLEASANT THOUGHT!)
BEHOLD! YOUR FIRST CHRISTMAS WITH UNCLE CHUCK AND SONIC!
Jingle Bots
Jingle Bots
OIL
FINISH TRIMMING THE TREE KIDS, WHILE I FIX YOU SOME LUNCH!
YES, UNCLE CHUCK!
HEE HEE HEE! I'LL USE UNCLE CHUCK'S TRACTOR TO KNOCK DOWN THE CHRISTMAS TREE!
THEN PIN THE BLAME ON SONIC!
CHARGE!
HAW! HAW! EVEN AS A BOY I WAS WONDERFULLY ROTTEN!
!!
End of Part I

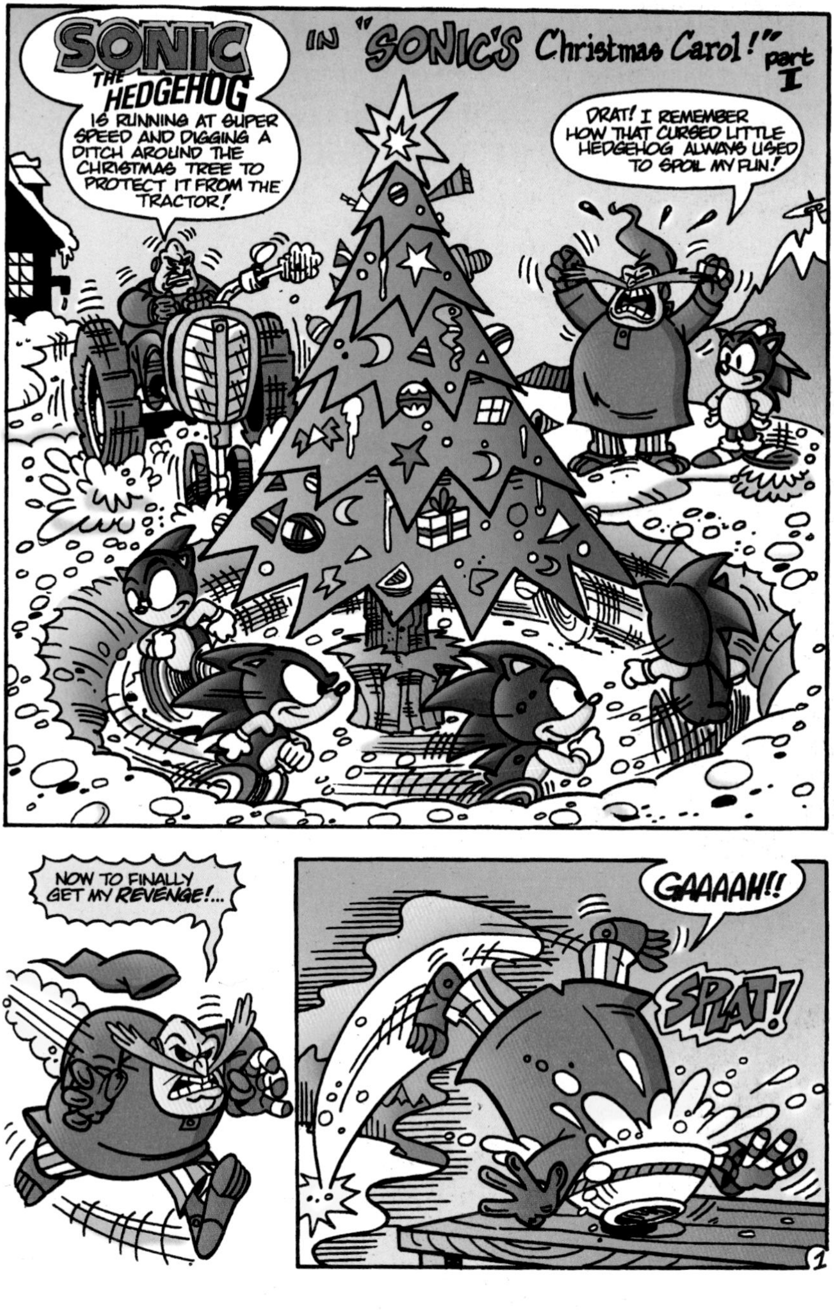
SONIC THE HEDGEHOG IN "SONIC'S Christmas Carol!" part I
SONIC THE HEDGEHOG IS RUNNING AT SUPER SPEED AND DIGGING A DITCH AROUND THE CHRISTMAS TREE TO PROTECT IT FROM THE TRACTOR!
DRAT! I REMEMBER HOW THAT CURSED LITTLE HEDGEHOG ALWAYS USED TO SPOIL MY FUN!
NOW TO FINALLY GET MY REVENGE!...
GAAAAH!!
SPLAT!

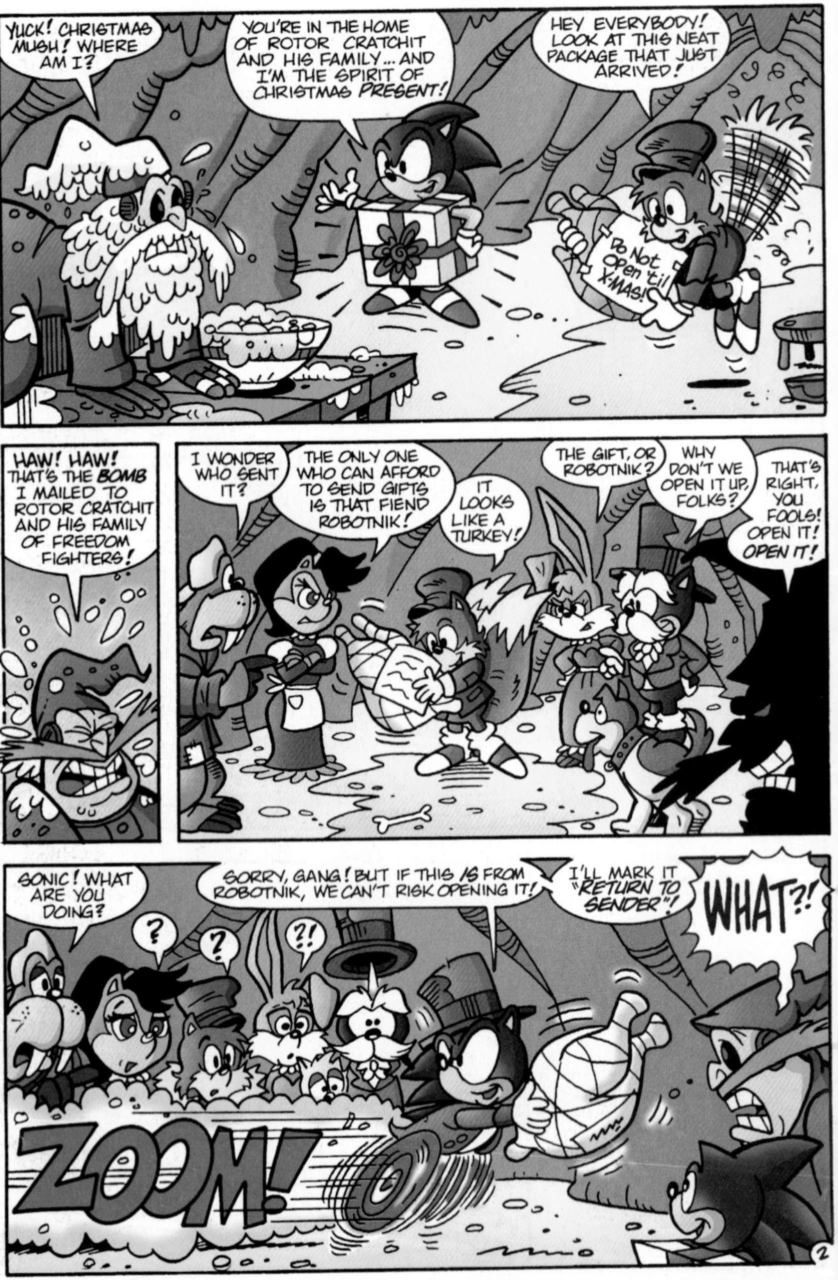

YUCK! CHRISTMAS MUSH! WHERE AM I?
YOU'RE IN THE HOME OF ROTOR CRATCHIT AND HIS FAMILY... AND I'M THE SPIRIT OF CHRISTMAS PRESENT!
HEY EVERYBODY! LOOK AT THIS NEAT PACKAGE THAT JUST ARRIVED!
Do Not Open 'til X-MAS!
HAW! HAW! THAT'S THE BOMB I MAILED TO ROTOR CRATCHIT AND HIS FAMILY OF FREEDOM FIGHTERS!
I WONDER WHO SENT IT?
THE ONLY ONE WHO CAN AFFORD TO SEND GIFTS IS THAT FIEND ROBOTNIK!
IT LOOKS LIKE A TURKEY!
THE GIFT, OR ROBOTNIK?
WHY DON'T WE OPEN IT UP, FOLKS?
THAT'S RIGHT, YOU FOOLS! OPEN IT! OPEN IT!
SONIC! WHAT ARE YOU DOING?
?
?
?!
SORRY, GANG! BUT IF THIS IS FROM ROBOTNIK, WE CAN'T RISK OPENING IT!
I'LL MARK IT "RETURN TO SENDER"!
WHAT?!
ZOOM!

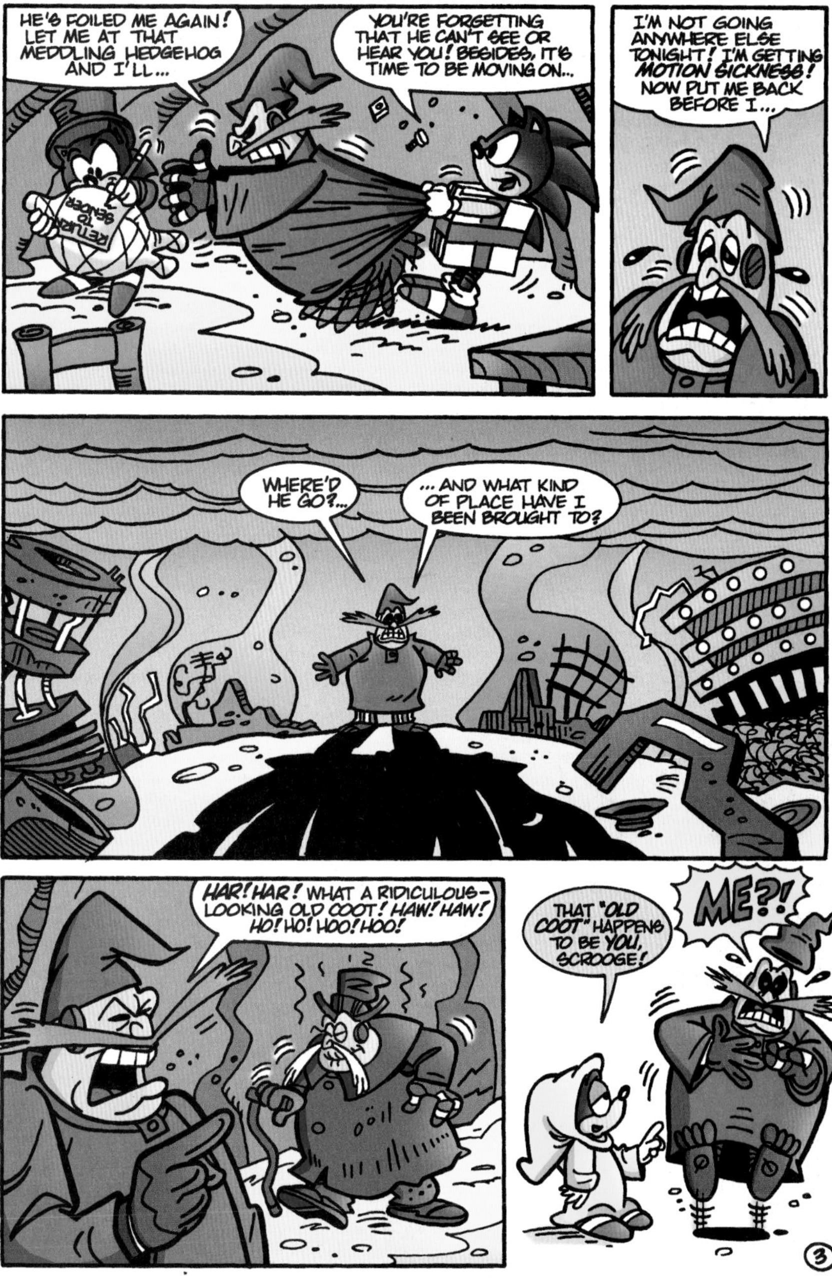
HE'S FOILED ME AGAIN! LET ME AT THAT MEDDLING HEDGEHOG AND I'LL...
YOU'RE FORGETTING THAT HE CAN'T SEE OR HEAR YOU! BESIDES, IT'S TIME TO BE MOVING ON...
RETURN TO SENDER
I'M NOT GOING ANYWHERE ELSE TONIGHT! I'M GETTING MOTION SICKNESS! NOW PUT ME BACK BEFORE I...
WHERE'D HE GO?...
...AND WHAT KIND OF PLACE HAVE I BEEN BROUGHT TO?
HAR! HAR! WHAT A RIDICULOUS-LOOKING OLD COOT! HAW! HAW! HO! HO! HOO! HOO!
THAT "OLD COOT" HAPPENS TO BE YOU, SCROOGE!
ME?!

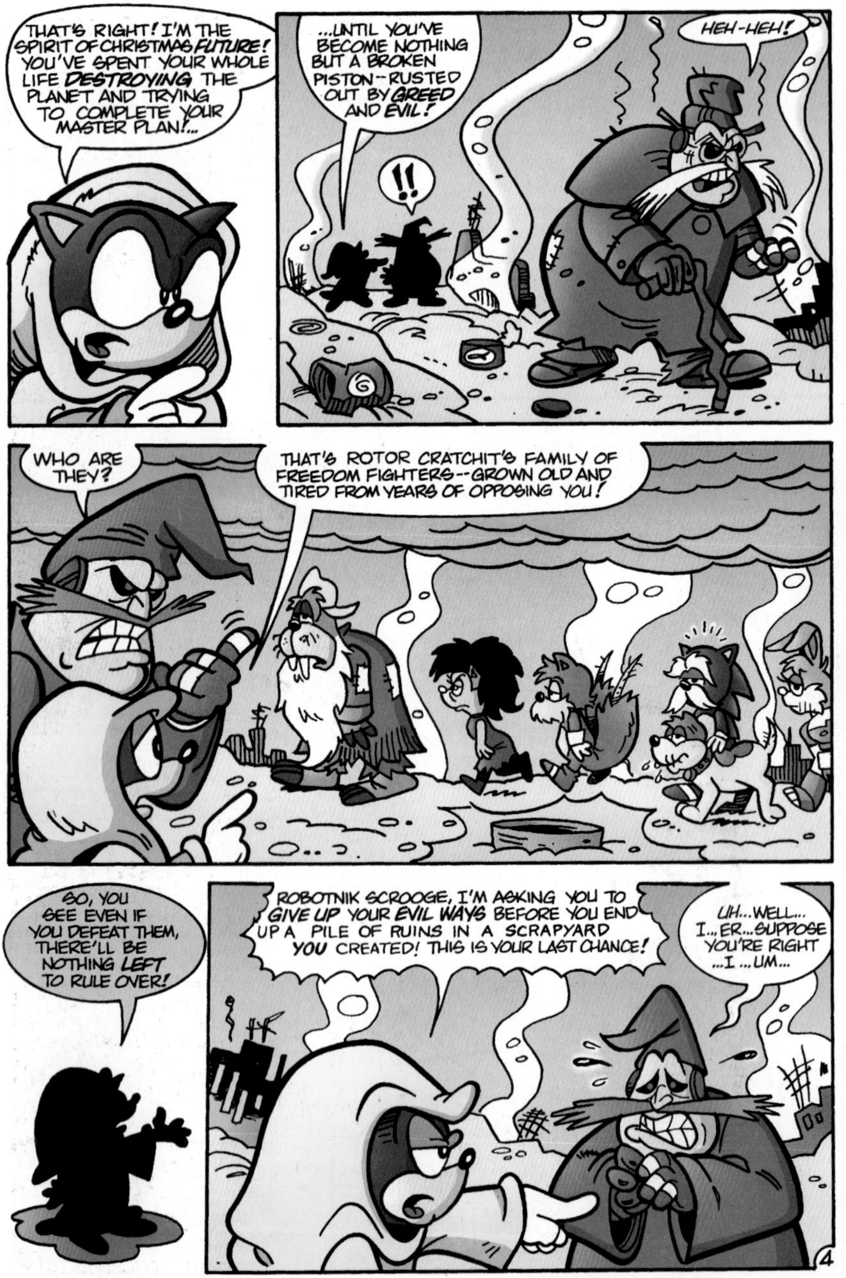

THAT'S RIGHT! I'M THE SPIRIT OF CHRISTMAS FUTURE! YOU'VE SPENT YOUR WHOLE LIFE DESTROYING THE PLANET AND TRYING TO COMPLETE YOUR MASTER PLAN!...
...UNTIL YOU'VE BECOME NOTHING BUT A BROKEN PISTON--RUSTED OUT BY GREED AND EVIL!
!!
HEH-HEH!
WHO ARE THEY?
THAT'S ROTOR CRATCHIT'S FAMILY OF FREEDOM FIGHTERS--GROWN OLD AND TIRED FROM YEARS OF OPPOSING YOU!
SO, YOU SEE EVEN IF YOU DEFEAT THEM, THERE'LL BE NOTHING LEFT TO RULE OVER!
ROBOTNIK SCROOGE, I'M ASKING YOU TO GIVE UP YOUR EVIL WAYS BEFORE YOU END UP A PILE OF RUINS IN A SCRAPYARD YOU CREATED! THIS IS YOUR LAST CHANCE!
UH...WELL... I...ER...SUPPOSE YOU'RE RIGHT ...I ...UM...

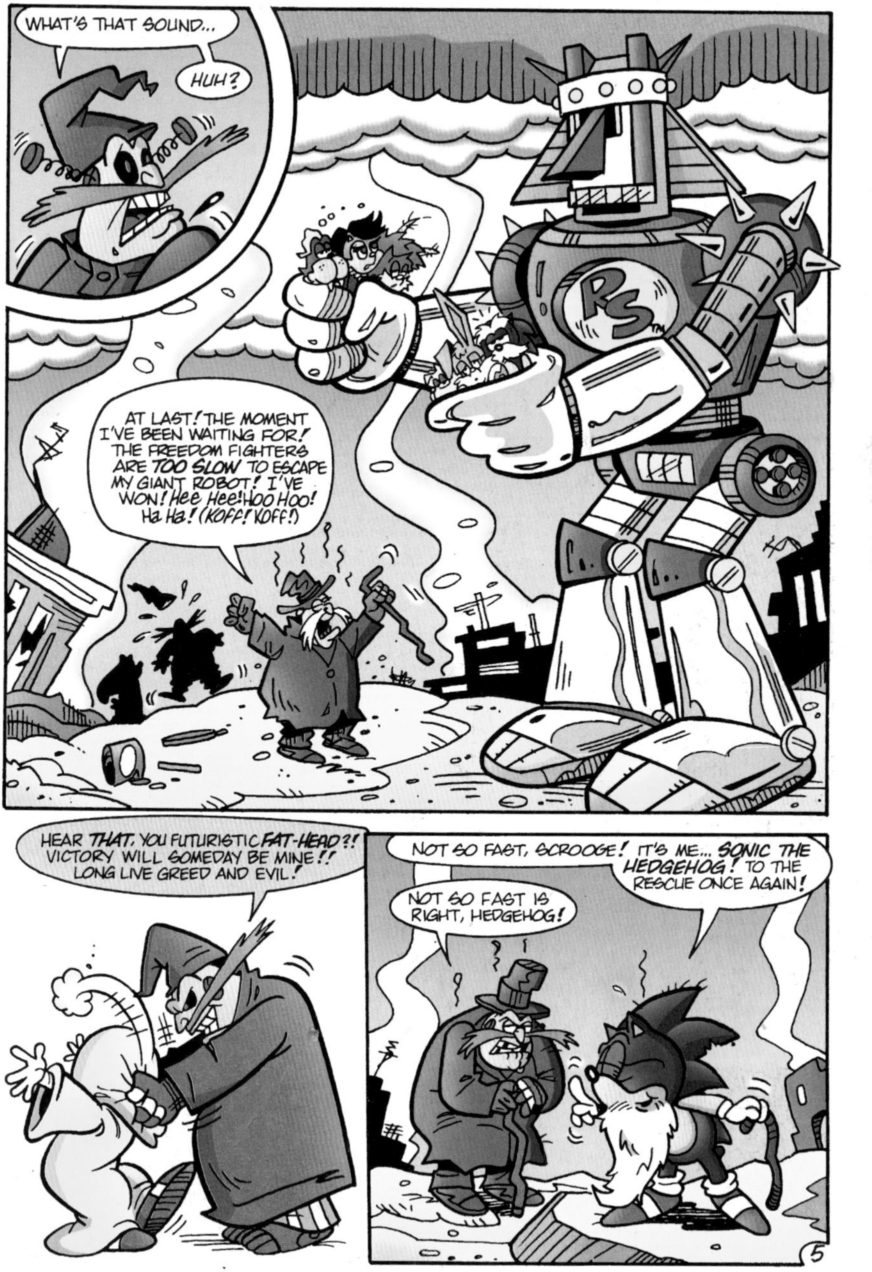

WHAT'S THAT SOUND...
HUH?
AT LAST! THE MOMENT I'VE BEEN WAITING FOR! THE FREEDOM FIGHTERS ARE TOO SLOW TO ESCAPE MY GIANT ROBOT! I'VE WON! Hee Hee! Hoo Hoo! Ha Ha! (KOFF! KOFF!)
HEAR THAT, YOU FUTURISTIC FAT-HEAD?! VICTORY WILL SOMEDAY BE MINE!! LONG LIVE GREED AND EVIL!
NOT SO FAST, SCROOGE! IT'S ME... SONIC THE HEDGEHOG! TO THE RESCUE ONCE AGAIN!
NOT SO FAST IS RIGHT, HEDGEHOG!

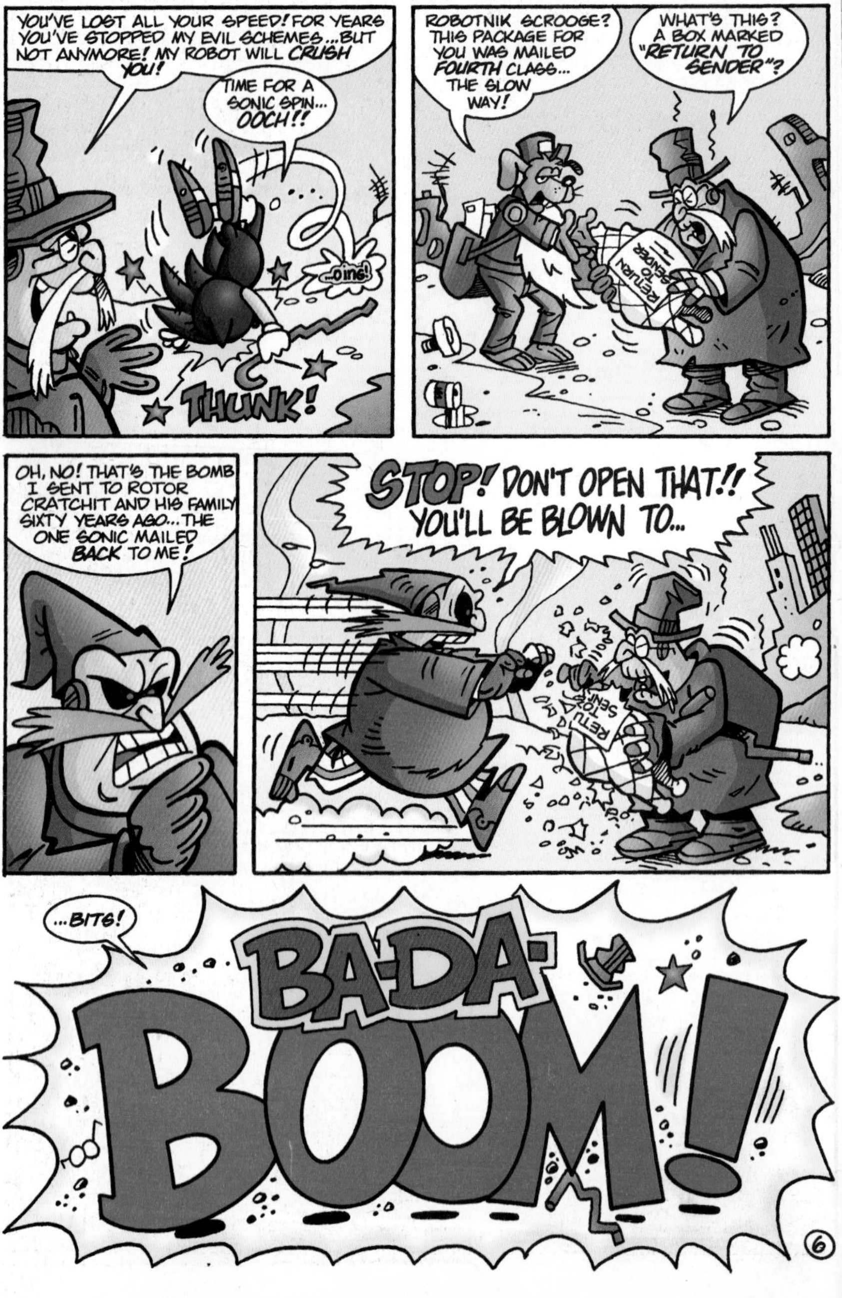
YOU'VE LOST ALL YOUR SPEED! FOR YEARS YOU'VE STOPPED MY EVIL SCHEMES...BUT NOT ANYMORE! MY ROBOT WILL CRUSH YOU!
TIME FOR A SONIC SPIN... OOCH!!
...oing!
THUNK!
ROBOTNIK SCROOGE? THIS PACKAGE FOR YOU WAS MAILED FOURTH CLASS... THE SLOW WAY!
WHAT'S THIS? A BOX MARKED "RETURN TO SENDER"?
RETURN TO SENDER
OH, NO! THAT'S THE BOMB I SENT TO ROTOR CRATCHIT AND HIS FAMILY SIXTY YEARS AGO...THE ONE SONIC MAILED BACK TO ME!
STOP! DON'T OPEN THAT!! YOU'LL BE BLOWN TO...
...BITS!
BA-DA-BOOM!
6

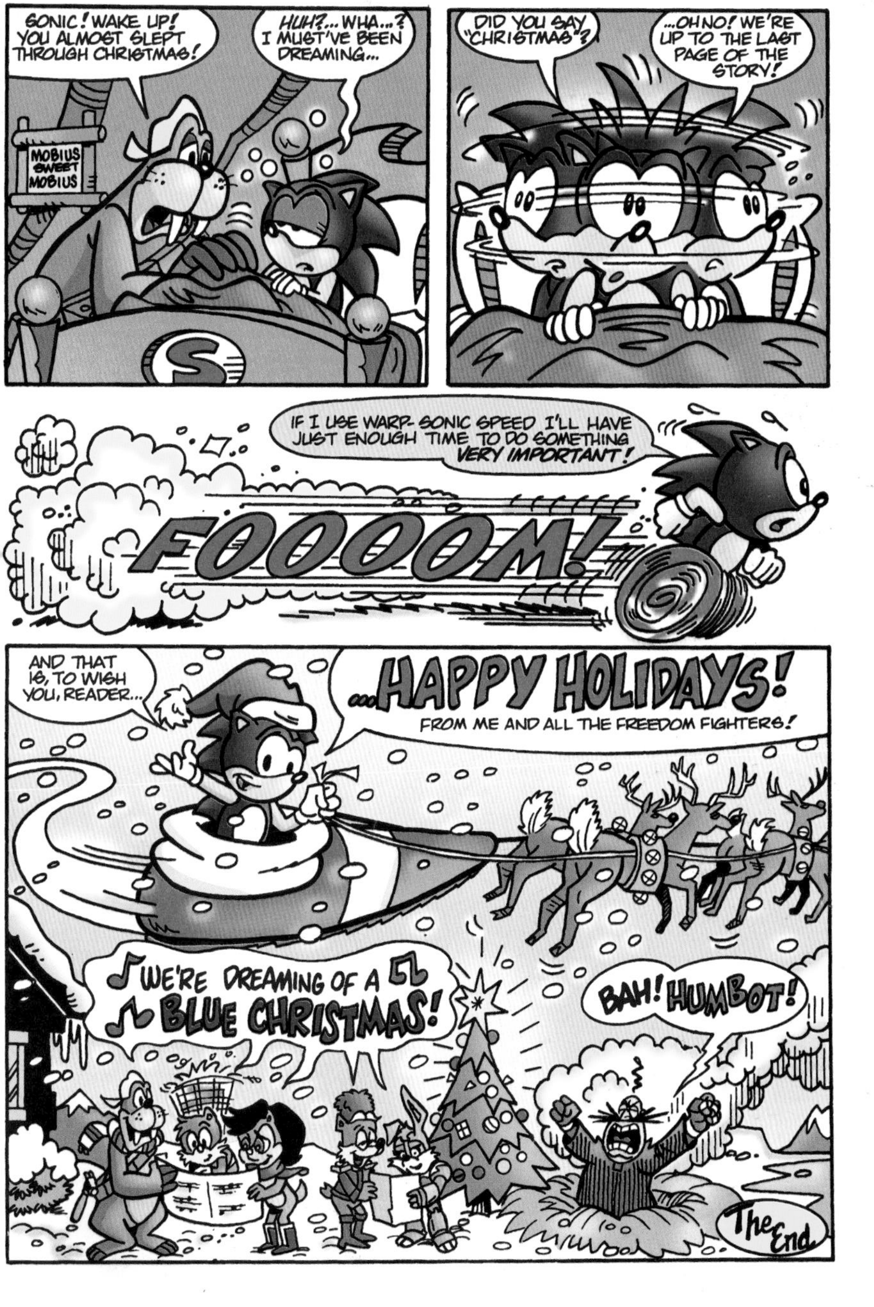
SONIC! WAKE UP! YOU ALMOST SLEPT THROUGH CHRISTMAS!
HUH?... WHA...? I MUST'VE BEEN DREAMING...
MOBIUS SWEET MOBIUS
DID YOU SAY "CHRISTMAS"?
...OH NO! WE'RE UP TO THE LAST PAGE OF THE STORY!
IF I USE WARP-SONIC SPEED I'LL HAVE JUST ENOUGH TIME TO DO SOMETHING VERY IMPORTANT!
FOOOOM!
AND THAT IS, TO WISH YOU, READER...
...HAPPY HOLIDAYS! FROM ME AND ALL THE FREEDOM FIGHTERS!
WE'RE DREAMING OF A BLUE CHRISTMAS!
BAH! HUMBOT!
The End

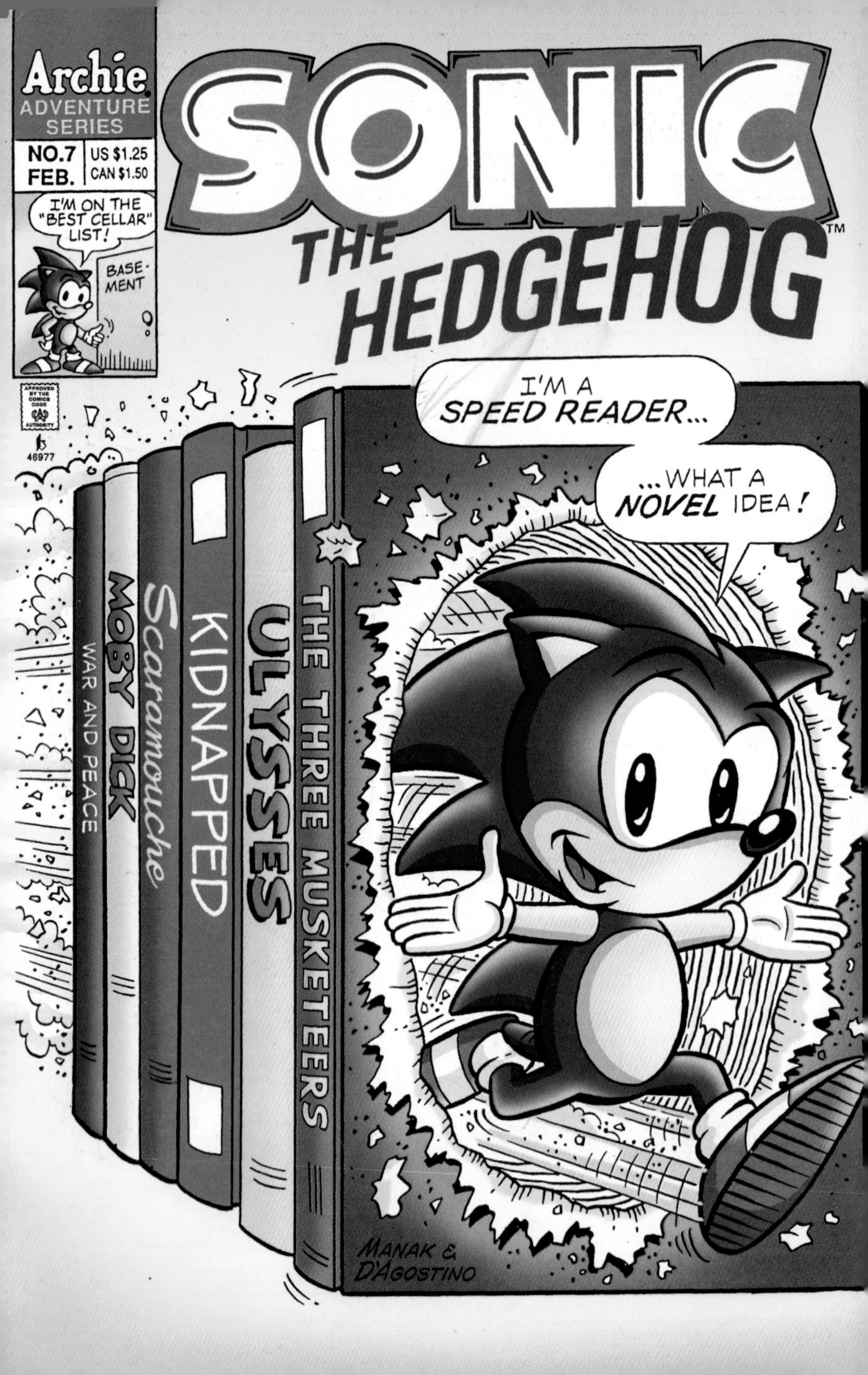
Archie ADVENTURE SERIES
NO.7 FEB.
US $1.25 CAN $1.50
I'M ON THE "BEST CELLAR" LIST!
BASE-MENT
SONIC THE HEDGEHOG™
APPROVED BY THE COMICS CODE AUTHORITY
46977
I'M A SPEED READER...
...WHAT A NOVEL IDEA!
WAR AND PEACE
MOBY DICK
Scaramouche
KIDNAPPED
ULYSSES
THE THREE MUSKETEERS
MANAK & D'AGOSTINO

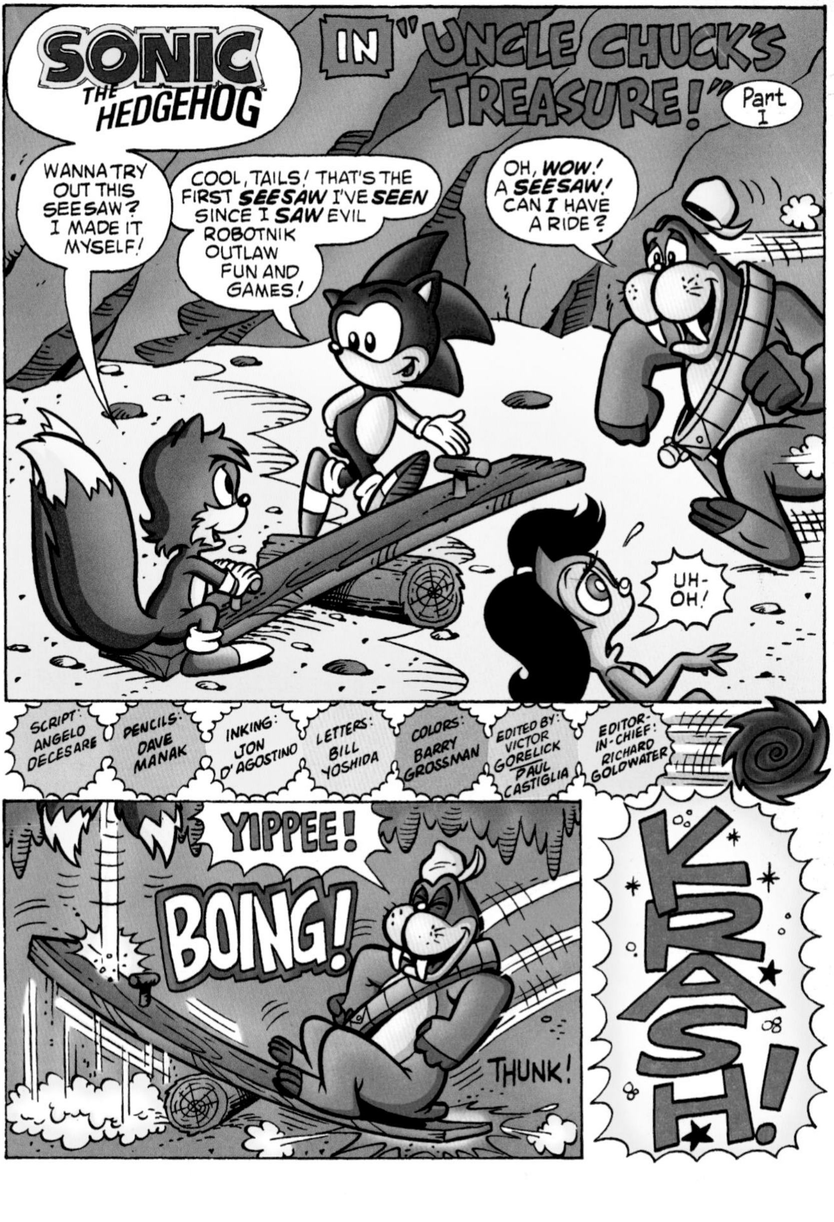
SONIC THE HEDGEHOG
IN "UNCLE CHUCK'S TREASURE!" Part I
WANNA TRY OUT THIS SEESAW? I MADE IT MYSELF!
COOL, TAILS! THAT'S THE FIRST SEESAW I'VE SEEN SINCE I SAW EVIL ROBOTNIK OUTLAW FUN AND GAMES!
OH, WOW! A SEESAW! CAN I HAVE A RIDE?
UH-OH!
SCRIPT: ANGELO DECESARE
PENCILS: DAVE MANAK
INKING: JON D'AGOSTINO
LETTERS: BILL YOSHIDA
COLORS: BARRY GROSSMAN
EDITED BY: VICTOR GORELICK PAUL CASTIGLIA
EDITOR-IN-CHIEF: RICHARD GOLDWATER
YIPPEE!
BOING!
THUNK!
KRASH!

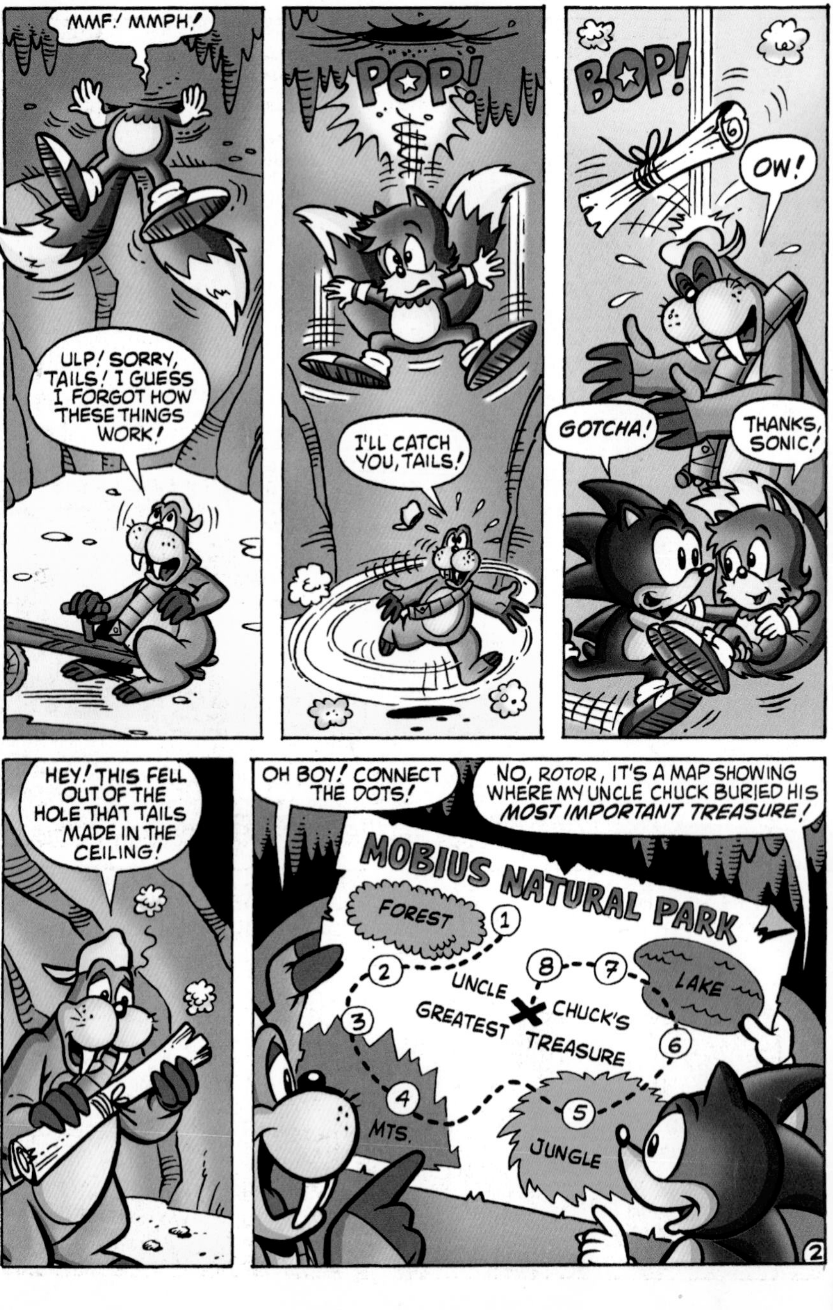
MMF! MMPH!
ULP! SORRY, TAILS! I GUESS I FORGOT HOW THESE THINGS WORK!
POP!
I'LL CATCH YOU, TAILS!
BOP!
OW!
GOTCHA!
THANKS, SONIC!
HEY! THIS FELL OUT OF THE HOLE THAT TAILS MADE IN THE CEILING!
OH BOY! CONNECT THE DOTS!
NO, ROTOR, IT'S A MAP SHOWING WHERE MY UNCLE CHUCK BURIED HIS MOST IMPORTANT TREASURE!
MOBIUS NATURAL PARK
FOREST
LAKE
UNCLE CHUCK'S GREATEST TREASURE
MTS.
JUNGLE
2

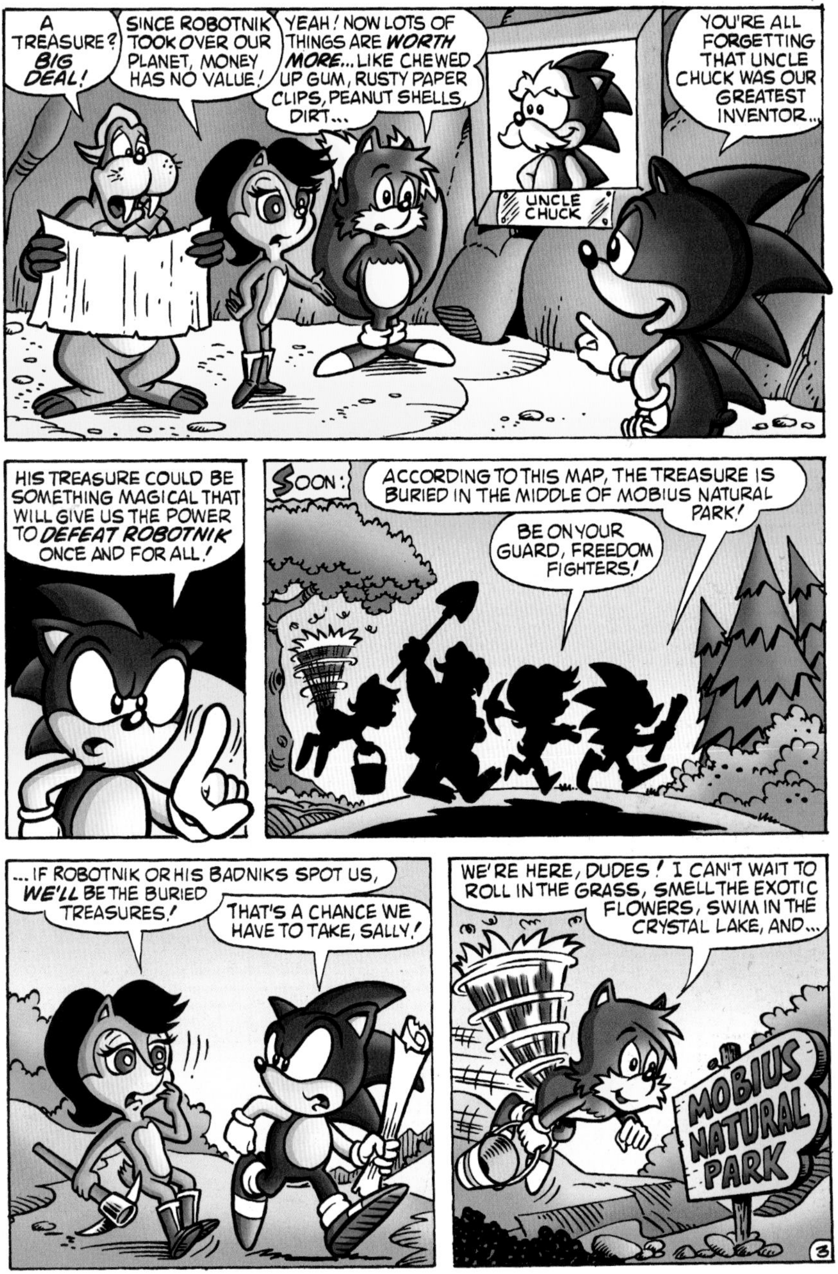
A TREASURE? BIG DEAL!
SINCE ROBOTNIK TOOK OVER OUR PLANET, MONEY HAS NO VALUE!
YEAH! NOW LOTS OF THINGS ARE WORTH MORE... LIKE CHEWED UP GUM, RUSTY PAPER CLIPS, PEANUT SHELLS, DIRT...
UNCLE CHUCK
YOU'RE ALL FORGETTING THAT UNCLE CHUCK WAS OUR GREATEST INVENTOR...
HIS TREASURE COULD BE SOMETHING MAGICAL THAT WILL GIVE US THE POWER TO DEFEAT ROBOTNIK ONCE AND FOR ALL!
SOON:
ACCORDING TO THIS MAP, THE TREASURE IS BURIED IN THE MIDDLE OF MOBIUS NATURAL PARK!
BE ON YOUR GUARD, FREEDOM FIGHTERS!
...IF ROBOTNIK OR HIS BADNIKS SPOT US, WE'LL BE THE BURIED TREASURES!
THAT'S A CHANCE WE HAVE TO TAKE, SALLY!
WE'RE HERE, DUDES! I CAN'T WAIT TO ROLL IN THE GRASS, SMELL THE EXOTIC FLOWERS, SWIM IN THE CRYSTAL LAKE, AND...
MOBIUS NATURAL PARK
3

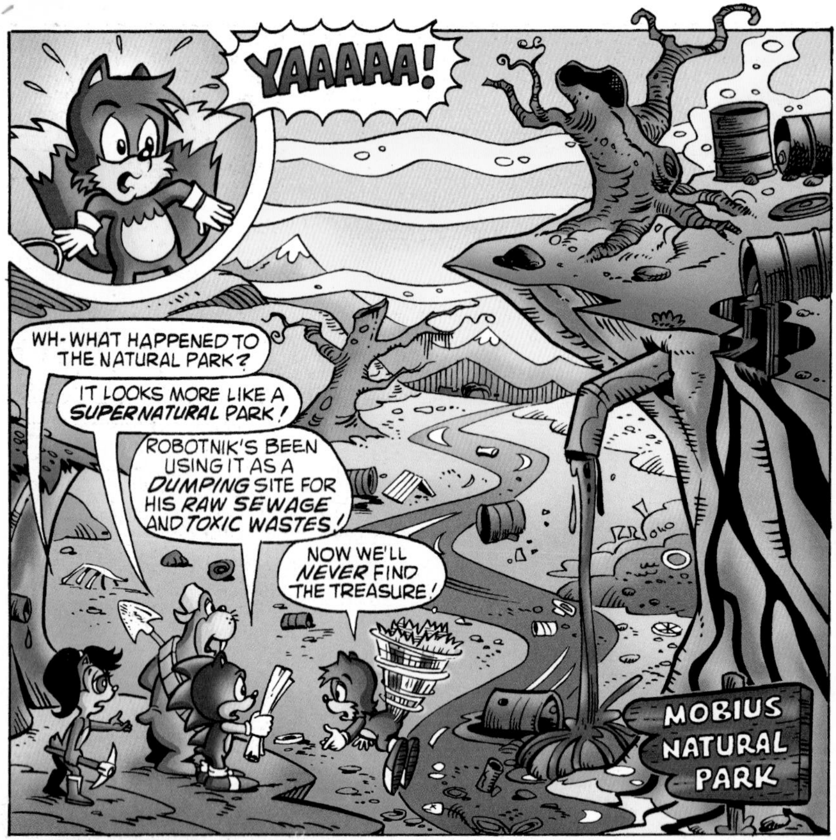
YAAAAA!
WH-WHAT HAPPENED TO THE NATURAL PARK?
IT LOOKS MORE LIKE A *SUPERNATURAL* PARK!
ROBOTNIK'S BEEN USING IT AS A *DUMPING* SITE FOR HIS *RAW SEWAGE* AND *TOXIC WASTES*!
NOW WE'LL *NEVER* FIND THE TREASURE!
MOBIUS NATURAL PARK

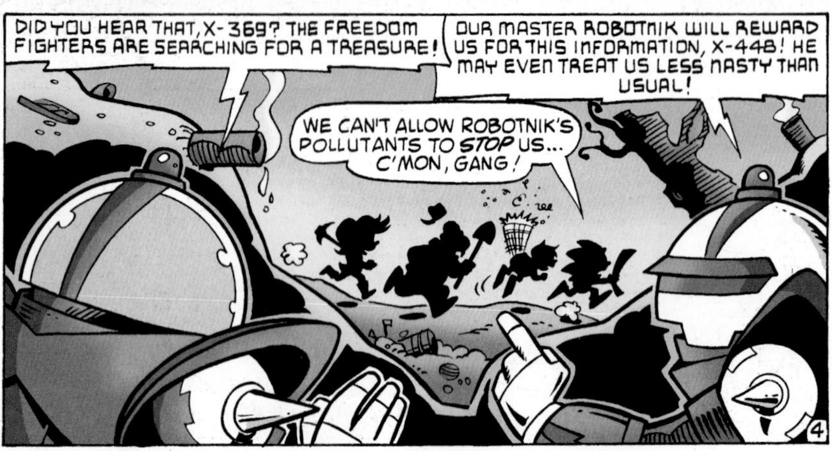
DID YOU HEAR THAT, X-369? THE FREEDOM FIGHTERS ARE SEARCHING FOR A TREASURE!
OUR MASTER ROBOTNIK WILL REWARD US FOR THIS INFORMATION, X-448! HE MAY EVEN TREAT US LESS NASTY THAN USUAL!
WE CAN'T ALLOW ROBOTNIK'S POLLUTANTS TO *STOP* US... C'MON, GANG!

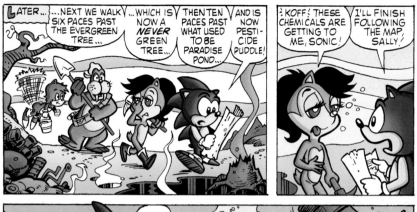

LATER... ...NEXT WE WALK SIX PACES PAST THE EVERGREEN TREE...

...WHICH IS NOW A *NEVER* GREEN TREE...

THEN TEN PACES PAST WHAT USED TO BE PARADISE POND...

AND IS NOW PESTICIDE PUDDLE!

KOFF! THESE CHEMICALS ARE GETTING TO ME, SONIC!

I'LL FINISH FOLLOWING THE MAP, SALLY!

AT...

...SUPER...

...SONIC...

...SPEED!

ZOOM!

ZOOM!

ZOOM!

SCREEEEECH!

MOBIUS NATURAL PARK

ALL *RIGHT*, THE "X" IS STILL HERE! LET'S START DIGGING!

CHECK IT OUT, GUYS!

A SINGLE FLOWER MANAGED TO SURVIVE THE POLLUTION!

!!

BLAM!

5

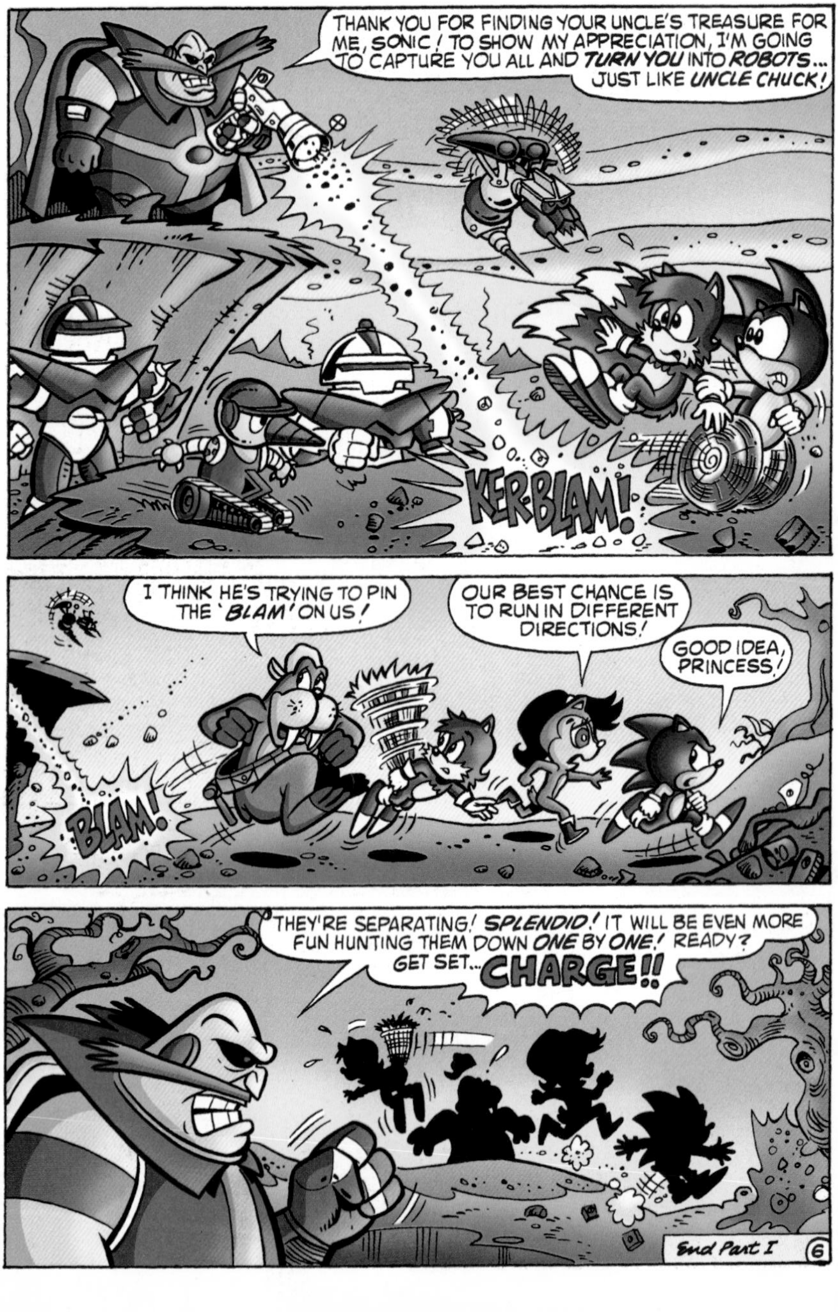
THANK YOU FOR FINDING YOUR UNCLE'S TREASURE FOR ME, SONIC! TO SHOW MY APPRECIATION, I'M GOING TO CAPTURE YOU ALL AND TURN YOU INTO ROBOTS... JUST LIKE UNCLE CHUCK!
KER-BLAM!
I THINK HE'S TRYING TO PIN THE 'BLAM' ON US!
OUR BEST CHANCE IS TO RUN IN DIFFERENT DIRECTIONS!
GOOD IDEA, PRINCESS!
BLAM!
THEY'RE SEPARATING! SPLENDID! IT WILL BE EVEN MORE FUN HUNTING THEM DOWN ONE BY ONE! READY? GET SET... CHARGE!!
End Part I
6

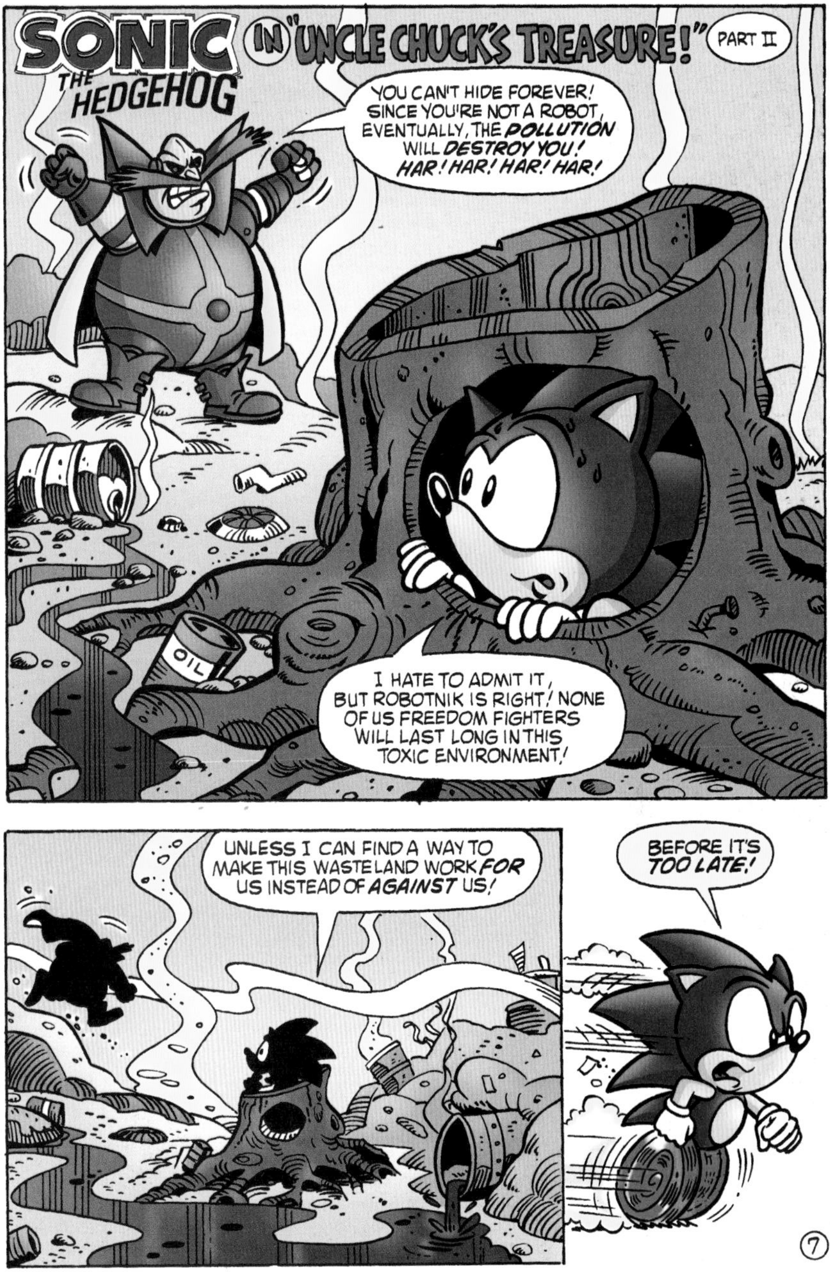
SONIC THE HEDGEHOG IN "UNCLE CHUCK'S TREASURE!" PART II
YOU CAN'T HIDE FOREVER! SINCE YOU'RE NOT A ROBOT, EVENTUALLY, THE POLLUTION WILL DESTROY YOU! HAR! HAR! HAR! HAR!
OIL
I HATE TO ADMIT IT, BUT ROBOTNIK IS RIGHT! NONE OF US FREEDOM FIGHTERS WILL LAST LONG IN THIS TOXIC ENVIRONMENT!
UNLESS I CAN FIND A WAY TO MAKE THIS WASTELAND WORK FOR US INSTEAD OF AGAINST US!
BEFORE IT'S TOO LATE!

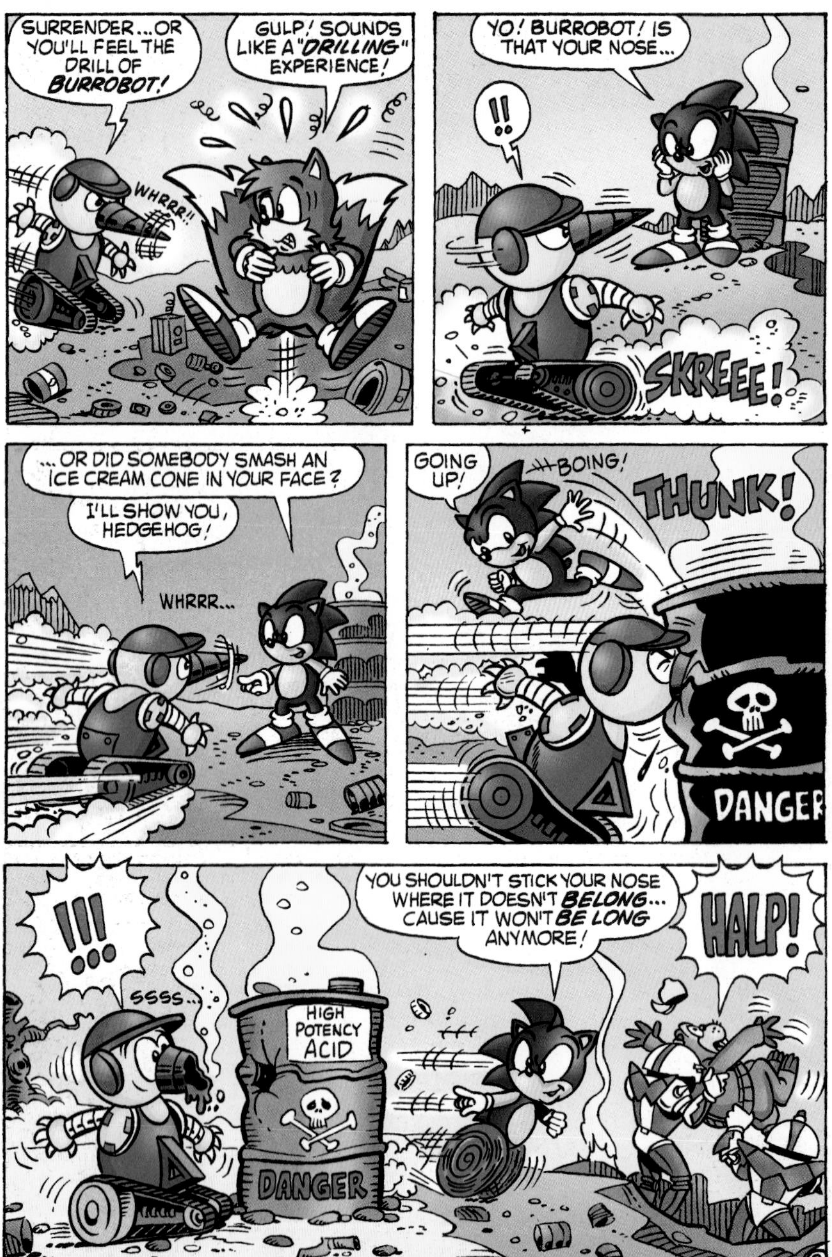

SURRENDER...OR YOU'LL FEEL THE DRILL OF BURROBOT!
GULP! SOUNDS LIKE A "DRILLING" EXPERIENCE!
WHRRR!!
YO! BURROBOT! IS THAT YOUR NOSE...
!!
SKREEEE!
...OR DID SOMEBODY SMASH AN ICE CREAM CONE IN YOUR FACE?
I'LL SHOW YOU, HEDGEHOG!
WHRRR...
GOING UP!
BOING!
THUNK!
DANGER
!!!
SSSS...
HIGH POTENCY ACID
DANGER
YOU SHOULDN'T STICK YOUR NOSE WHERE IT DOESN'T BELONG... CAUSE IT WON'T BE LONG ANYMORE!
HALP!

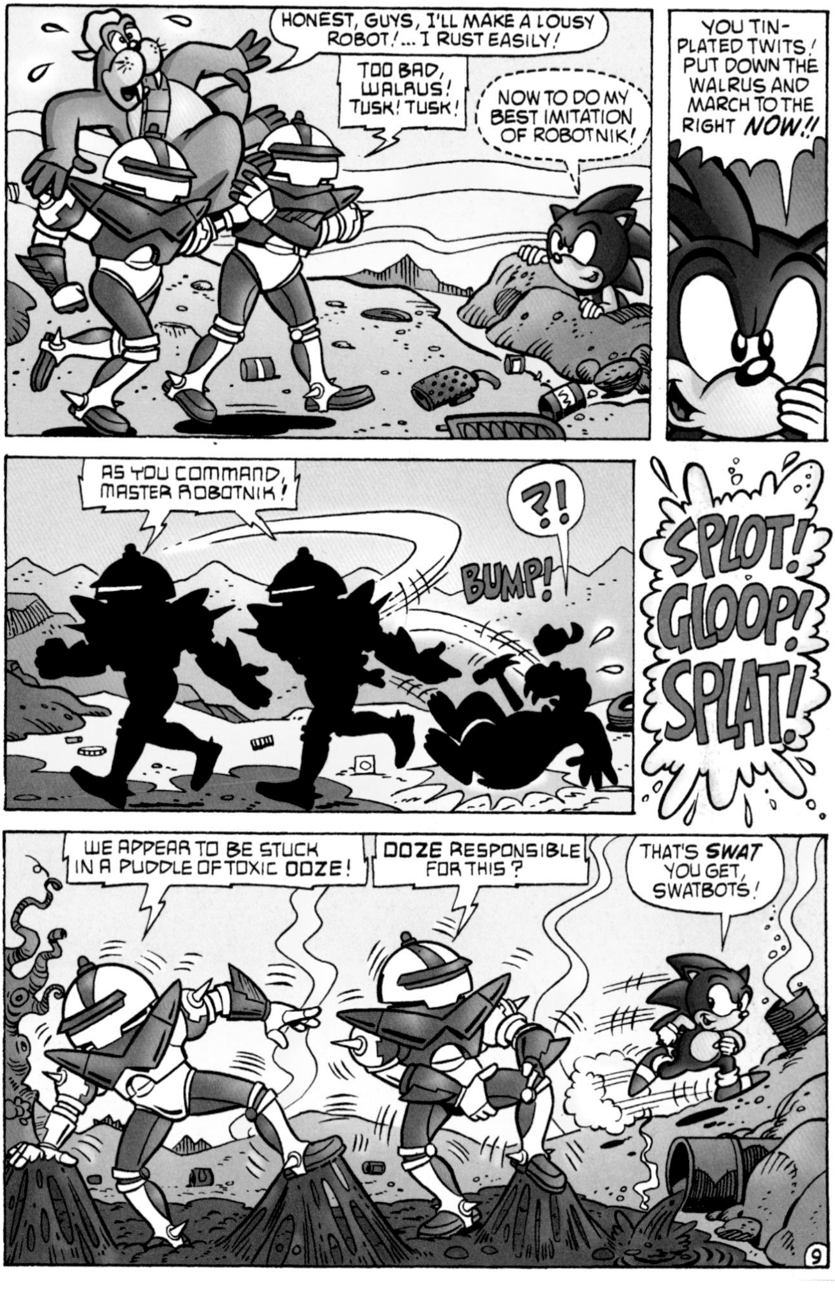

HONEST, GUYS, I'LL MAKE A LOUSY ROBOT!... I RUST EASILY!
TOO BAD, WALRUS! TUSK! TUSK!
NOW TO DO MY BEST IMITATION OF ROBOTNIK!
YOU TIN-PLATED TWITS! PUT DOWN THE WALRUS AND MARCH TO THE RIGHT NOW!!
AS YOU COMMAND, MASTER ROBOTNIK!
?!
BUMP!
SPLOT! GLOOP! SPLAT!
WE APPEAR TO BE STUCK IN A PUDDLE OF TOXIC OOZE!
OOZE RESPONSIBLE FOR THIS?
THAT'S SWAT YOU GET, SWATBOTS!

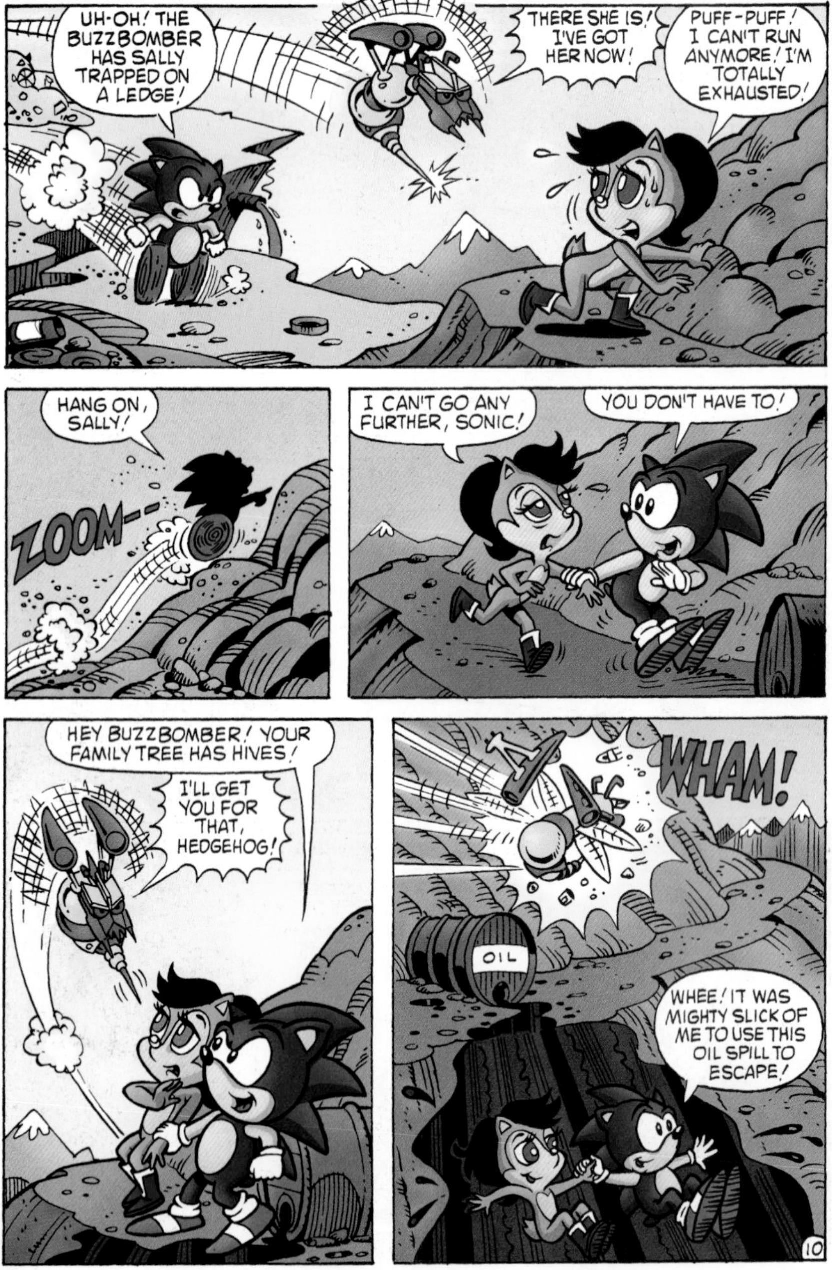
UH-OH! THE BUZZBOMBER HAS SALLY TRAPPED ON A LEDGE!
THERE SHE IS! I'VE GOT HER NOW!
PUFF-PUFF! I CAN'T RUN ANYMORE! I'M TOTALLY EXHAUSTED!
HANG ON, SALLY!
ZOOM--
I CAN'T GO ANY FURTHER, SONIC!
YOU DON'T HAVE TO!
HEY BUZZBOMBER! YOUR FAMILY TREE HAS HIVES!
I'LL GET YOU FOR THAT, HEDGEHOG!
WHAM!
OIL
WHEE! IT WAS MIGHTY SLICK OF ME TO USE THIS OIL SPILL TO ESCAPE!

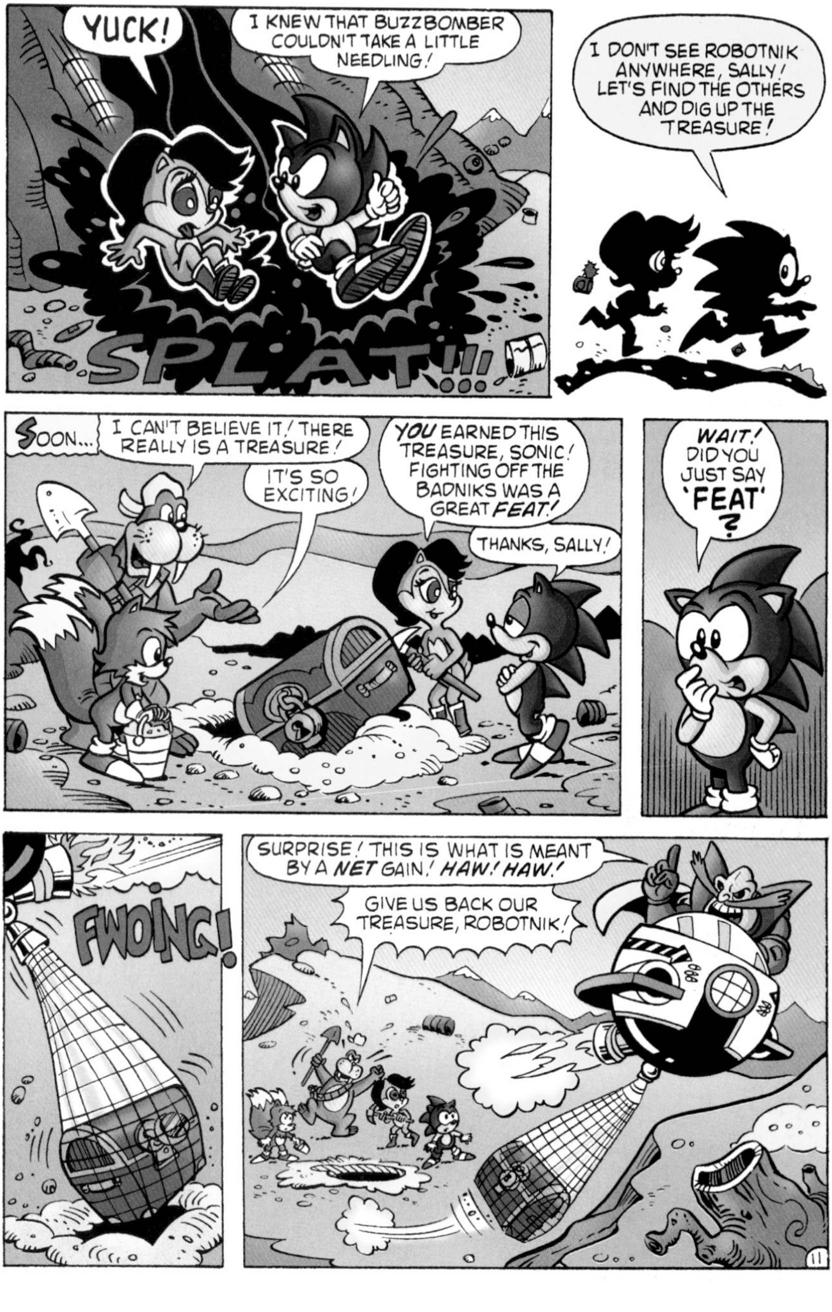
YUCK!
I KNEW THAT BUZZBOMBER COULDN'T TAKE A LITTLE NEEDLING!
SPLAT!!!
I DON'T SEE ROBOTNIK ANYWHERE, SALLY! LET'S FIND THE OTHERS AND DIG UP THE TREASURE!
SOON...
I CAN'T BELIEVE IT! THERE REALLY IS A TREASURE!
IT'S SO EXCITING!
YOU EARNED THIS TREASURE, SONIC! FIGHTING OFF THE BADNIKS WAS A GREAT FEAT!
THANKS, SALLY!
WAIT! DID YOU JUST SAY 'FEAT'?
FWOING!
SURPRISE! THIS IS WHAT IS MEANT BY A NET GAIN! HAW! HAW!
GIVE US BACK OUR TREASURE, ROBOTNIK!

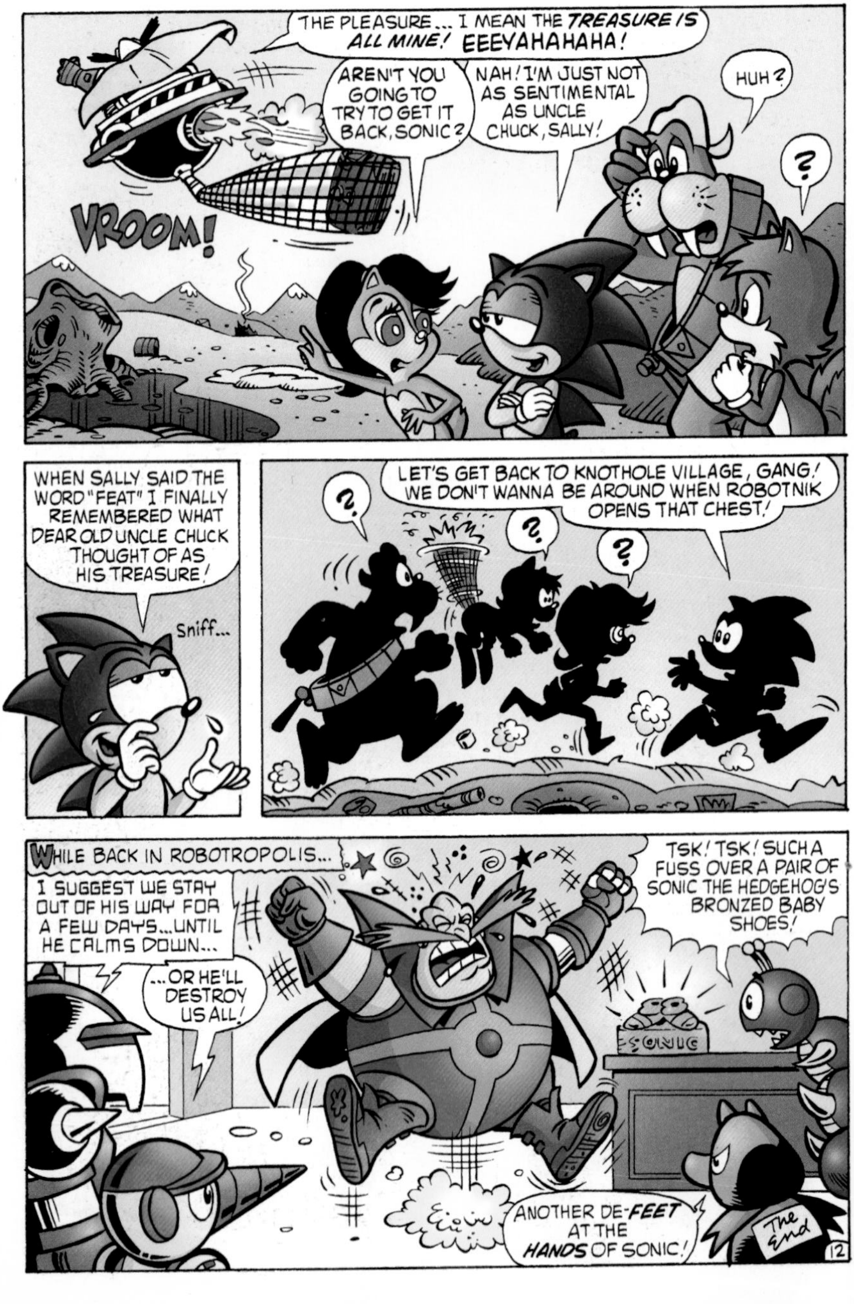
THE PLEASURE... I MEAN THE TREASURE IS ALL MINE! EEEYAHAHAHAHA!
ARE'NT YOU GOING TO TRY TO GET IT BACK, SONIC?
NAH! I'M JUST NOT AS SENTIMENTAL AS UNCLE CHUCK, SALLY!
HUH?
?
VROOM!
WHEN SALLY SAID THE WORD "FEAT" I FINALLY REMEMBERED WHAT DEAR OLD UNCLE CHUCK THOUGHT OF AS HIS TREASURE!
Sniff...
LET'S GET BACK TO KNOTHOLE VILLAGE, GANG! WE DON'T WANNA BE AROUND WHEN ROBOTNIK OPENS THAT CHEST!
?
?
?
WHILE BACK IN ROBOTROPOLIS...
I SUGGEST WE STAY OUT OF HIS WAY FOR A FEW DAYS...UNTIL HE CALMS DOWN...
...OR HE'LL DESTROY US ALL!
TSK! TSK! SUCH A FUSS OVER A PAIR OF SONIC THE HEDGEHOG'S BRONZED BABY SHOES!
SONIC
ANOTHER DE-FEET AT THE HANDS OF SONIC!
The End
12

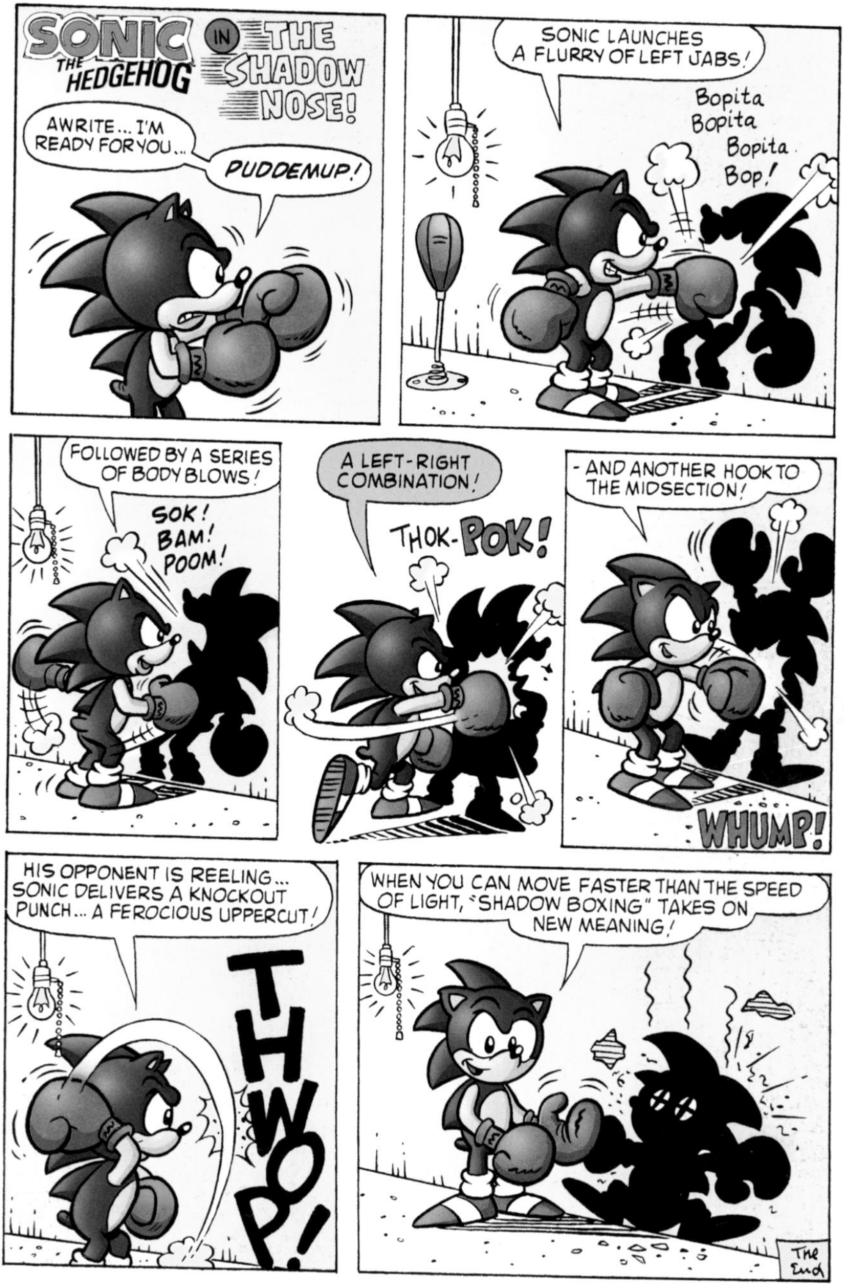
SONIC THE HEDGEHOG IN THE SHADOW NOSE!
AWRITE... I'M READY FOR YOU...
PUDDEMUP!
SONIC LAUNCHES A FLURRY OF LEFT JABS!
Bopita Bopita Bopita Bop!
FOLLOWED BY A SERIES OF BODY BLOWS!
SOK! BAM! POOM!
A LEFT-RIGHT COMBINATION!
THOK-POK!
- AND ANOTHER HOOK TO THE MIDSECTION!
WHUMP!
HIS OPPONENT IS REELING... SONIC DELIVERS A KNOCKOUT PUNCH... A FEROCIOUS UPPERCUT!
THWOP!
WHEN YOU CAN MOVE FASTER THAN THE SPEED OF LIGHT, "SHADOW BOXING" TAKES ON NEW MEANING!
The End

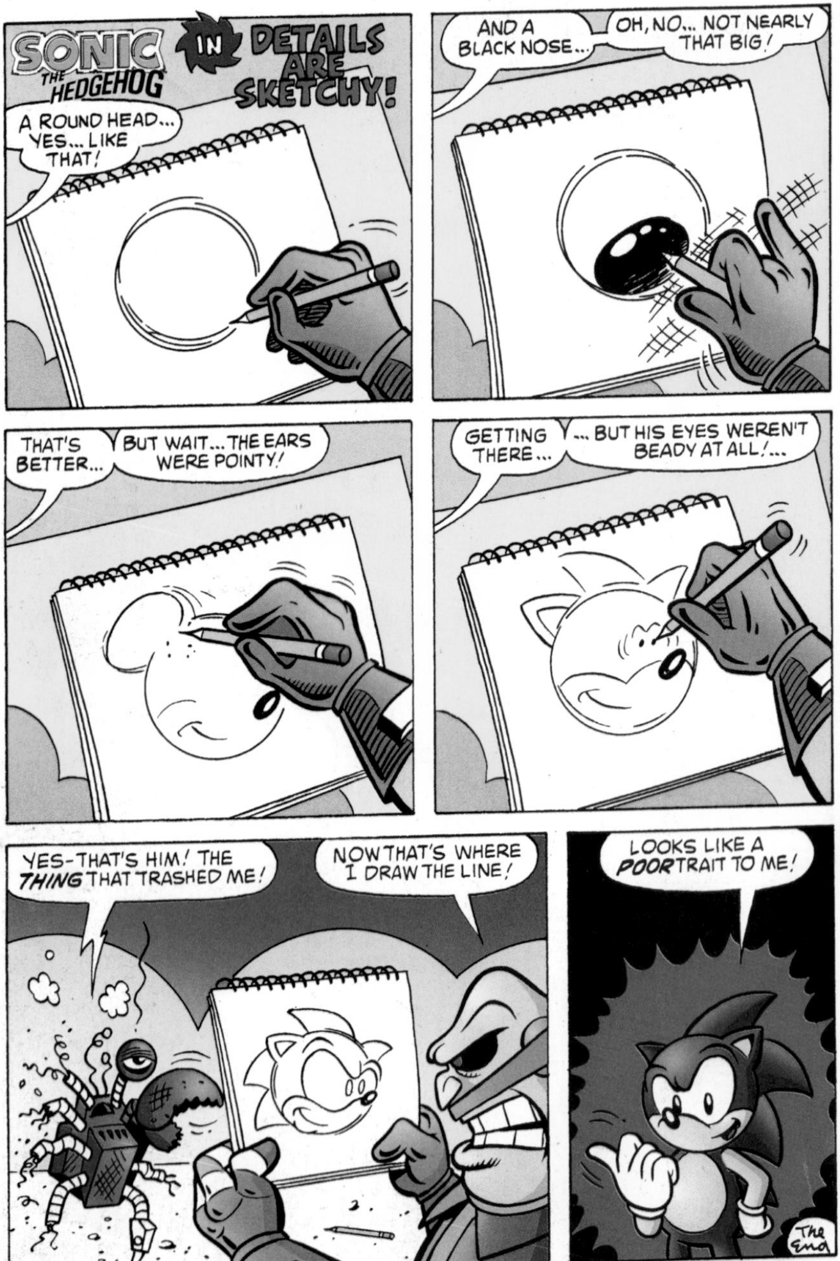
SONIC THE HEDGEHOG
IN
DETAILS ARE SKETCHY!
A ROUND HEAD... YES... LIKE THAT!
AND A BLACK NOSE...
OH, NO... NOT NEARLY THAT BIG!
THAT'S BETTER...
BUT WAIT... THE EARS WERE POINTY!
GETTING THERE...
... BUT HIS EYES WEREN'T BEADY AT ALL!...
YES-THAT'S HIM! THE THING THAT TRASHED ME!
NOW THAT'S WHERE I DRAW THE LINE!
LOOKS LIKE A POORTRAIT TO ME!
The End

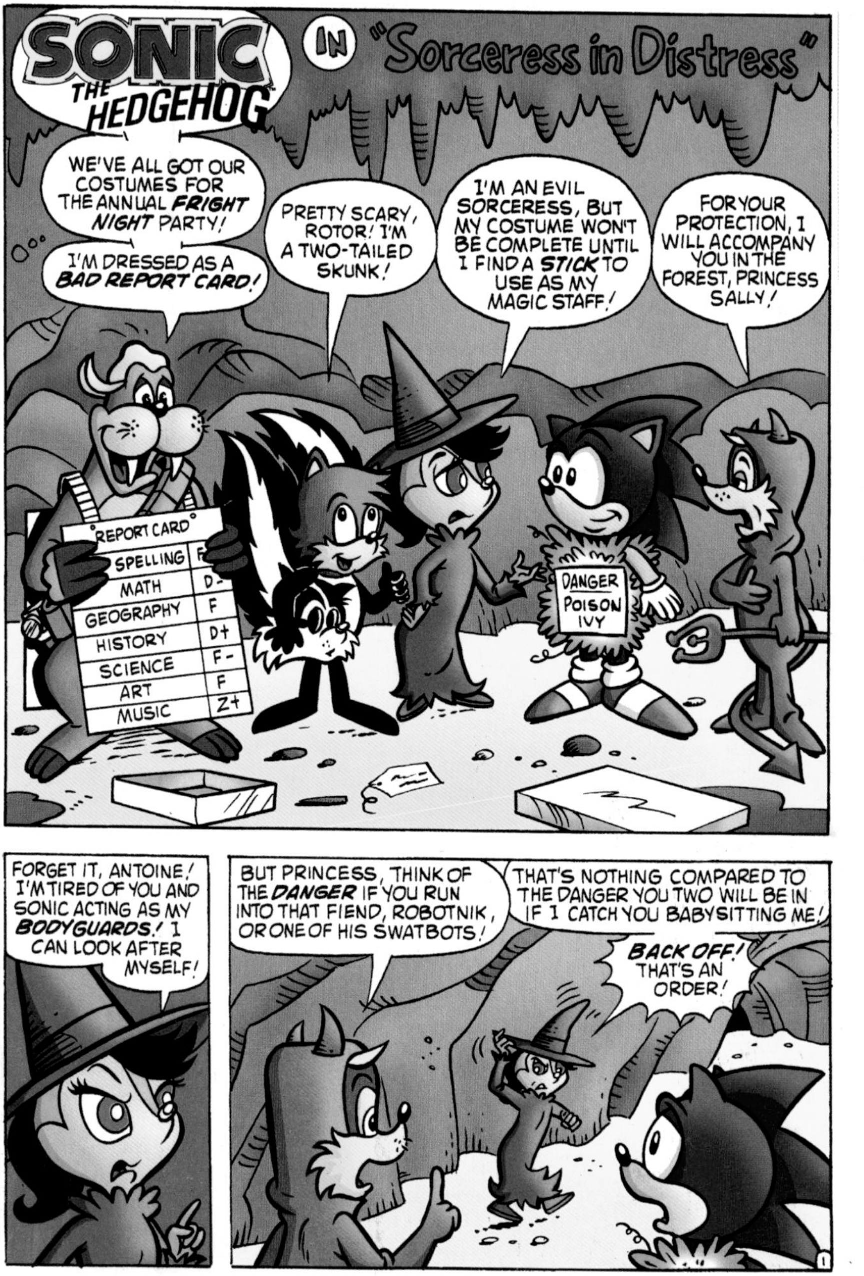
SONIC THE HEDGEHOG
IN "Sorceress in Distress"
WE'VE ALL GOT OUR COSTUMES FOR THE ANNUAL FRIGHT NIGHT PARTY!
I'M DRESSED AS A BAD REPORT CARD!
PRETTY SCARY, ROTOR! I'M A TWO-TAILED SKUNK!
I'M AN EVIL SORCERESS, BUT MY COSTUME WON'T BE COMPLETE UNTIL I FIND A STICK TO USE AS MY MAGIC STAFF!
FOR YOUR PROTECTION, I WILL ACCOMPANY YOU IN THE FOREST, PRINCESS SALLY!
REPORT CARD
SPELLING F
MATH D-
GEOGRAPHY F
HISTORY D+
SCIENCE F-
ART F
MUSIC Z+
DANGER POISON IVY
FORGET IT, ANTOINE! I'M TIRED OF YOU AND SONIC ACTING AS MY BODYGUARDS! I CAN LOOK AFTER MYSELF!
BUT PRINCESS, THINK OF THE DANGER IF YOU RUN INTO THAT FIEND, ROBOTNIK, OR ONE OF HIS SWATBOTS!
THAT'S NOTHING COMPARED TO THE DANGER YOU TWO WILL BE IN IF I CATCH YOU BABYSITTING ME!
BACK OFF! THAT'S AN ORDER!
1

SOON... THIS IS EXACTLY THE KIND OF STICK I WAS LOOKING FOR! HEE! HEE! MAYBE IT *REALLY* IS A MAGIC STAFF...

...THAT A *REAL* SORCERESS DROPPED WHILE SHE WAS WALKING IN THE WOODS! THAT WOULD BE *SO* COOL!

UNKNOWN TO SALLY AT THAT MOMENT, AN UNDERGROUND GEYSER IS ABOUT TO BURST FORTH FROM BENEATH A NEARBY ROCK!

ROCK

SSSHHH! SLEEPING GOPHER!

GEYSER

Z

IF THIS *WERE* A MAGIC STAFF I'D SAY TO THAT ROCK, "ARISE, ROCK, I COMMAND *YOU*!" AND UP IT WOULD...

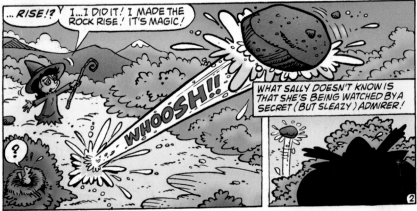

...*RISE!?* I...I DID IT! I MADE THE ROCK RISE! IT'S MAGIC!

WHOOSH!!

?

WHAT SALLY DOESN'T KNOW IS THAT SHE'S BEING WATCHED BY A SECRET (BUT SLEAZY) ADMIRER!

2

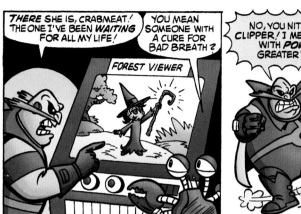

THERE SHE IS, CRABMEAT! THE ONE I'VE BEEN **WAITING** FOR ALL MY LIFE!

FOREST VIEWER

YOU MEAN SOMEONE WITH A CURE FOR BAD BREATH?

NO, YOU NIT-WITTED NAIL CLIPPER! I MEAN A WOMAN WITH **POWER** EVEN GREATER THAN **MINE**!

WHAM!

WITH SUCH POWER AT MY DISPOSAL, I COULD FINALLY SLAM-DUNK SONIC THE HEDGEHOG AND HIS FREEDOM FIGHTERS...

I COULD TAKE OVER THE ENTIRE UNIVERSE...

...MAYBE I COULD EVEN STAR IN MY **OWN** COMIC BOOK AND TV SERIES!

WHY, I THINK I'M IN **LOVE**!

SOON...

...I SAID, "ARISE, LOG!"

"**ARISE! ARISE!**" OKAY, FORGET IT!

YEAH, THIS IS REALLY A MAGIC STAFF... **NOT!**

MAYBE I HAVEN'T BEEN SAYING THE RIGHT MAGIC WORDS! MAYBE I SHOULD SAY...

3

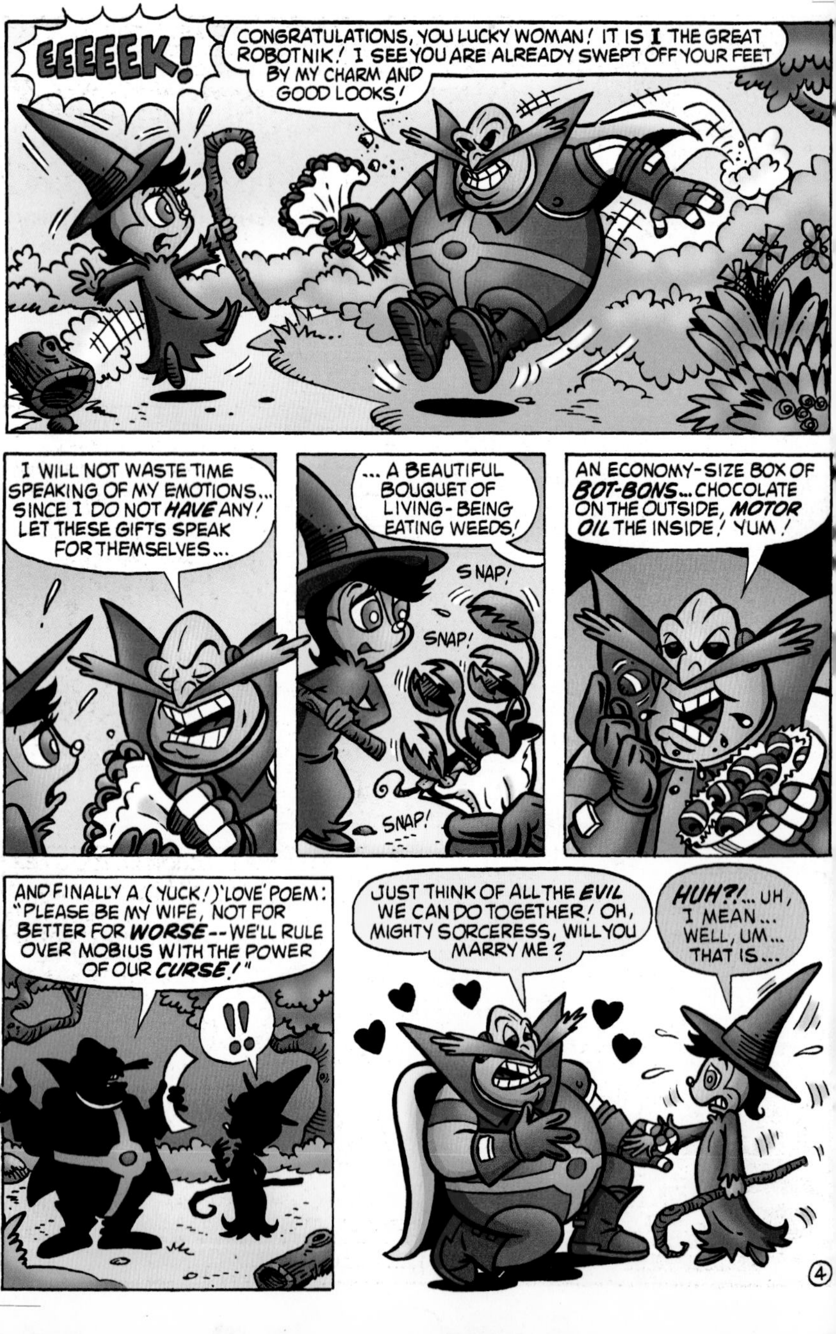
EEEEEK!
CONGRATULATIONS, YOU LUCKY WOMAN! IT IS I THE GREAT ROBOTNIK! I SEE YOU ARE ALREADY SWEPT OFF YOUR FEET BY MY CHARM AND GOOD LOOKS!
I WILL NOT WASTE TIME SPEAKING OF MY EMOTIONS... SINCE I DO NOT HAVE ANY! LET THESE GIFTS SPEAK FOR THEMSELVES...
... A BEAUTIFUL BOUQUET OF LIVING-BEING EATING WEEDS!
SNAP!
SNAP!
SNAP!
AN ECONOMY-SIZE BOX OF BOT-BONS... CHOCOLATE ON THE OUTSIDE, MOTOR OIL THE INSIDE! YUM!
AND FINALLY A (YUCK!) 'LOVE' POEM: "PLEASE BE MY WIFE, NOT FOR BETTER FOR WORSE--WE'LL RULE OVER MOBIUS WITH THE POWER OF OUR CURSE!"
!!
JUST THINK OF ALL THE EVIL WE CAN DO TOGETHER! OH, MIGHTY SORCERESS, WILL YOU MARRY ME?
HUH?!... UH, I MEAN... WELL, UM... THAT IS...

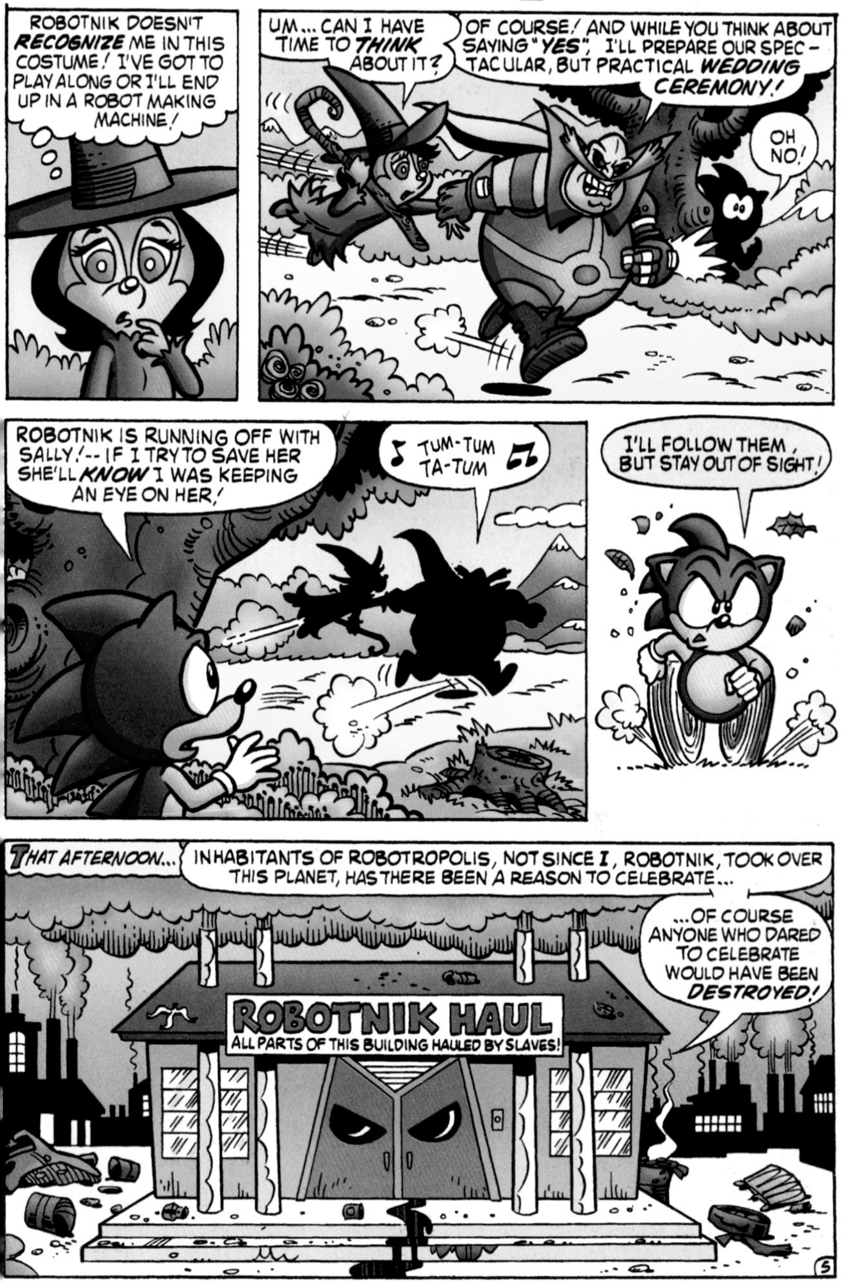
ROBOTNIK DOESN'T RECOGNIZE ME IN THIS COSTUME! I'VE GOT TO PLAY ALONG OR I'LL END UP IN A ROBOT MAKING MACHINE!
UM... CAN I HAVE TIME TO THINK ABOUT IT?
OF COURSE! AND WHILE YOU THINK ABOUT SAYING "YES", I'LL PREPARE OUR SPEC-TACULAR, BUT PRACTICAL WEDDING CEREMONY!
OH NO!
ROBOTNIK IS RUNNING OFF WITH SALLY!-- IF I TRY TO SAVE HER SHE'LL KNOW I WAS KEEPING AN EYE ON HER!
TUM-TUM TA-TUM
I'LL FOLLOW THEM, BUT STAY OUT OF SIGHT!
THAT AFTERNOON...
INHABITANTS OF ROBOTROPOLIS, NOT SINCE I, ROBOTNIK, TOOK OVER THIS PLANET, HAS THERE BEEN A REASON TO CELEBRATE...
...OF COURSE ANYONE WHO DARED TO CELEBRATE WOULD HAVE BEEN DESTROYED!
ROBOTNIK HAUL
ALL PARTS OF THIS BUILDING HAULED BY SLAVES!
5

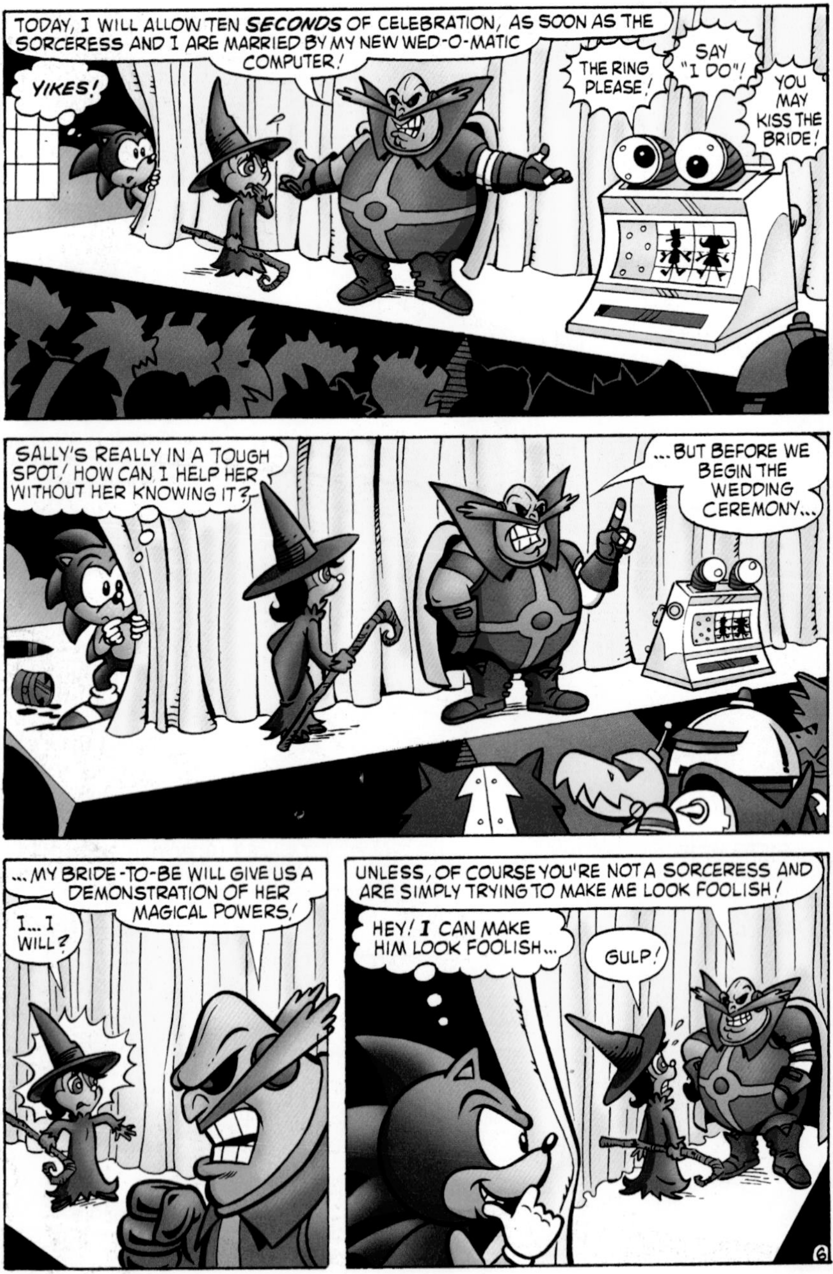
TODAY, I WILL ALLOW TEN SECONDS OF CELEBRATION, AS SOON AS THE SORCERESS AND I ARE MARRIED BY MY NEW WED-O-MATIC COMPUTER!
YIKES!
THE RING PLEASE!
SAY "I DO"!
YOU MAY KISS THE BRIDE!
SALLY'S REALLY IN A TOUGH SPOT! HOW CAN I HELP HER WITHOUT HER KNOWING IT?
...BUT BEFORE WE BEGIN THE WEDDING CEREMONY...
...MY BRIDE-TO-BE WILL GIVE US A DEMONSTRATION OF HER MAGICAL POWERS!
I... I WILL?
UNLESS, OF COURSE YOU'RE NOT A SORCERESS AND ARE SIMPLY TRYING TO MAKE ME LOOK FOOLISH!
HEY! I CAN MAKE HIM LOOK FOOLISH...
GULP!
6

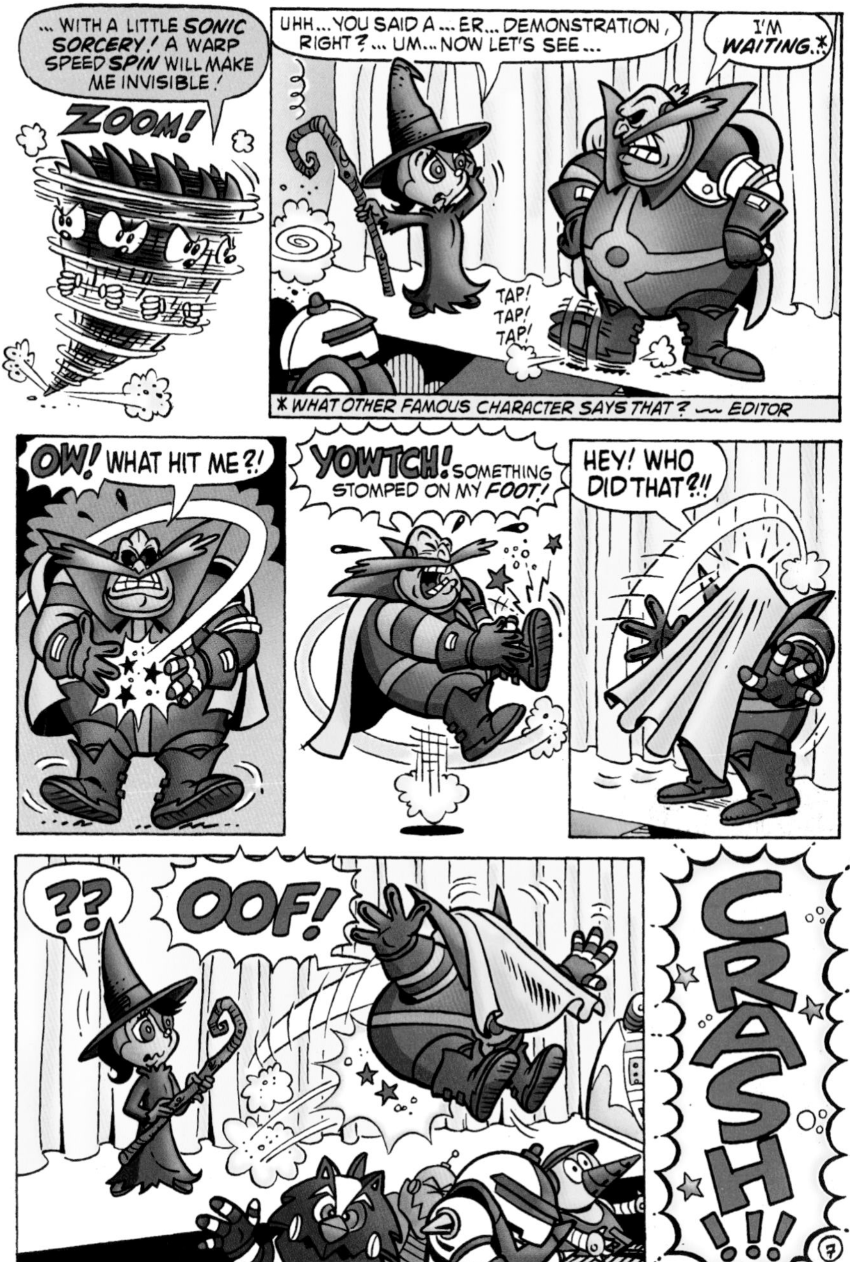
... WITH A LITTLE SONIC SORCERY! A WARP SPEED SPIN WILL MAKE ME INVISIBLE!
ZOOM!
UHH... YOU SAID A ... ER... DEMONSTRATION, RIGHT? ... UM... NOW LET'S SEE ...
I'M WAITING..*
TAP! TAP! TAP!
* WHAT OTHER FAMOUS CHARACTER SAYS THAT? — EDITOR
OW! WHAT HIT ME?!
YOWTCH! SOMETHING STOMPED ON MY FOOT!
HEY! WHO DID THAT?!!
??
OOF!
CRASH!!!

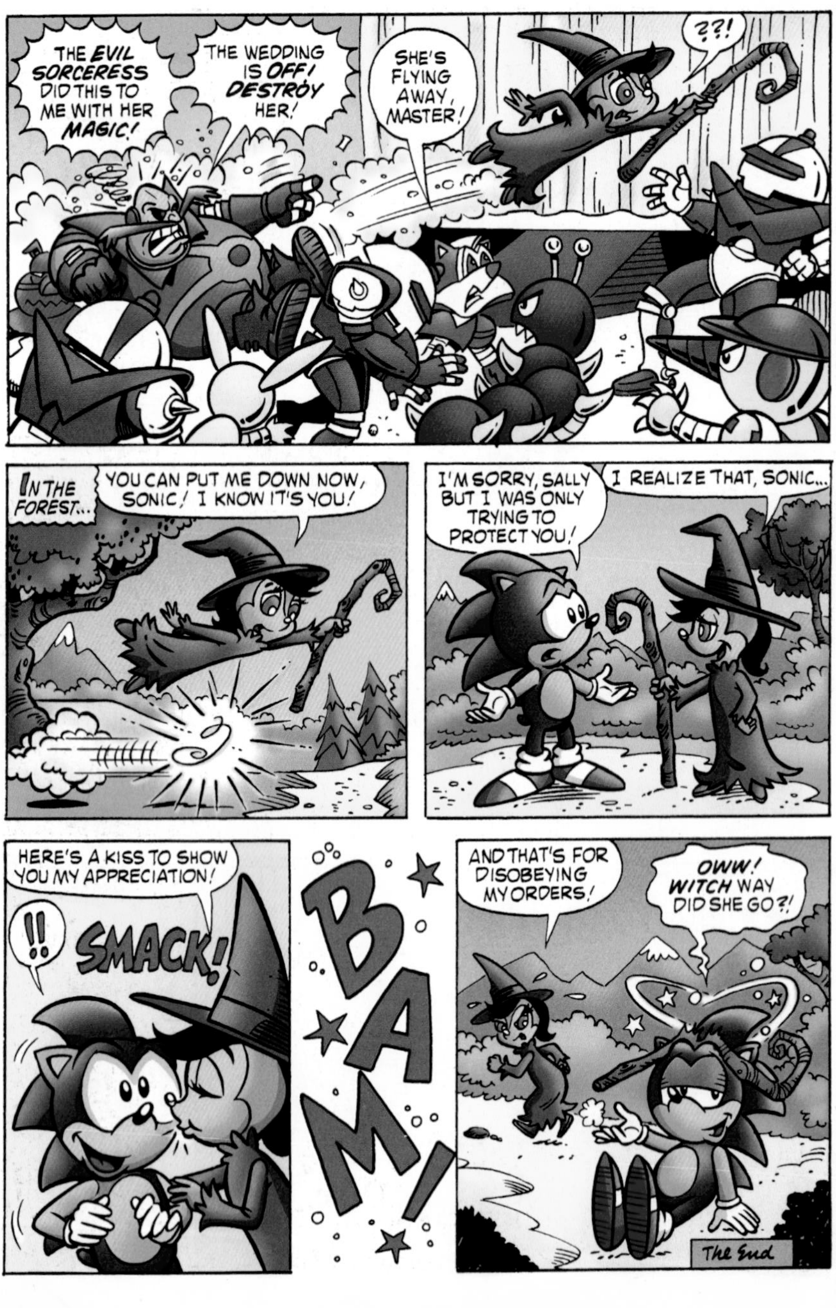
THE EVIL SORCERESS DID THIS TO ME WITH HER MAGIC!
THE WEDDING IS OFF! DESTROY HER!
SHE'S FLYING AWAY, MASTER!
??!
IN THE FOREST...
YOU CAN PUT ME DOWN NOW, SONIC! I KNOW IT'S YOU!
I'M SORRY, SALLY BUT I WAS ONLY TRYING TO PROTECT YOU!
I REALIZE THAT, SONIC...
HERE'S A KISS TO SHOW YOU MY APPRECIATION!
!!
SMACK!
BAM!
AND THAT'S FOR DISOBEYING MY ORDERS!
OWW! WITCH WAY DID SHE GO?!
The End

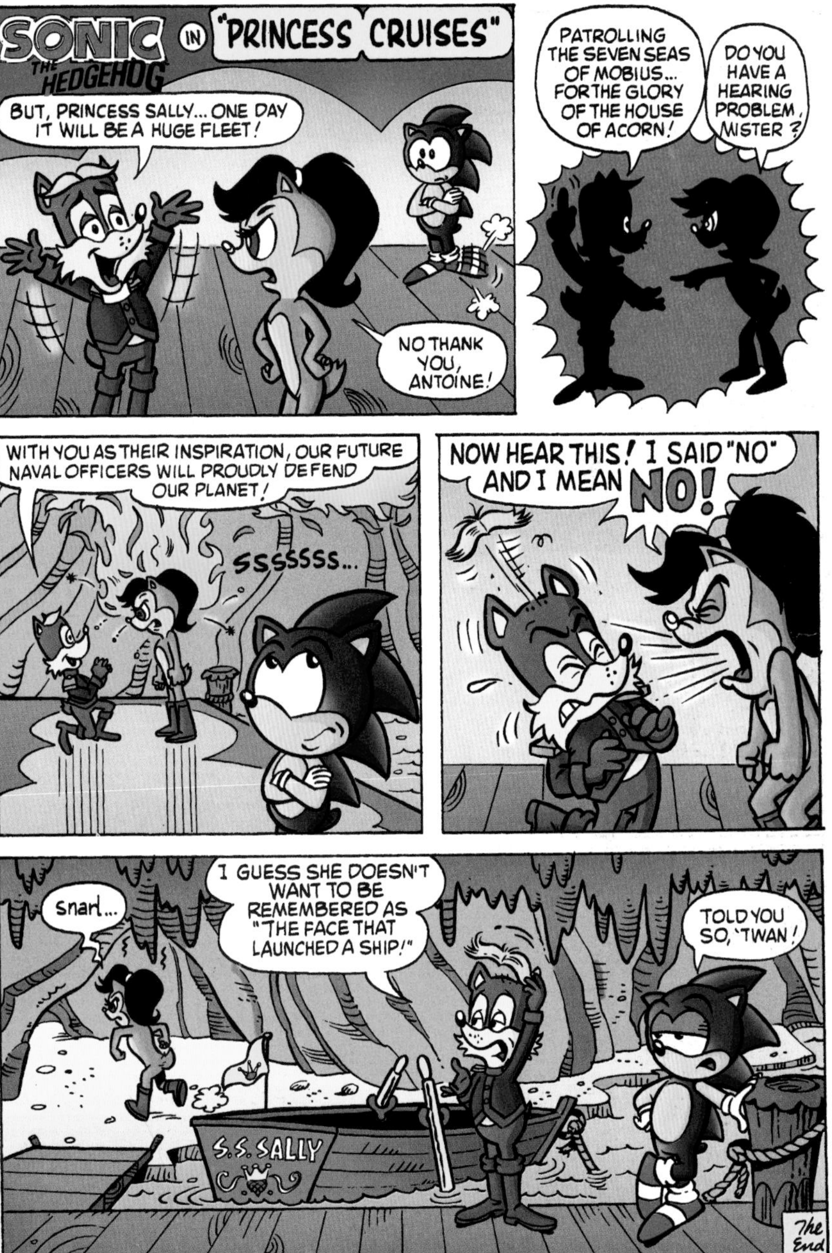
SONIC THE HEDGEHOG IN "PRINCESS CRUISES"
BUT, PRINCESS SALLY... ONE DAY IT WILL BE A HUGE FLEET!
NO THANK YOU, ANTOINE!
PATROLLING THE SEVEN SEAS OF MOBIUS... FOR THE GLORY OF THE HOUSE OF ACORN!
DO YOU HAVE A HEARING PROBLEM, MISTER?
WITH YOU AS THEIR INSPIRATION, OUR FUTURE NAVAL OFFICERS WILL PROUDLY DEFEND OUR PLANET!
SSSSSSS...
NOW HEAR THIS! I SAID "NO" AND I MEAN NO!
snarl...
I GUESS SHE DOESN'T WANT TO BE REMEMBERED AS "THE FACE THAT LAUNCHED A SHIP!"
TOLD YOU SO, 'TWAN!
S.S. SALLY
The End

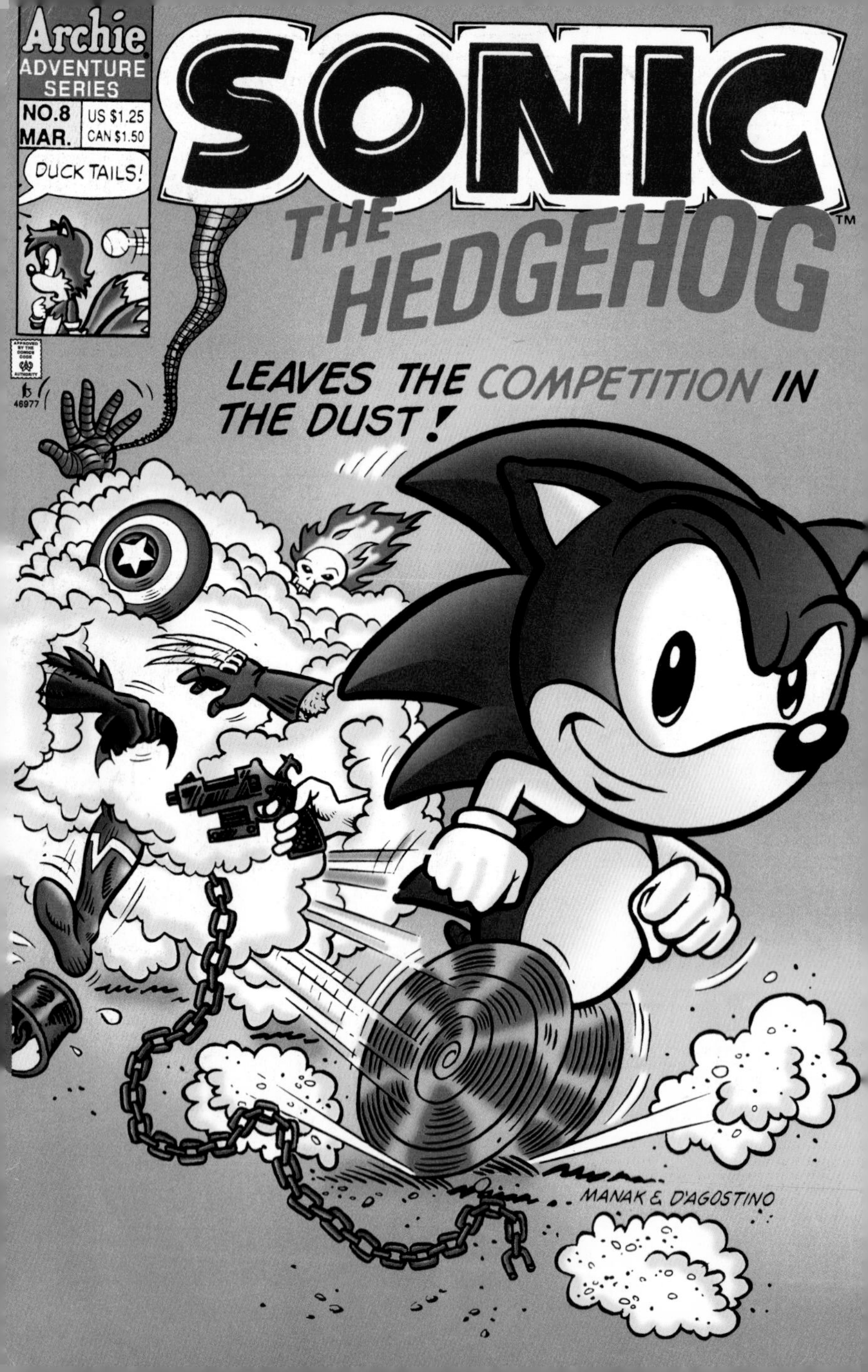
Archie
ADVENTURE SERIES
NO.8
MAR.
US $1.25
CAN $1.50
DUCK TAILS!
SONIC THE HEDGEHOG™
LEAVES THE COMPETITION IN THE DUST!
46977
MANAK & D'AGOSTINO

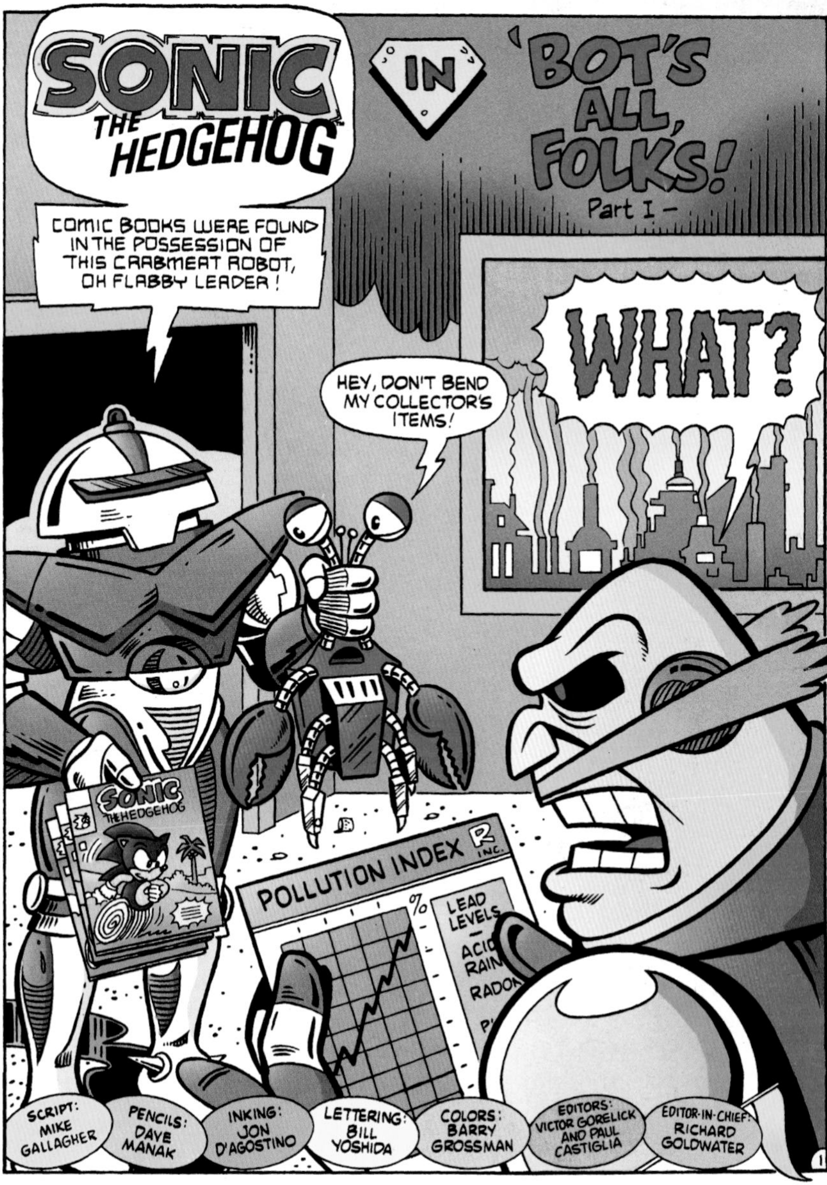
SONIC THE HEDGEHOG
IN
'BOT'S ALL, FOLKS!
Part I -
COMIC BOOKS WERE FOUND IN THE POSSESSION OF THIS CRABMEAT ROBOT, OH FLABBY LEADER!
HEY, DON'T BEND MY COLLECTOR'S ITEMS!
WHAT?
POLLUTION INDEX
LEAD LEVELS
ACID RAIN
RADON
SCRIPT: MIKE GALLAGHER
PENCILS: DAVE MANAK
INKING: JON D'AGOSTINO
LETTERING: BILL YOSHIDA
COLORS: BARRY GROSSMAN
EDITORS: VICTOR GORELICK AND PAUL CASTIGLIA
EDITOR-IN-CHIEF: RICHARD GOLDWATER

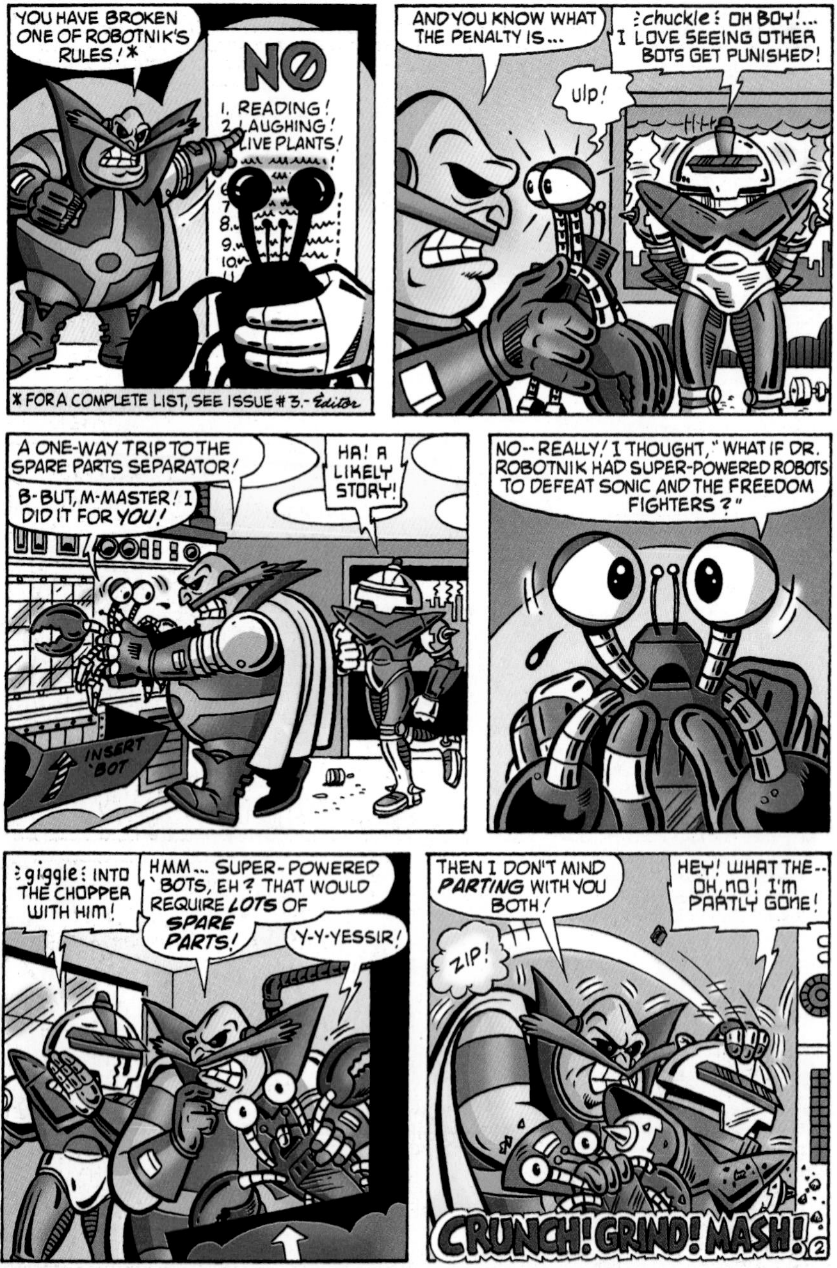
YOU HAVE BROKEN ONE OF ROBOTNIK'S RULES! *
NO
1. READING!
2. LAUGHING!
3. LIVE PLANTS!
* FOR A COMPLETE LIST, SEE ISSUE # 3. - Editor
AND YOU KNOW WHAT THE PENALTY IS...
:chuckle: OH BOY!... I LOVE SEEING OTHER BOTS GET PUNISHED!
ulp!
A ONE-WAY TRIP TO THE SPARE PARTS SEPARATOR!
B-BUT, M-MASTER! I DID IT FOR YOU!
HA! A LIKELY STORY!
INSERT 'BOT
NO-- REALLY! I THOUGHT, "WHAT IF DR. ROBOTNIK HAD SUPER-POWERED ROBOTS TO DEFEAT SONIC AND THE FREEDOM FIGHTERS?"
:giggle: INTO THE CHOPPER WITH HIM!
HMM... SUPER-POWERED 'BOTS, EH? THAT WOULD REQUIRE LOTS OF SPARE PARTS!
Y-Y-YESSIR!
THEN I DON'T MIND PARTING WITH YOU BOTH!
HEY! WHAT THE-- OH, NO! I'M PARTLY GONE!
ZIP!
CRUNCH! GRIND! MASH!
2

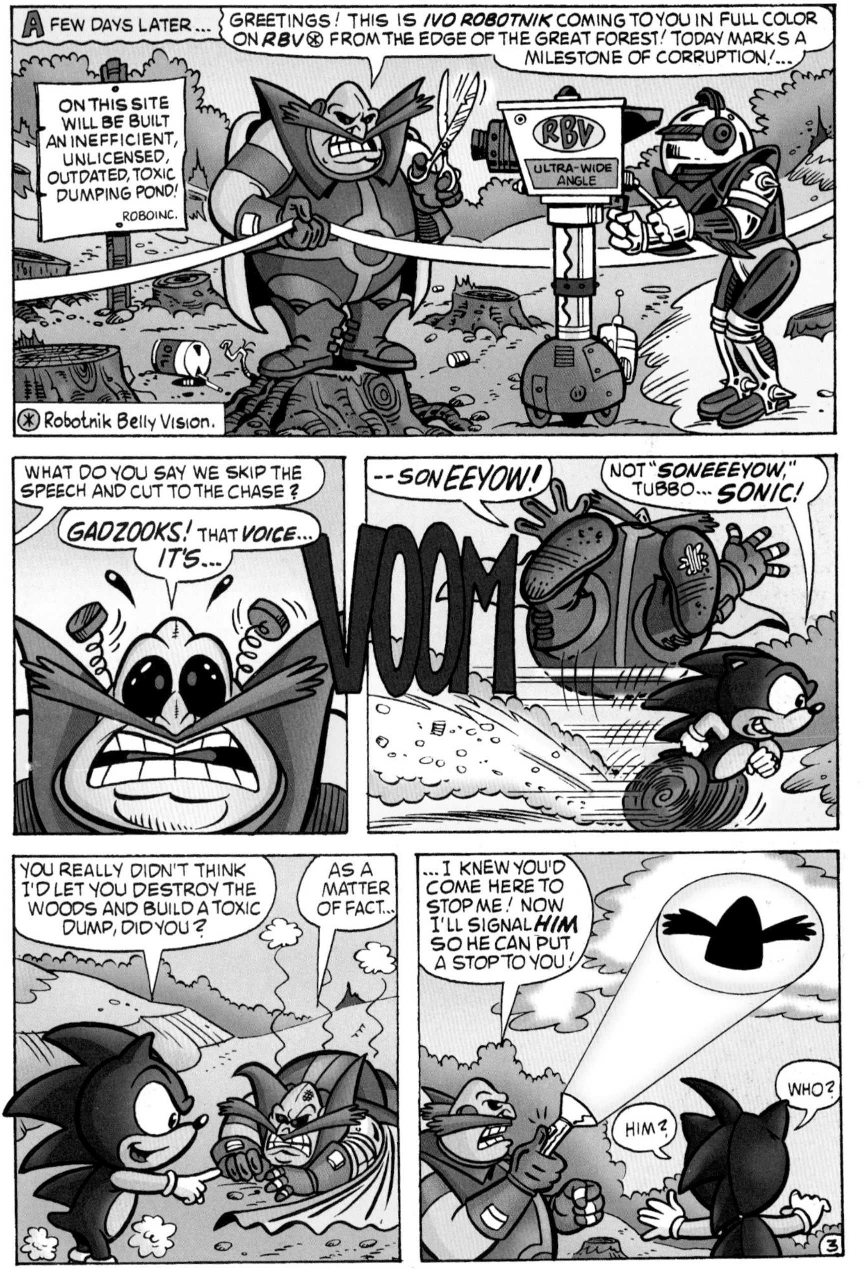
A FEW DAYS LATER...
GREETINGS! THIS IS IVO ROBOTNIK COMING TO YOU IN FULL COLOR ON RBV(*) FROM THE EDGE OF THE GREAT FOREST! TODAY MARKS A MILESTONE OF CORRUPTION!...
ON THIS SITE WILL BE BUILT AN INEFFICIENT, UNLICENSED, OUTDATED, TOXIC DUMPING POND! ROBOINC.
RBV
ULTRA-WIDE ANGLE
(*) Robotnik Belly Vision.
WHAT DO YOU SAY WE SKIP THE SPEECH AND CUT TO THE CHASE?
GADZOOKS! THAT VOICE... IT'S...
VOOM
--SONEEYOW!
NOT "SONEEEYOW," TUBBO... SONIC!
YOU REALLY DIDN'T THINK I'D LET YOU DESTROY THE WOODS AND BUILD A TOXIC DUMP, DID YOU?
AS A MATTER OF FACT...
...I KNEW YOU'D COME HERE TO STOP ME! NOW I'LL SIGNAL HIM SO HE CAN PUT A STOP TO YOU!
HIM?
WHO?
3

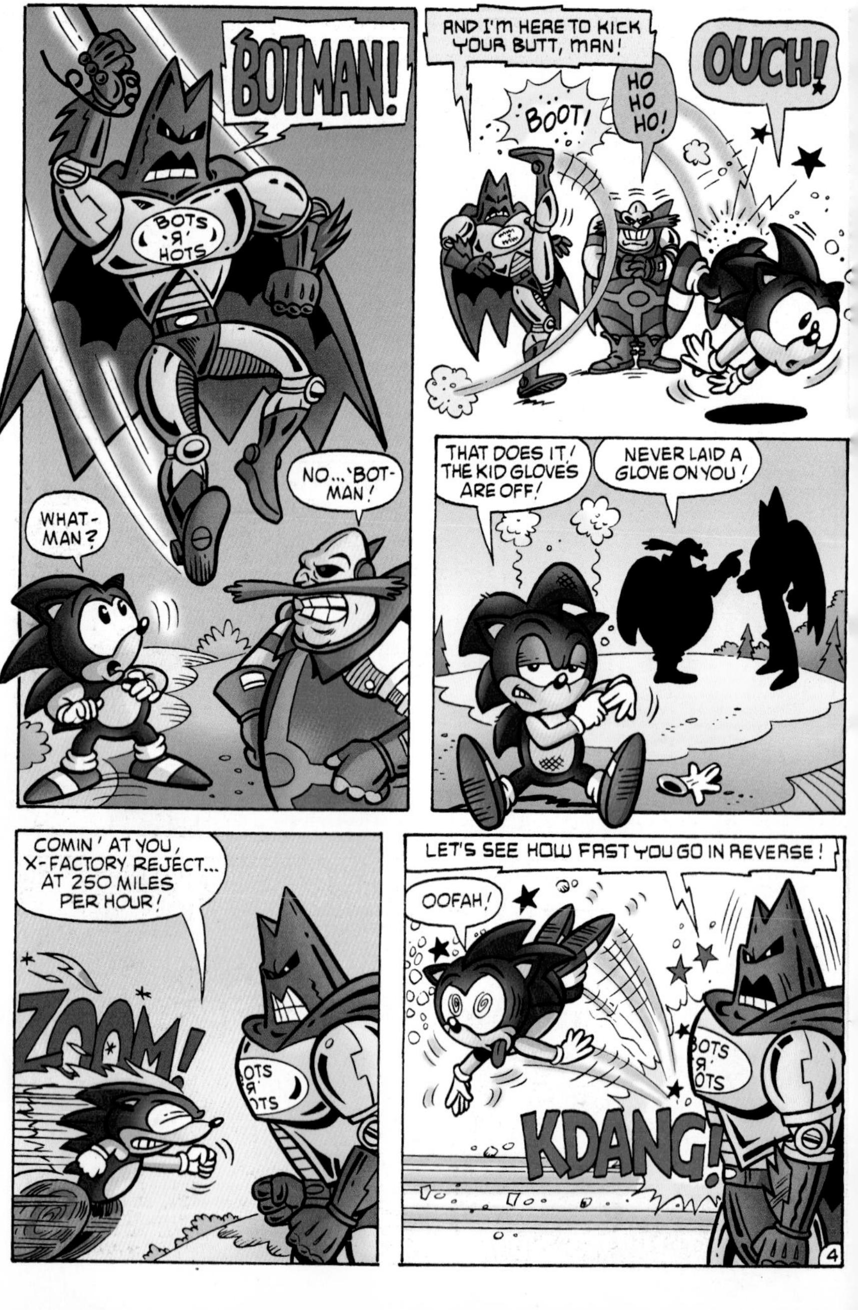
BOTMAN!
WHAT-MAN?
NO...'BOT-MAN!
AND I'M HERE TO KICK YOUR BUTT, MAN!
BOOT!
HO HO HO!
OUCH!
THAT DOES IT! THE KID GLOVES ARE OFF!
NEVER LAID A GLOVE ON YOU!
COMIN' AT YOU, X-FACTORY REJECT... AT 250 MILES PER HOUR!
ZOOM!
LET'S SEE HOW FAST YOU GO IN REVERSE!
OOFAH!
KDANG!

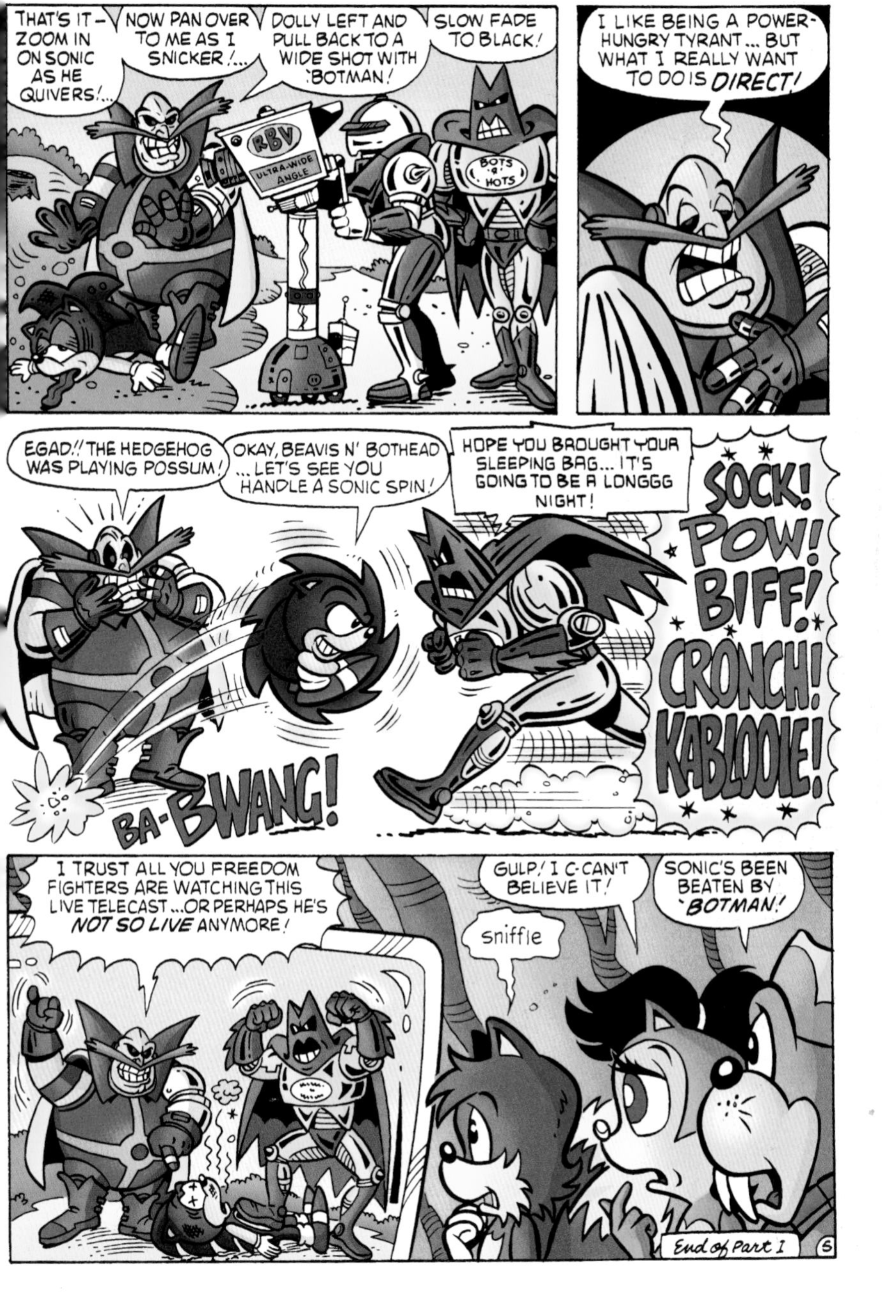
THAT'S IT — ZOOM IN ON SONIC AS HE QUIVERS!...
NOW PAN OVER TO ME AS I SNICKER!...
DOLLY LEFT AND PULL BACK TO A WIDE SHOT WITH 'BOTMAN!
SLOW FADE TO BLACK!
RBV
ULTRA-WIDE ANGLE
BOTS 'R' HOTS
I LIKE BEING A POWER-HUNGRY TYRANT ... BUT WHAT I REALLY WANT TO DO IS DIRECT!
EGAD!! THE HEDGEHOG WAS PLAYING POSSUM!
OKAY, BEAVIS N' BOTHEAD ... LET'S SEE YOU HANDLE A SONIC SPIN!
HOPE YOU BROUGHT YOUR SLEEPING BAG... IT'S GOING TO BE A LONGGG NIGHT!
SOCK! POW! BIFF! CRONCH! KABLOOIE!
BA-BWANG!
I TRUST ALL YOU FREEDOM FIGHTERS ARE WATCHING THIS LIVE TELECAST ...OR PERHAPS HE'S NOT SO LIVE ANYMORE!
GULP! I C-CAN'T BELIEVE IT!
SONIC'S BEEN BEATEN BY 'BOTMAN!
sniffle
End of Part I
5

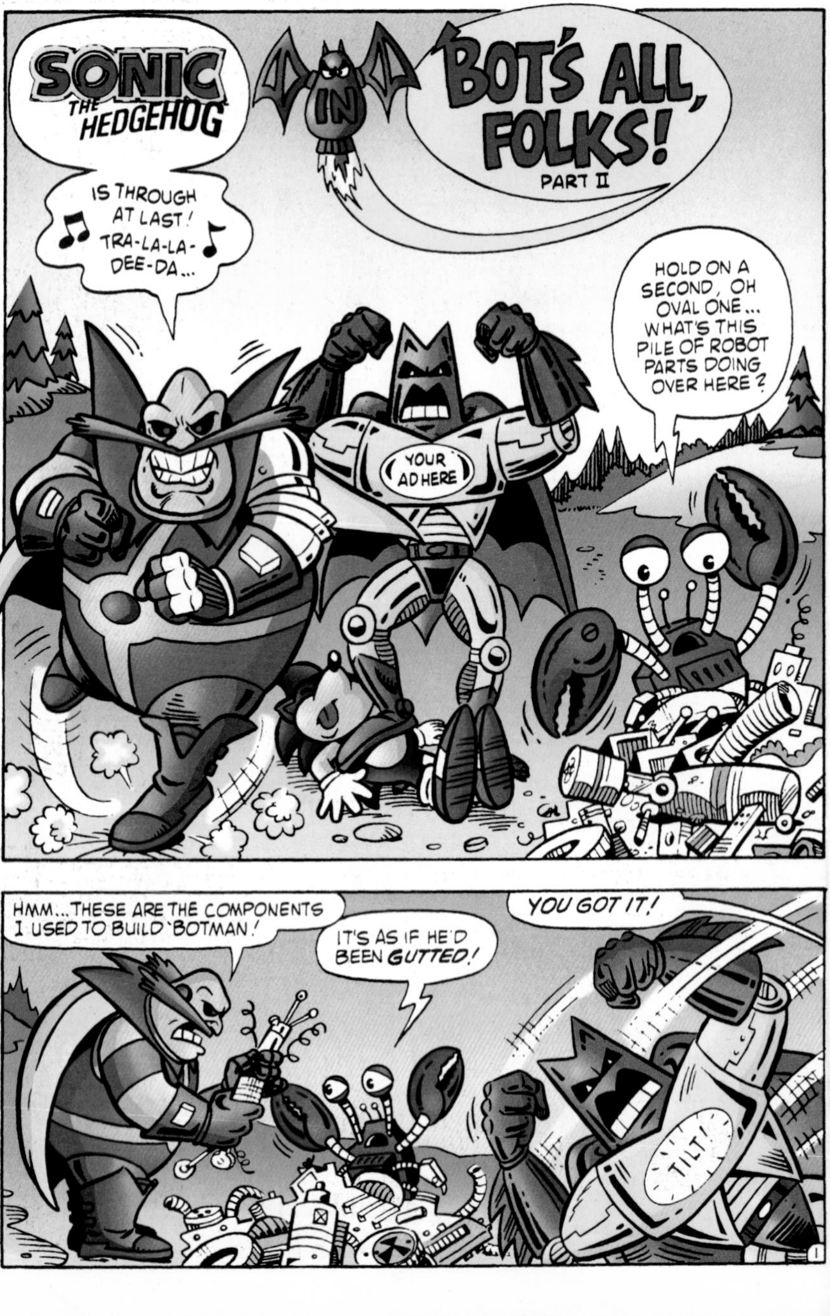
SONIC THE HEDGEHOG
IN
'BOT'S ALL, FOLKS! PART II
IS THROUGH AT LAST! TRA-LA-LA-DEE-DA...
HOLD ON A SECOND, OH OVAL ONE... WHAT'S THIS PILE OF ROBOT PARTS DOING OVER HERE?
YOUR AD HERE
HMM... THESE ARE THE COMPONENTS I USED TO BUILD 'BOTMAN!
IT'S AS IF HE'D BEEN GUTTED!
YOU GOT IT!
TILT!

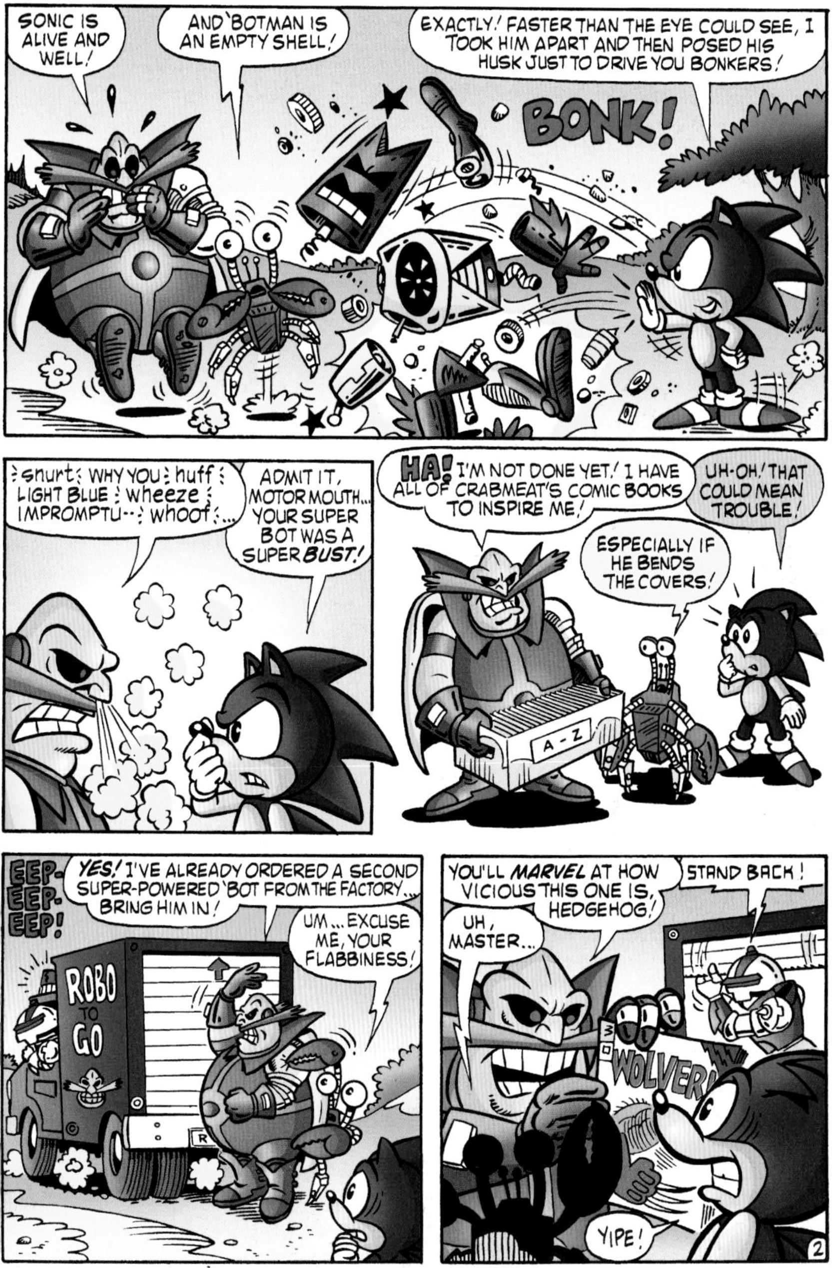
SONIC IS ALIVE AND WELL!
AND 'BOTMAN IS AN EMPTY SHELL!
EXACTLY! FASTER THAN THE EYE COULD SEE, I TOOK HIM APART AND THEN POSED HIS HUSK JUST TO DRIVE YOU BONKERS!
BONK!
:snurt: WHY YOU :huff: LIGHT BLUE :wheeze: IMPROMPTU-- :whoof:...
ADMIT IT, MOTOR MOUTH... YOUR SUPER BOT WAS A SUPER BUST!
HA! I'M NOT DONE YET! I HAVE ALL OF CRABMEAT'S COMIC BOOKS TO INSPIRE ME!
UH-OH! THAT COULD MEAN TROUBLE!
ESPECIALLY IF HE BENDS THE COVERS!
A - Z
EEP- EEP- EEP!
YES! I'VE ALREADY ORDERED A SECOND SUPER-POWERED 'BOT FROM THE FACTORY... BRING HIM IN!
UM... EXCUSE ME, YOUR FLABBINESS!
ROBO TO GO
YOU'LL MARVEL AT HOW VICIOUS THIS ONE IS, HEDGEHOG!
STAND BACK!
UH, MASTER...
WOLVERI
YIPE!

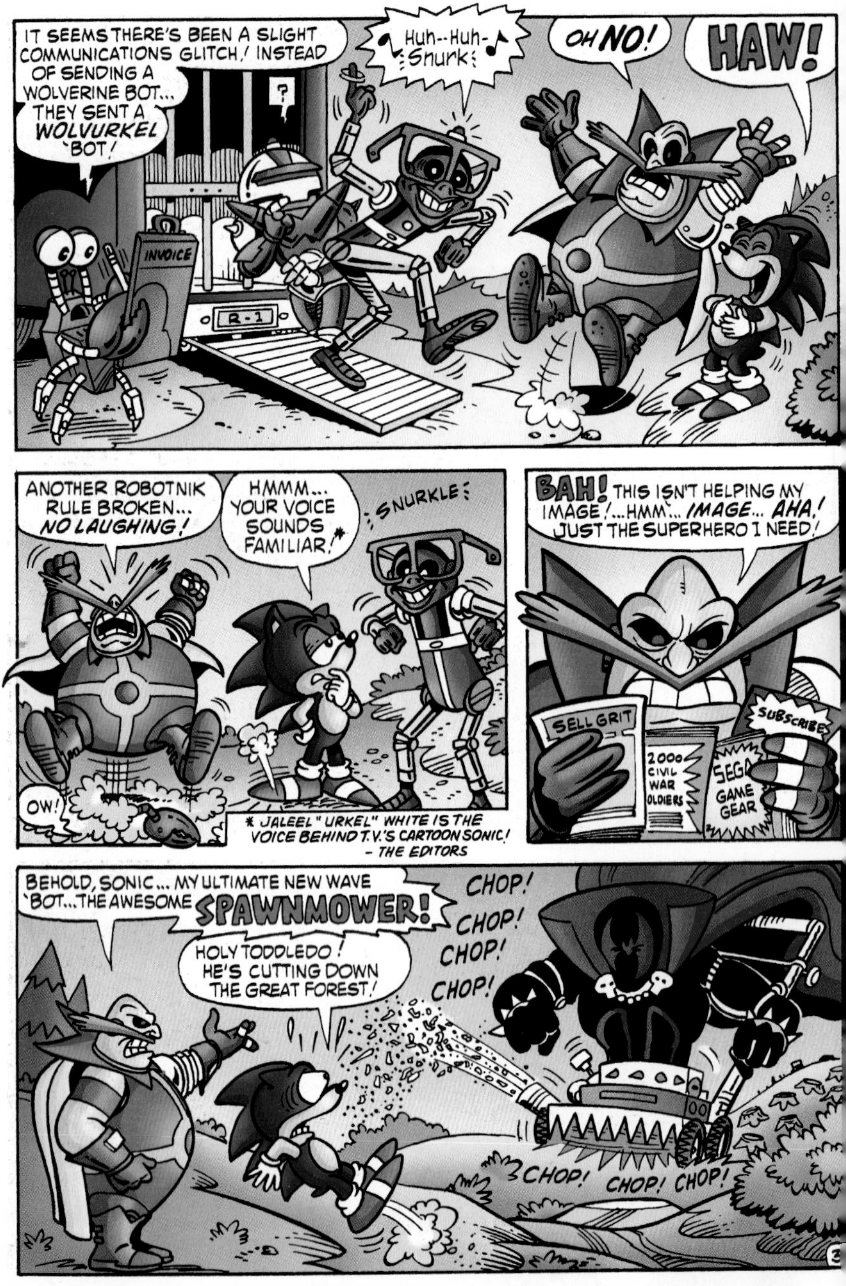
IT SEEMS THERE'S BEEN A SLIGHT COMMUNICATIONS GLITCH! INSTEAD OF SENDING A WOLVERINE BOT... THEY SENT A WOLVURKEL 'BOT!
Huh--Huh-Snurk
?
INVOICE
R-1
OH NO!
HAW!
ANOTHER ROBOTNIK RULE BROKEN... NO LAUGHING!
HMMM... YOUR VOICE SOUNDS FAMILIAR!*
SNURKLE
OW!
* JALEEL "URKEL" WHITE IS THE VOICE BEHIND T.V.'S CARTOON SONIC! - THE EDITORS
BAH! THIS ISN'T HELPING MY IMAGE!...HMM... IMAGE... AHA! JUST THE SUPERHERO I NEED!
SELL GRIT
2000 CIVIL WAR OLDIERS
SUBSCRIBE
SEGA GAME GEAR
BEHOLD, SONIC... MY ULTIMATE NEW WAVE 'BOT...THE AWESOME SPAWNMOWER!
HOLY TODDLEDO! HE'S CUTTING DOWN THE GREAT FOREST!
CHOP! CHOP! CHOP! CHOP!
CHOP! CHOP! CHOP!

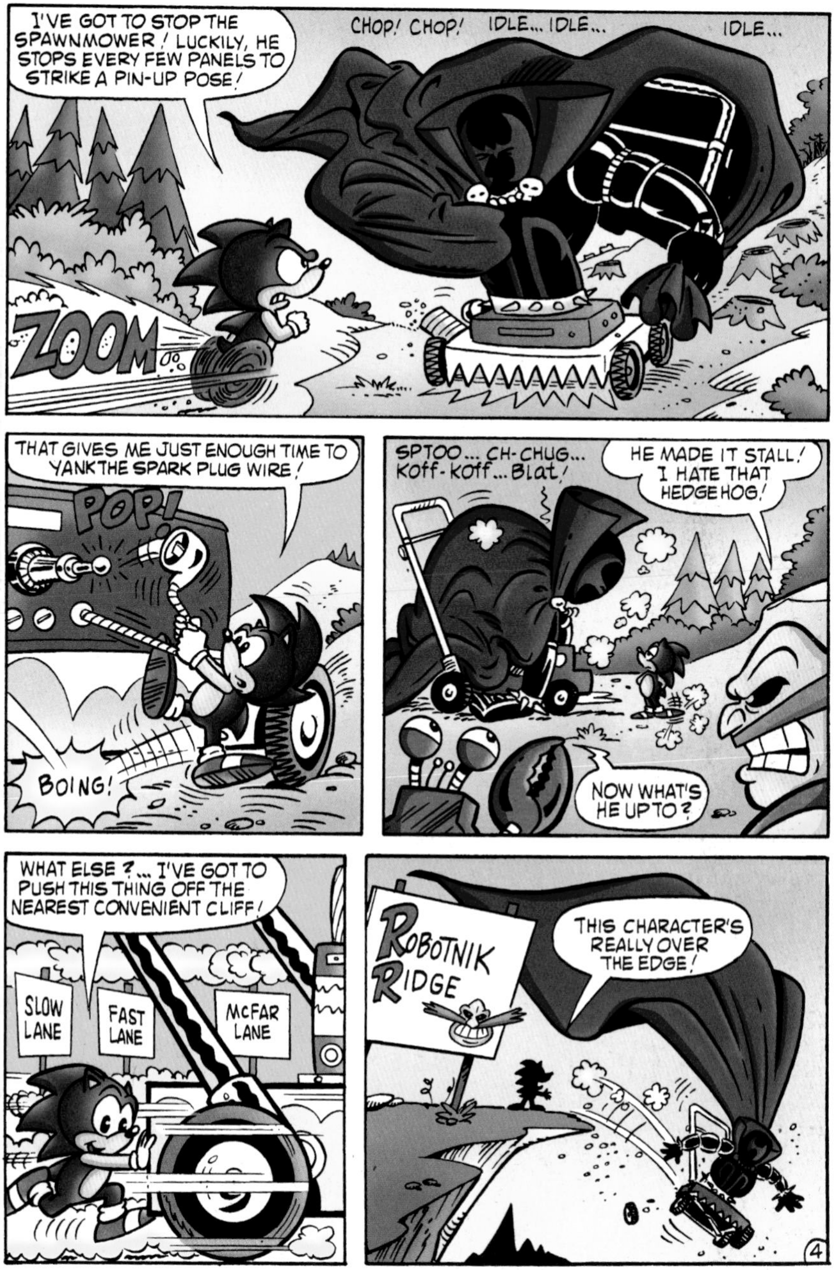
I'VE GOT TO STOP THE SPAWNMOWER! LUCKILY, HE STOPS EVERY FEW PANELS TO STRIKE A PIN-UP POSE!
CHOP! CHOP! IDLE... IDLE... IDLE...
ZOOM
THAT GIVES ME JUST ENOUGH TIME TO YANK THE SPARK PLUG WIRE!
POP!
BOING!
SPTOO... CH-CHUG... Koff-koff... Blat!
HE MADE IT STALL! I HATE THAT HEDGEHOG!
NOW WHAT'S HE UP TO?
WHAT ELSE?... I'VE GOT TO PUSH THIS THING OFF THE NEAREST CONVENIENT CLIFF!
SLOW LANE
FAST LANE
MCFAR LANE
ROBOTNIK RIDGE
THIS CHARACTER'S REALLY OVER THE EDGE!
4

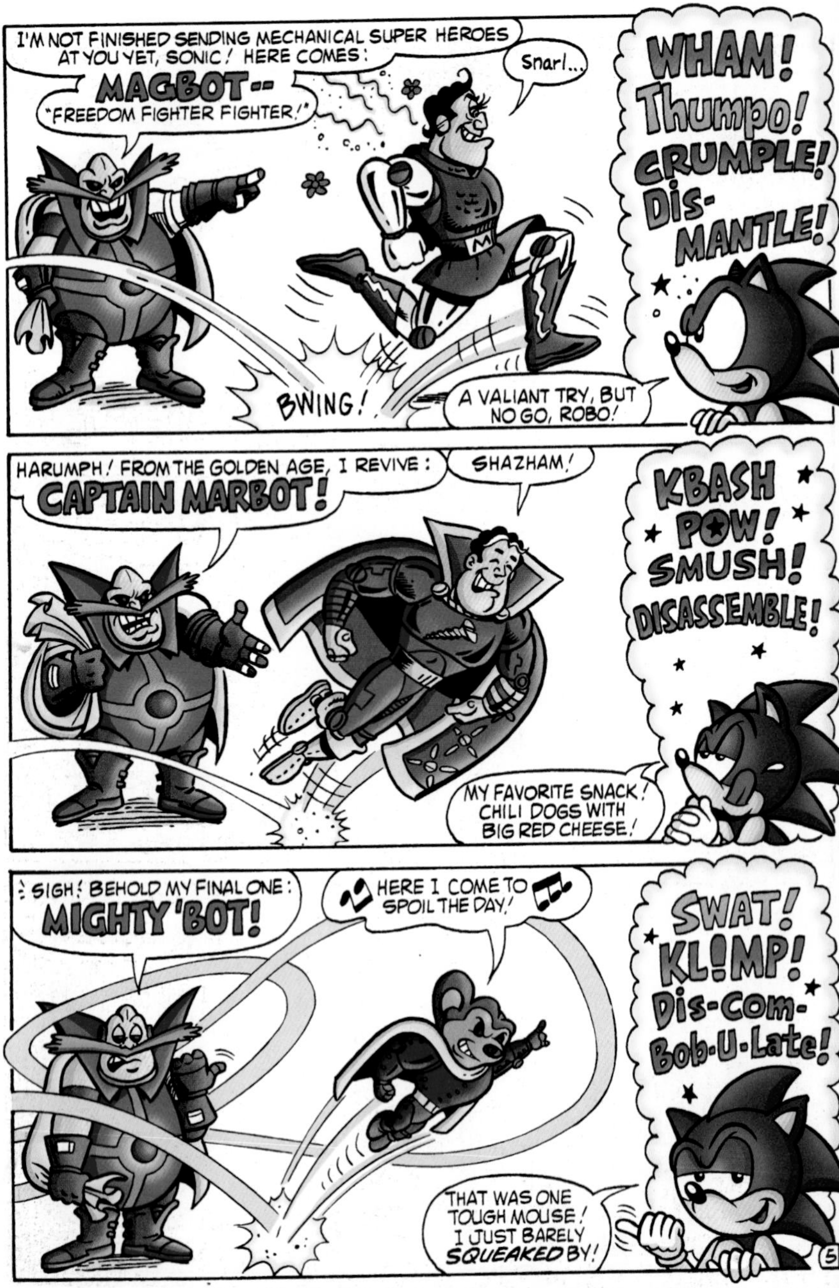
I'M NOT FINISHED SENDING MECHANICAL SUPER HEROES AT YOU YET, SONIC! HERE COMES:
MAGBOT-- "FREEDOM FIGHTER FIGHTER!"
Snarl...
WHAM! Thumpo! CRUMPLE! Dis-MANTLE!
BWING!
A VALIANT TRY, BUT NO GO, ROBO!
HARUMPH! FROM THE GOLDEN AGE, I REVIVE:
CAPTAIN MARBOT!
SHAZHAM!
KBASH POW! SMUSH! DISASSEMBLE!
MY FAVORITE SNACK! CHILI DOGS WITH BIG RED CHEESE!
SIGH! BEHOLD MY FINAL ONE:
MIGHTY 'BOT!
HERE I COME TO SPOIL THE DAY!
SWAT! KL!MP! Dis-Com-Bob-U-Late!
THAT WAS ONE TOUGH MOUSE! I JUST BARELY SQUEAKED BY!

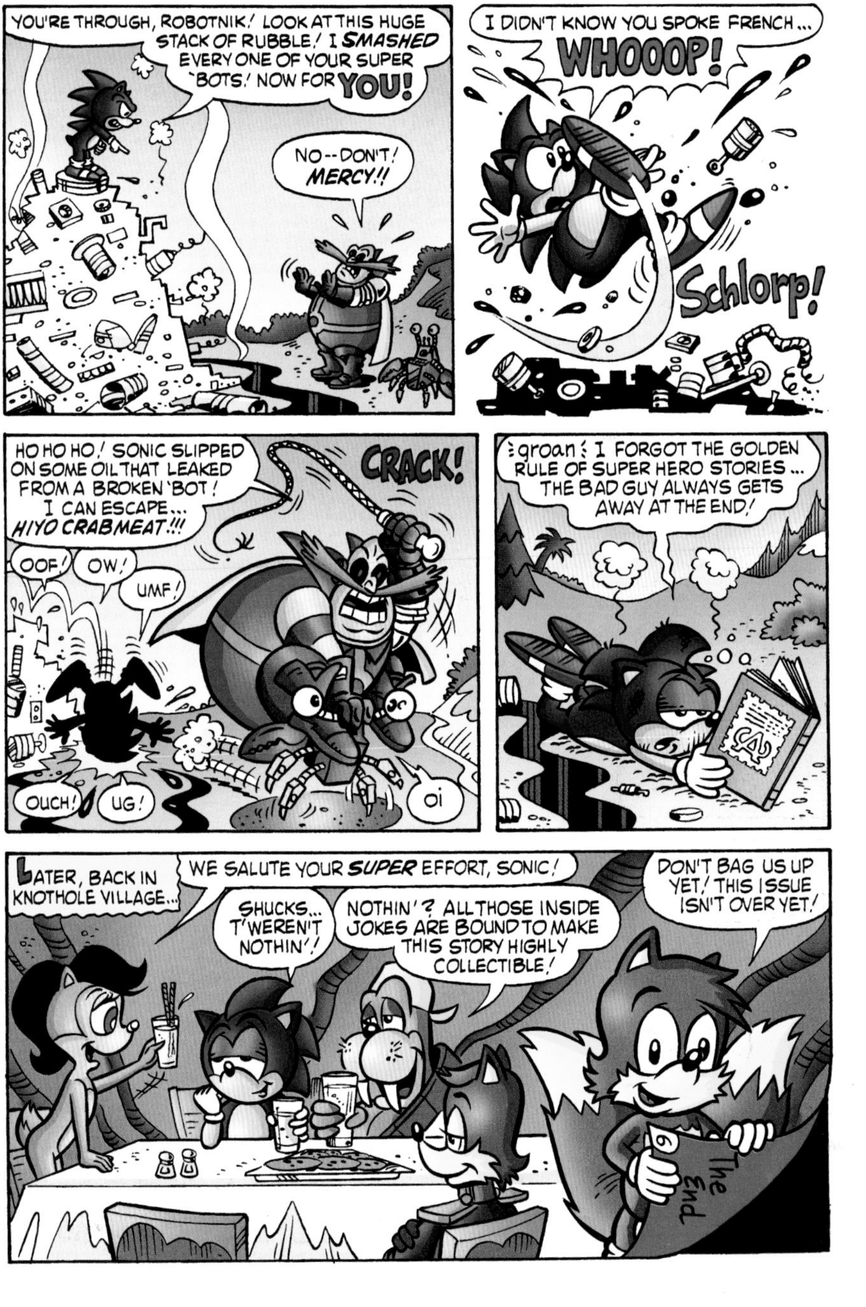
YOU'RE THROUGH, ROBOTNIK! LOOK AT THIS HUGE STACK OF RUBBLE! I *SMASHED* EVERY ONE OF YOUR SUPER 'BOTS! NOW FOR **YOU!**
NO--DON'T! *MERCY!!*
I DIDN'T KNOW YOU SPOKE FRENCH...
WHOOOP!
Schlorp!
HO HO HO! SONIC SLIPPED ON SOME OIL THAT LEAKED FROM A BROKEN 'BOT! I CAN ESCAPE... *HIYO CRABMEAT!!!*
CRACK!
OOF!
OW!
UMF!
OUCH!
UG!
OI
:groan: I FORGOT THE GOLDEN RULE OF SUPER HERO STORIES ... THE BAD GUY ALWAYS GETS AWAY AT THE END!
LATER, BACK IN KNOTHOLE VILLAGE...
WE SALUTE YOUR *SUPER* EFFORT, SONIC!
SHUCKS... T'WEREN'T NOTHIN'!
NOTHIN'? ALL THOSE INSIDE JOKES ARE BOUND TO MAKE THIS STORY HIGHLY COLLECTIBLE!
DON'T BAG US UP YET! THIS ISSUE ISN'T OVER YET!
The End

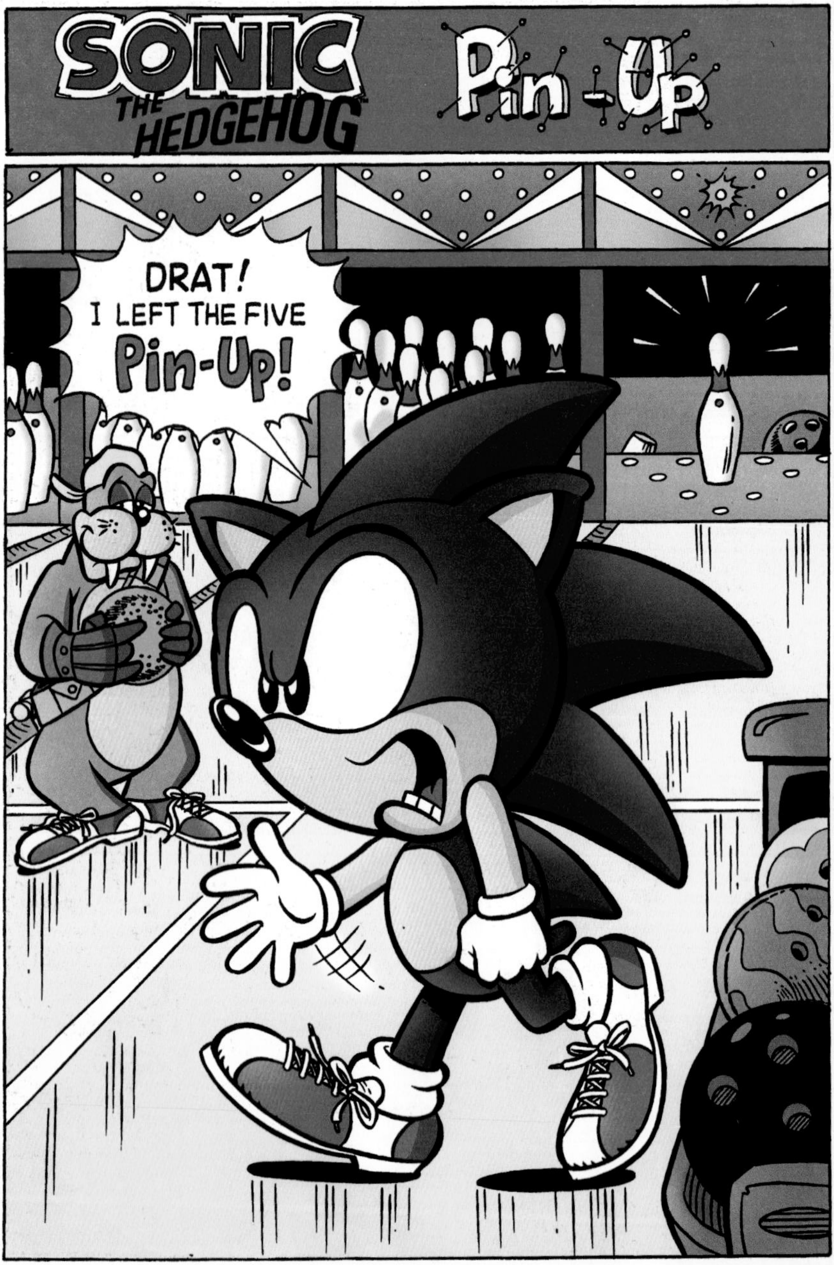
SONIC THE HEDGEHOG
Pin-Up
DRAT! I LEFT THE FIVE Pin-Up!

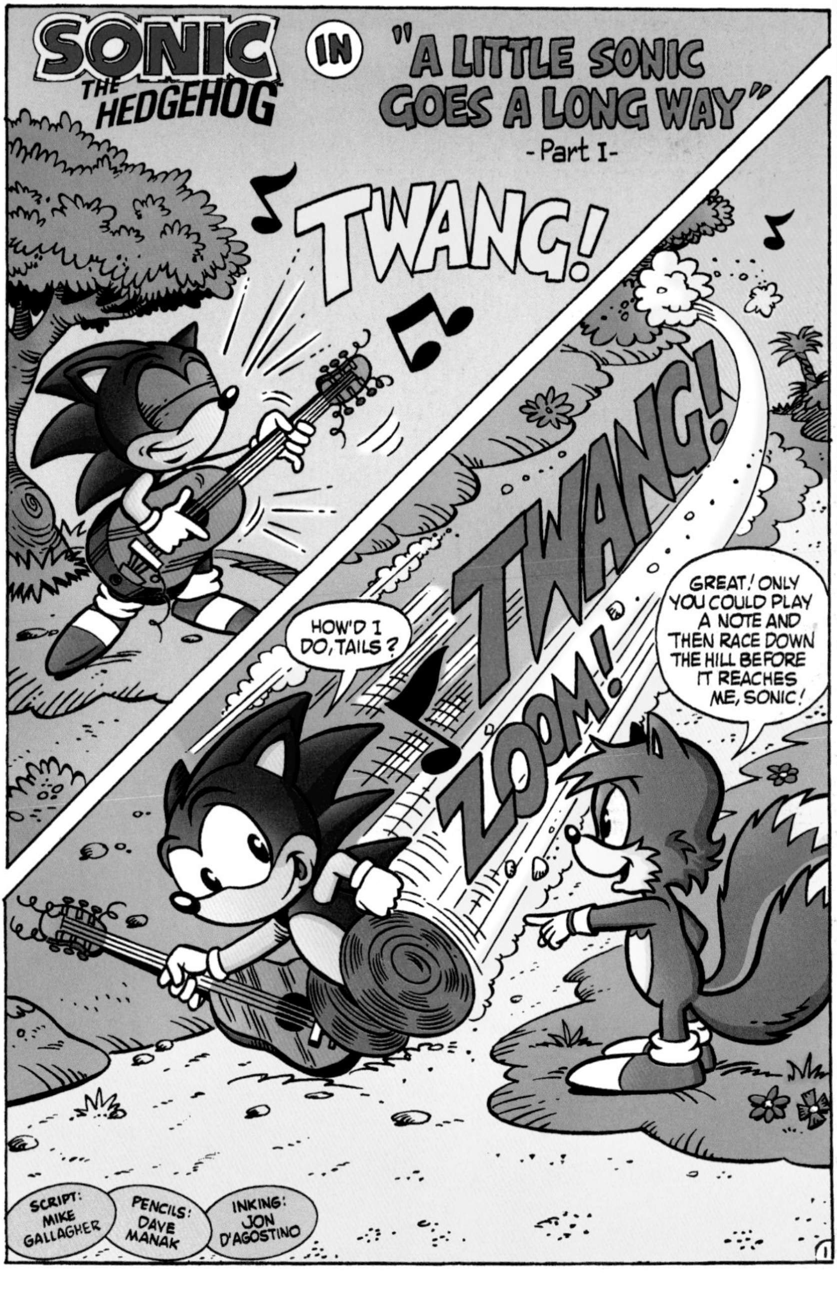
SONIC THE HEDGEHOG IN
"A LITTLE SONIC GOES A LONG WAY"
-Part I-
TWANG!
TWANG!
ZOOM!
HOW'D I DO, TAILS?
GREAT! ONLY YOU COULD PLAY A NOTE AND THEN RACE DOWN THE HILL BEFORE IT REACHES ME, SONIC!
SCRIPT: MIKE GALLAGHER
PENCILS: DAVE MANAK
INKING: JON D'AGOSTINO
1

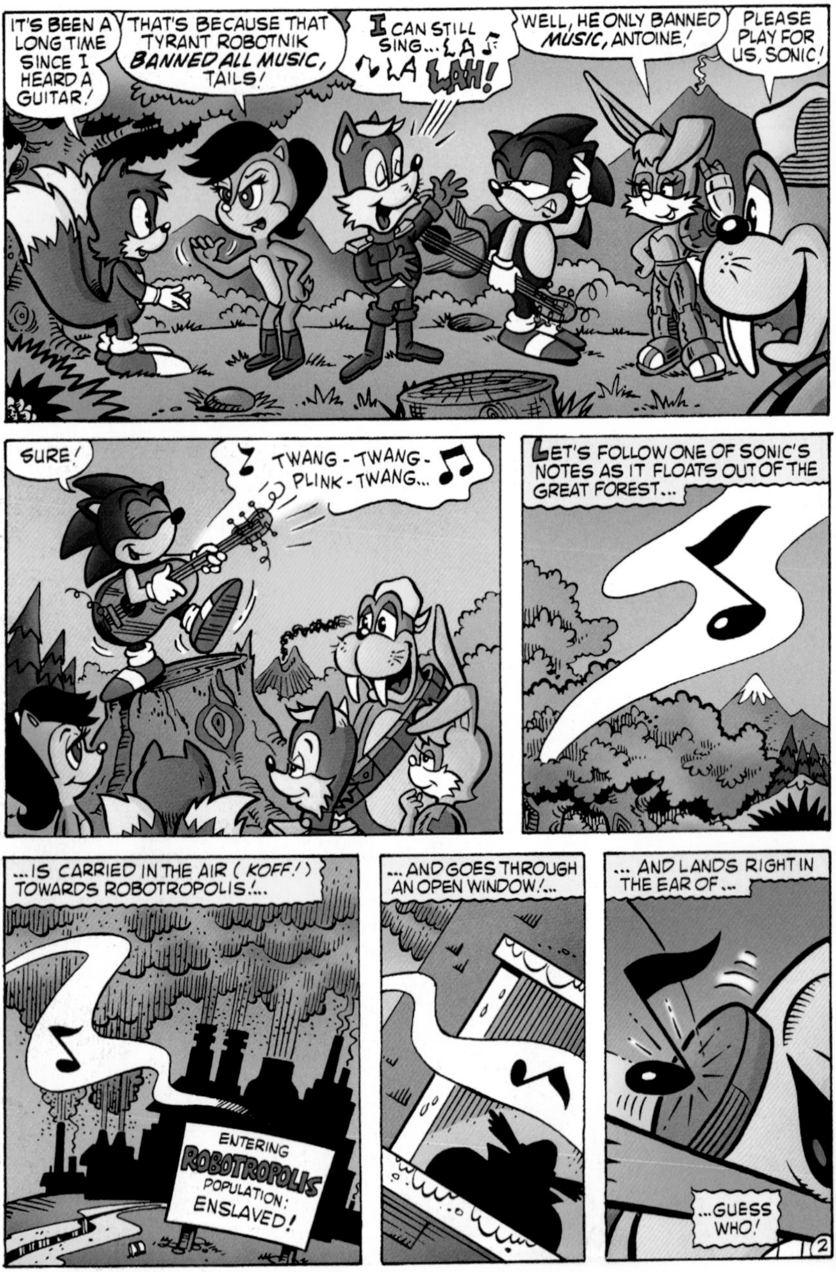
IT'S BEEN A LONG TIME SINCE I HEARD A GUITAR!
THAT'S BECAUSE THAT TYRANT ROBOTNIK BANNED ALL MUSIC, TAILS!
I CAN STILL SING... LA LA LAH!
WELL, HE ONLY BANNED MUSIC, ANTOINE!
PLEASE PLAY FOR US, SONIC!
SURE!
TWANG - TWANG - PLINK - TWANG...
LET'S FOLLOW ONE OF SONIC'S NOTES AS IT FLOATS OUT OF THE GREAT FOREST...
...IS CARRIED IN THE AIR (KOFF!) TOWARDS ROBOTROPOLIS!...
ENTERING ROBOTROPOLIS POPULATION: ENSLAVED!
... AND GOES THROUGH AN OPEN WINDOW!...
... AND LANDS RIGHT IN THE EAR OF...
...GUESS WHO!
2

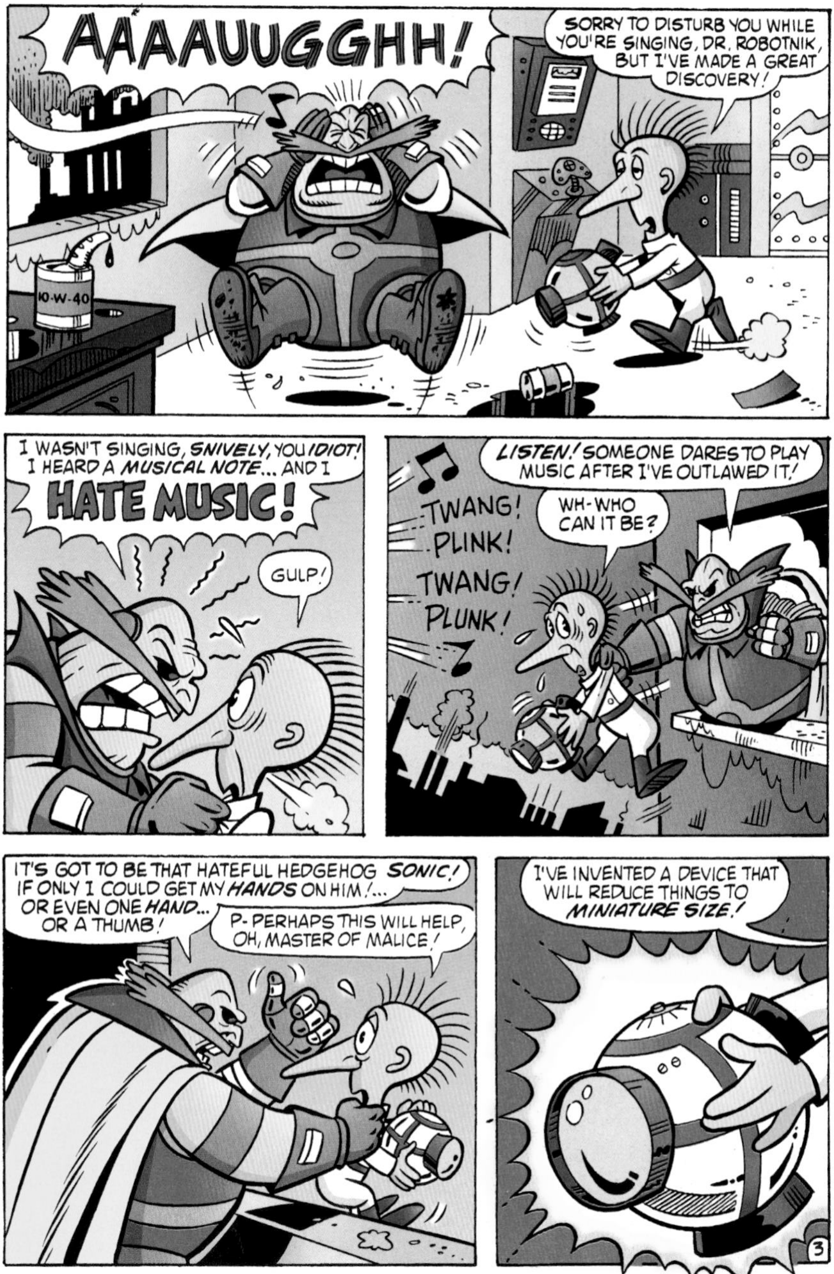
AAAAUUGGHH!
SORRY TO DISTURB YOU WHILE YOU'RE SINGING, DR. ROBOTNIK, BUT I'VE MADE A GREAT DISCOVERY!
10-W-40
I WASN'T SINGING, SNIVELY, YOU IDIOT! I HEARD A MUSICAL NOTE... AND I HATE MUSIC!
GULP!
LISTEN! SOMEONE DARES TO PLAY MUSIC AFTER I'VE OUTLAWED IT!
TWANG! PLINK! TWANG! PLUNK!
WH-WHO CAN IT BE?
IT'S GOT TO BE THAT HATEFUL HEDGEHOG SONIC! IF ONLY I COULD GET MY HANDS ON HIM!... OR EVEN ONE HAND... OR A THUMB!
P-PERHAPS THIS WILL HELP, OH, MASTER OF MALICE!
I'VE INVENTED A DEVICE THAT WILL REDUCE THINGS TO MINIATURE SIZE!

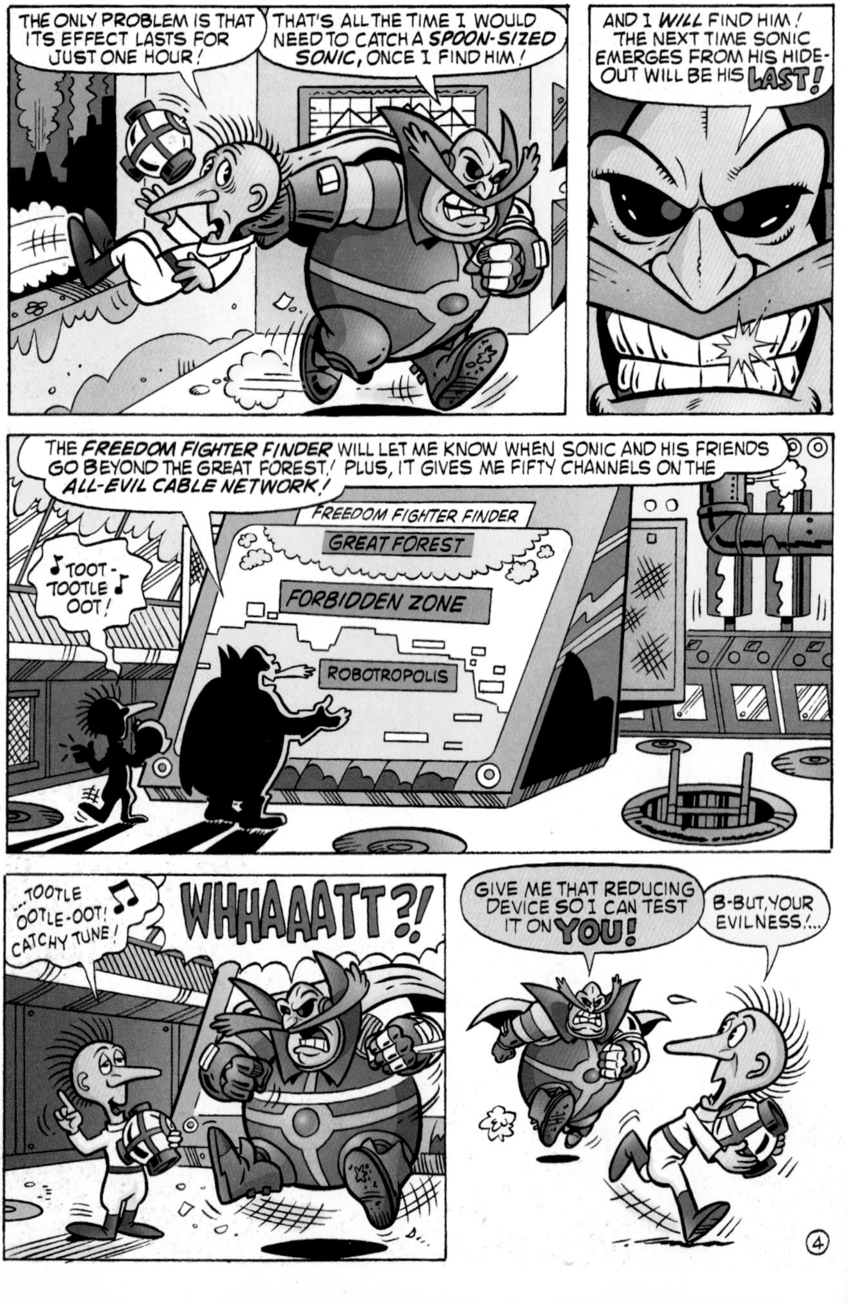

THE ONLY PROBLEM IS THAT ITS EFFECT LASTS FOR JUST ONE HOUR!
THAT'S ALL THE TIME I WOULD NEED TO CATCH A SPOON-SIZED SONIC, ONCE I FIND HIM!
AND I WILL FIND HIM! THE NEXT TIME SONIC EMERGES FROM HIS HIDE-OUT WILL BE HIS LAST!
THE FREEDOM FIGHTER FINDER WILL LET ME KNOW WHEN SONIC AND HIS FRIENDS GO BEYOND THE GREAT FOREST! PLUS, IT GIVES ME FIFTY CHANNELS ON THE ALL-EVIL CABLE NETWORK!
FREEDOM FIGHTER FINDER
GREAT FOREST
FORBIDDEN ZONE
ROBOTROPOLIS
♪ TOOT-TOOTLE ♪ OOT!
...TOOTLE OOTLE-OOT! CATCHY TUNE!
WHHAAATT?!
GIVE ME THAT REDUCING DEVICE SO I CAN TEST IT ON YOU!
B-BUT, YOUR EVILNESS!...

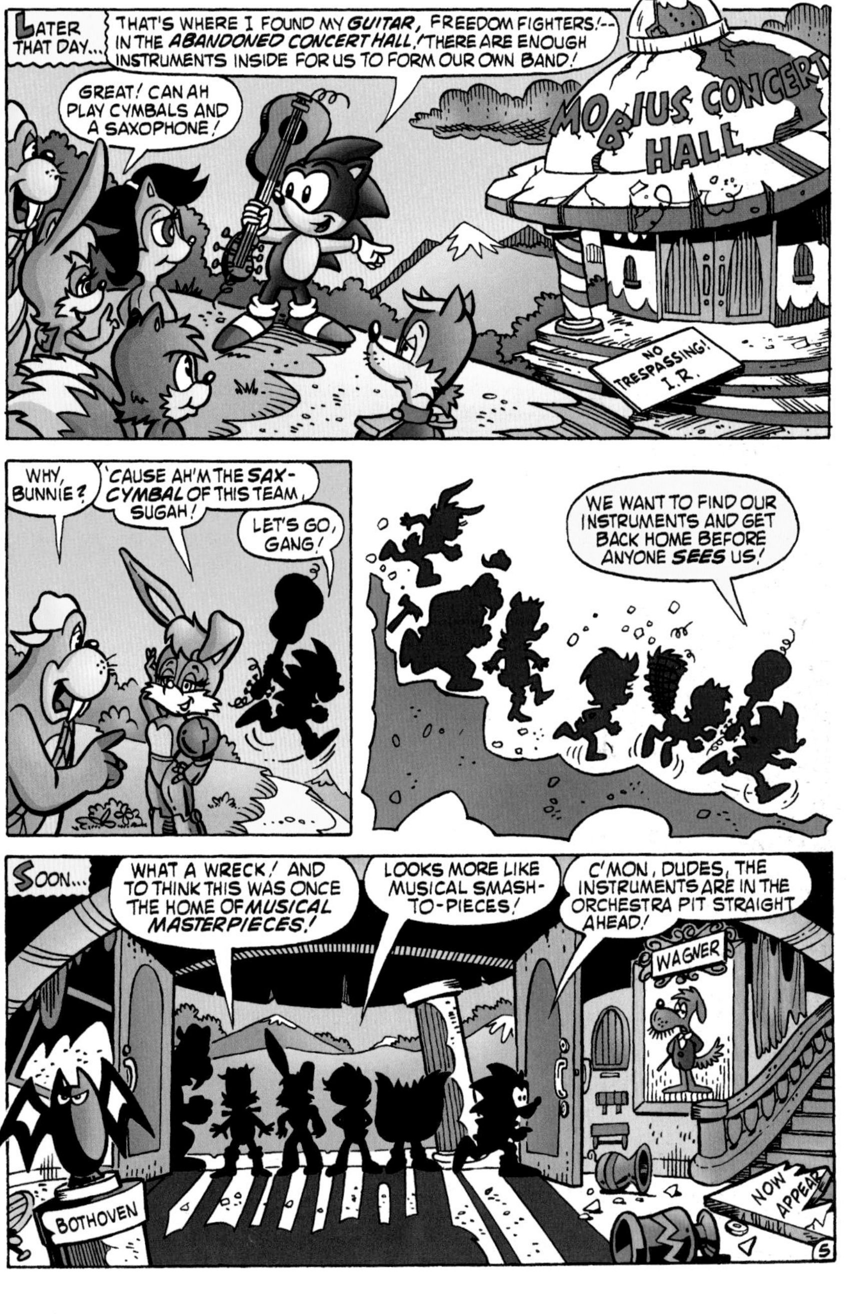
LATER THAT DAY...
THAT'S WHERE I FOUND MY GUITAR, FREEDOM FIGHTERS!--IN THE ABANDONED CONCERT HALL! THERE ARE ENOUGH INSTRUMENTS INSIDE FOR US TO FORM OUR OWN BAND!
GREAT! CAN AH PLAY CYMBALS AND A SAXOPHONE!
MOBIUS CONCERT HALL
NO TRESPASSING! I.R.
WHY, BUNNIE?
'CAUSE AH'M THE SAX-CYMBAL OF THIS TEAM, SUGAH!
LET'S GO, GANG!
WE WANT TO FIND OUR INSTRUMENTS AND GET BACK HOME BEFORE ANYONE SEES US!
SOON...
WHAT A WRECK! AND TO THINK THIS WAS ONCE THE HOME OF MUSICAL MASTERPIECES!
LOOKS MORE LIKE MUSICAL SMASH-TO-PIECES!
C'MON, DUDES, THE INSTRUMENTS ARE IN THE ORCHESTRA PIT STRAIGHT AHEAD!
WAGNER
BOTHOVEN
NOW APPEAR
5

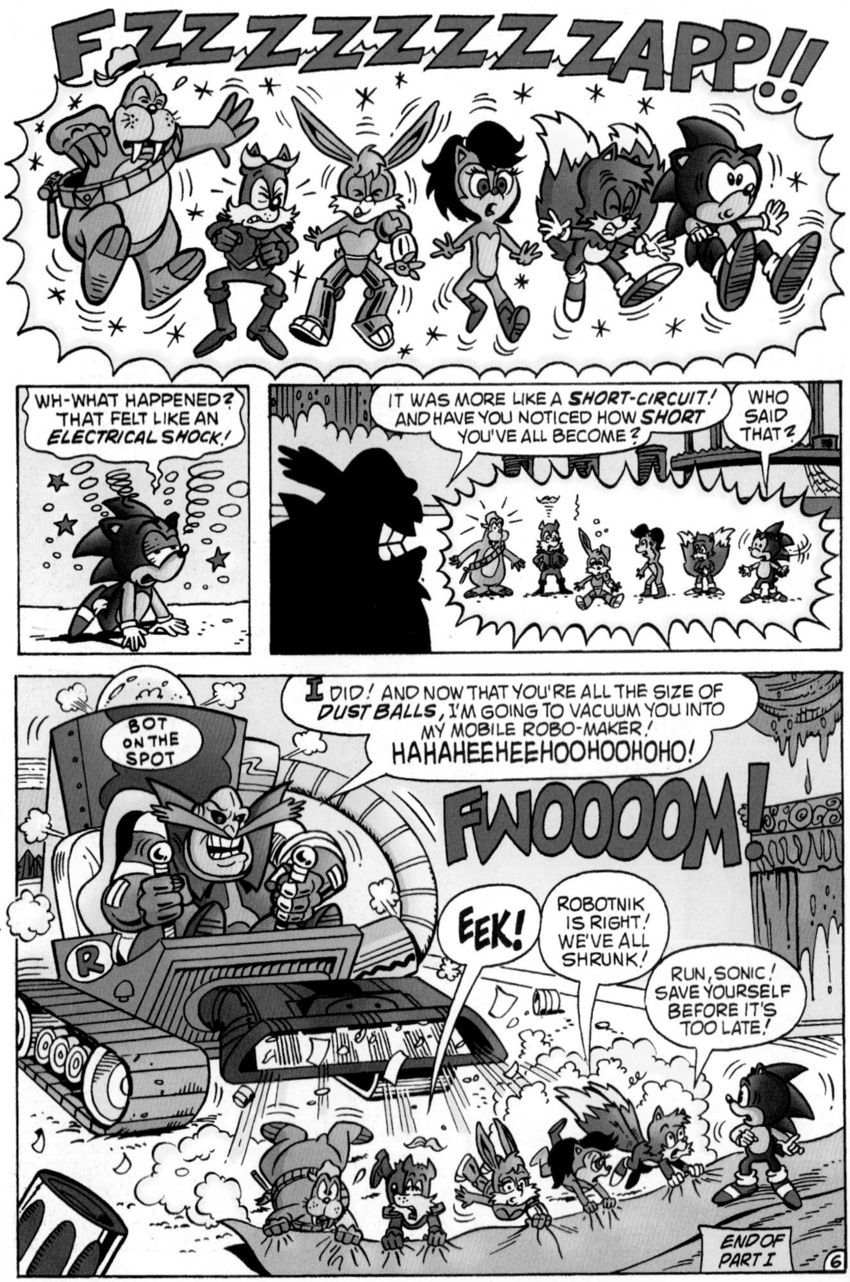
FZZZZZZZZZZAPP!!
WH-WHAT HAPPENED? THAT FELT LIKE AN ELECTRICAL SHOCK!
IT WAS MORE LIKE A SHORT-CIRCUIT! AND HAVE YOU NOTICED HOW SHORT YOU'VE ALL BECOME?
WHO SAID THAT?
I DID! AND NOW THAT YOU'RE ALL THE SIZE OF DUST BALLS, I'M GOING TO VACUUM YOU INTO MY MOBILE ROBO-MAKER! HAHAHEEHEEHOOHOOHOHO!
BOT ON THE SPOT
FWOOOOM!
EEK!
ROBOTNIK IS RIGHT! WE'VE ALL SHRUNK!
RUN, SONIC! SAVE YOURSELF BEFORE IT'S TOO LATE!
END OF PART I

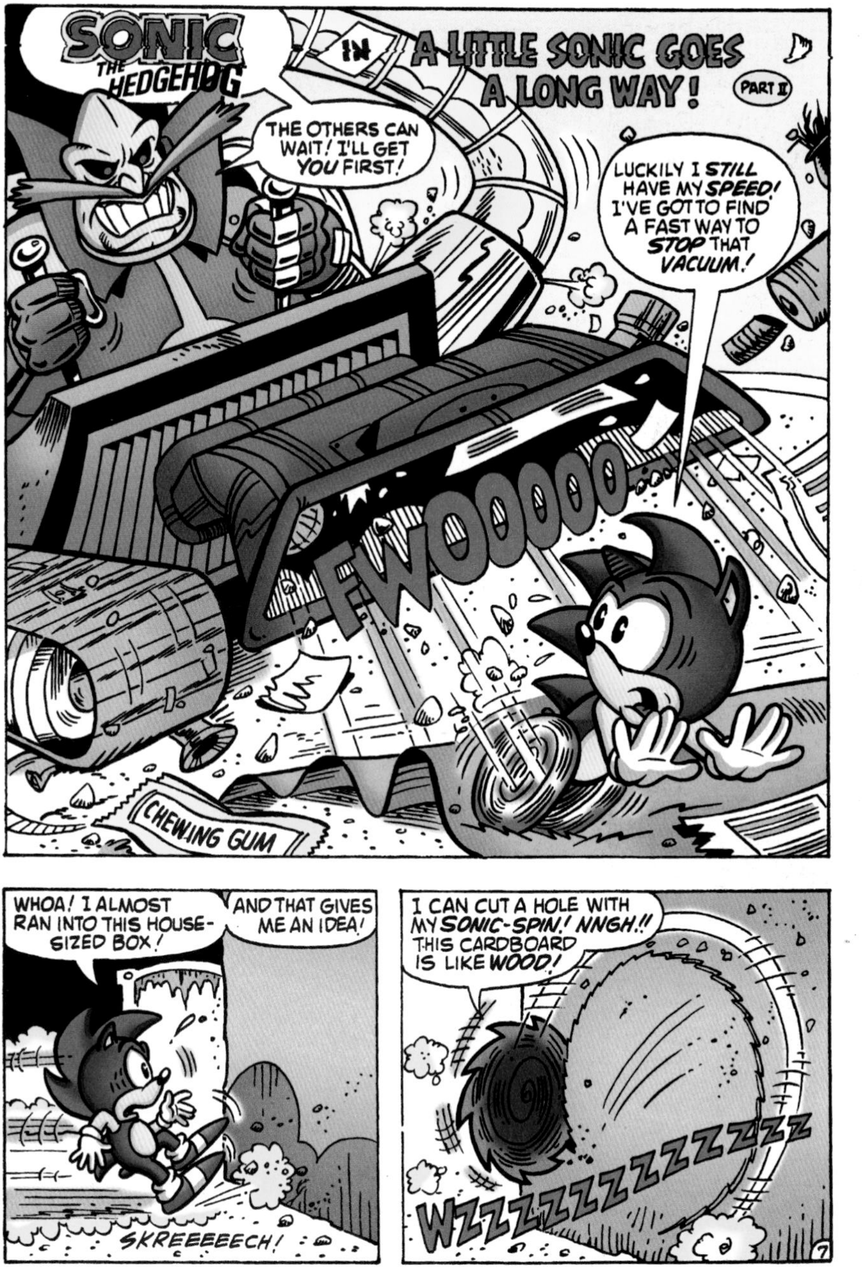
SONIC THE HEDGEHOG
IN
A LITTLE SONIC GOES A LONG WAY!
PART II
THE OTHERS CAN WAIT! I'LL GET YOU FIRST!
LUCKILY I STILL HAVE MY SPEED! I'VE GOT TO FIND A FAST WAY TO STOP THAT VACUUM!
FWOOOOO
CHEWING GUM
WHOA! I ALMOST RAN INTO THIS HOUSE-SIZED BOX!
AND THAT GIVES ME AN IDEA!
SKREEEEECH!
I CAN CUT A HOLE WITH MY SONIC-SPIN! NNGH!! THIS CARDBOARD IS LIKE WOOD!
WZZZZZZZZZZZ

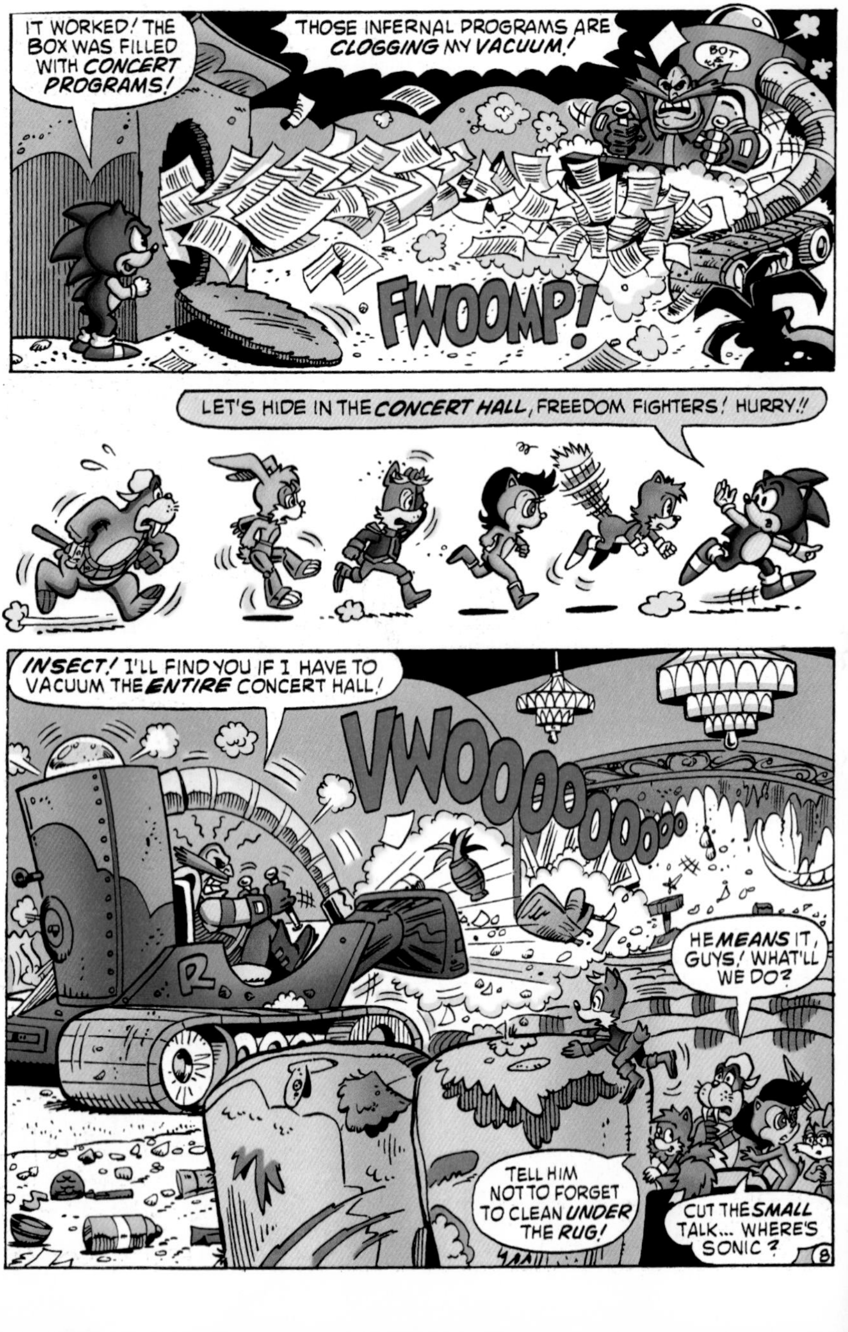
IT WORKED! THE BOX WAS FILLED WITH CONCERT PROGRAMS!
THOSE INFERNAL PROGRAMS ARE CLOGGING MY VACUUM!
FWOOMP!
LET'S HIDE IN THE CONCERT HALL, FREEDOM FIGHTERS! HURRY!!
INSECT! I'LL FIND YOU IF I HAVE TO VACUUM THE ENTIRE CONCERT HALL!
VWOOOOOOOOOO
HE MEANS IT, GUYS! WHAT'LL WE DO?
TELL HIM NOT TO FORGET TO CLEAN UNDER THE RUG!
CUT THE SMALL TALK... WHERE'S SONIC?
8

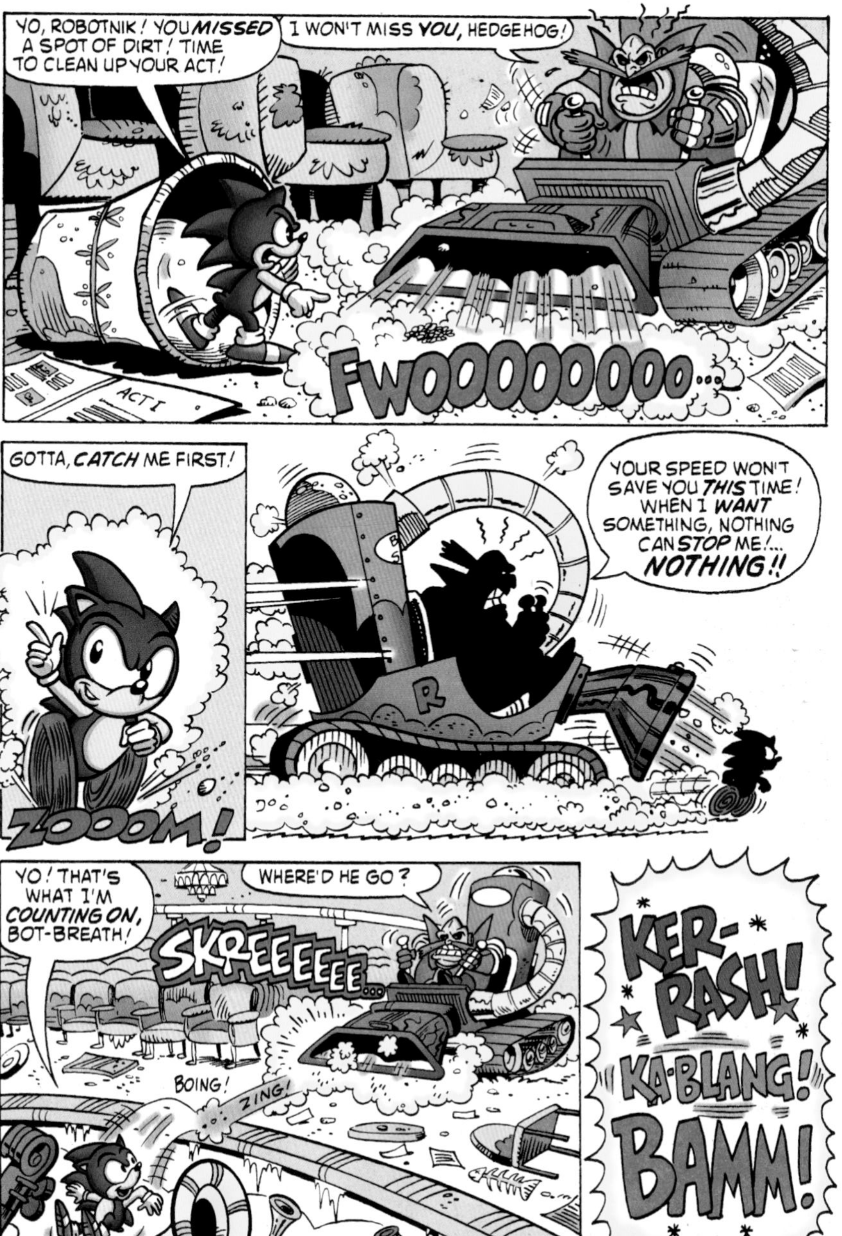
YO, ROBOTNIK! YOU MISSED A SPOT OF DIRT! TIME TO CLEAN UP YOUR ACT!
I WON'T MISS YOU, HEDGEHOG!
ACT I
FWOOOOOOOOO...
GOTTA, CATCH ME FIRST!
YOUR SPEED WON'T SAVE YOU THIS TIME! WHEN I WANT SOMETHING, NOTHING CAN STOP ME!... NOTHING!!
R
ZOOOM!
YO! THAT'S WHAT I'M COUNTING ON, BOT-BREATH!
WHERE'D HE GO?
SKREEEEEEE...
BOING!
ZING!
KER-RASH!
KA-BLANG!
BAMM!

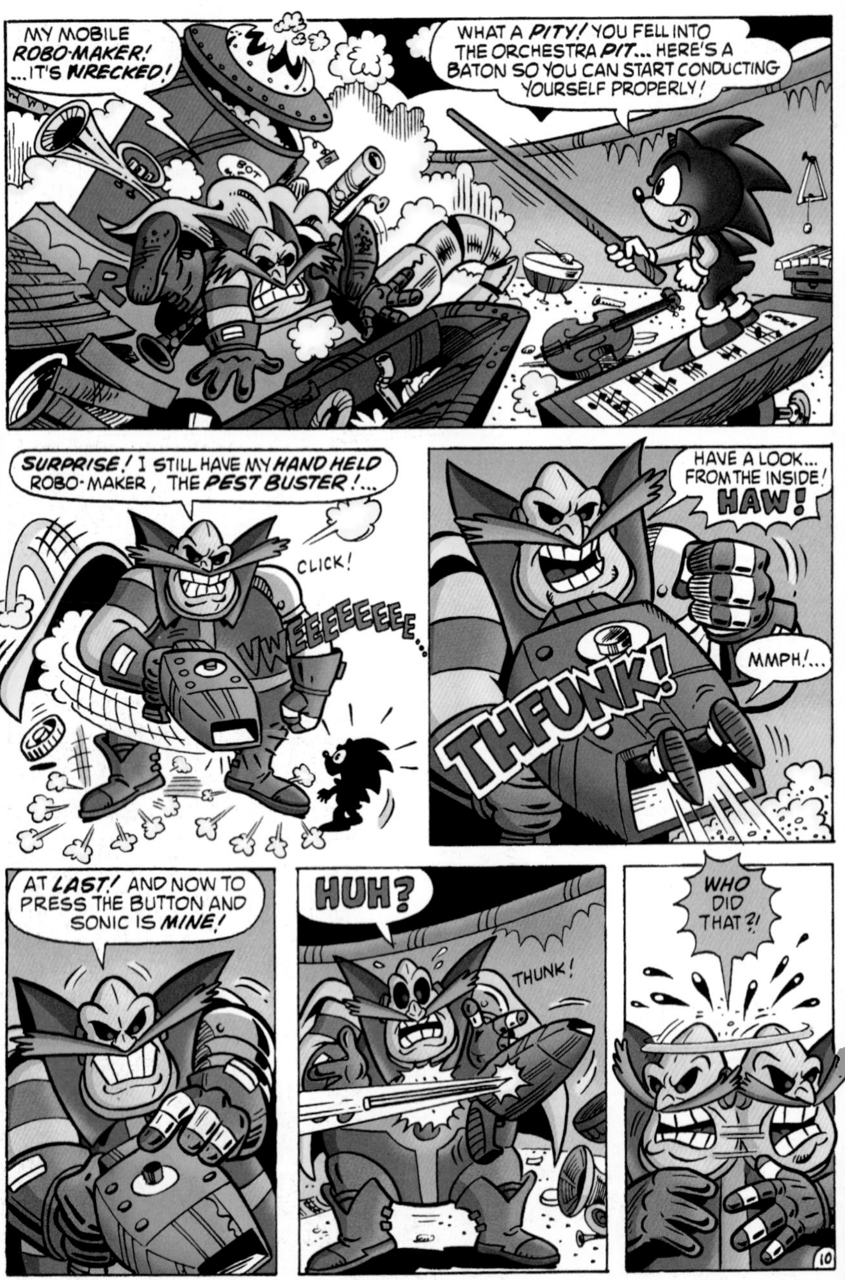
MY MOBILE ROBO-MAKER! ...IT'S WRECKED!
WHAT A PITY! YOU FELL INTO THE ORCHESTRA PIT... HERE'S A BATON SO YOU CAN START CONDUCTING YOURSELF PROPERLY!
SURPRISE! I STILL HAVE MY HAND HELD ROBO-MAKER, THE PEST BUSTER!...
CLICK!
VWEEEEEEEEE...
HAVE A LOOK... FROM THE INSIDE! HAW!
MMPH!...
THFUNK!
AT LAST! AND NOW TO PRESS THE BUTTON AND SONIC IS MINE!
HUH?
THUNK!
WHO DID THAT?!
10

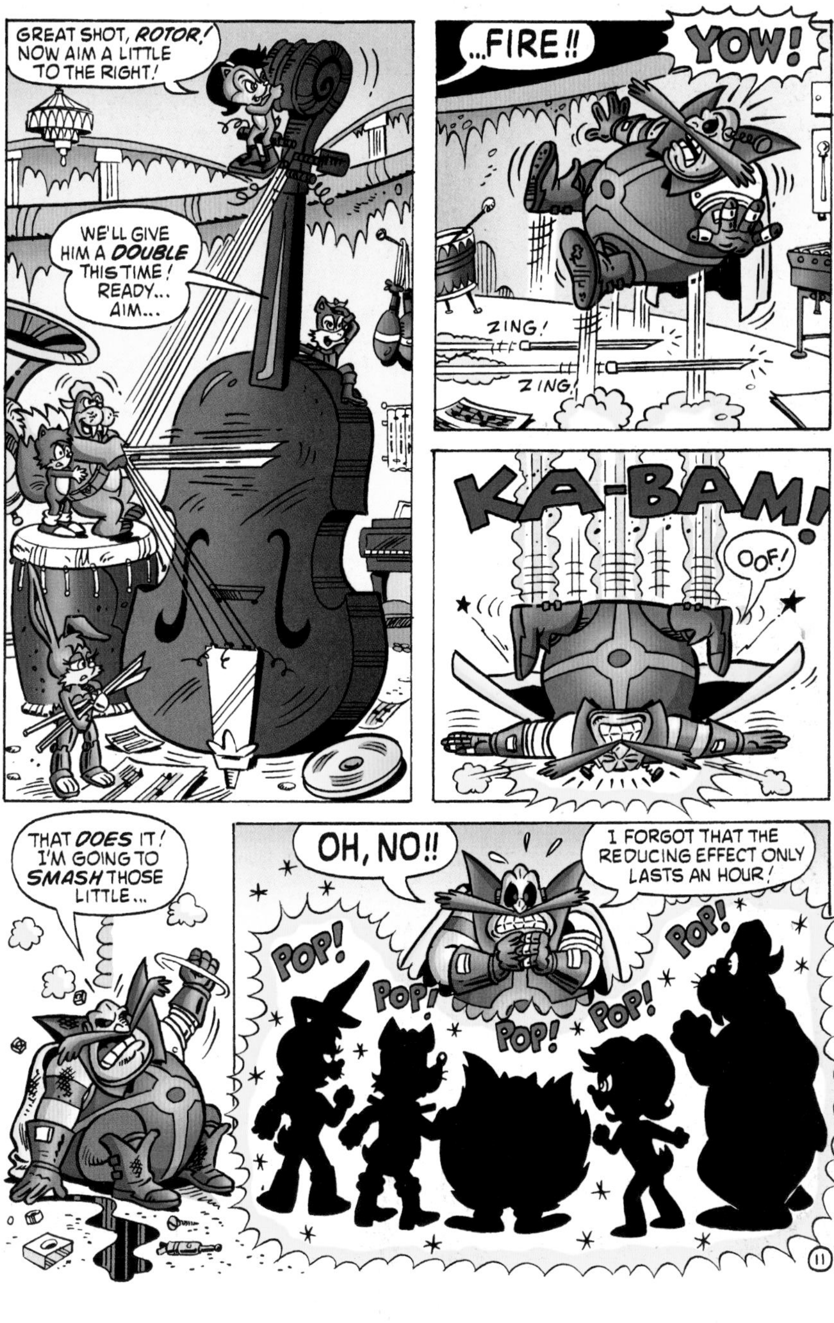
GREAT SHOT, ROTOR! NOW AIM A LITTLE TO THE RIGHT!
WE'LL GIVE HIM A DOUBLE THIS TIME! READY... AIM...
...FIRE!!
YOW!
ZING!
ZING!
KA-BAM!
OOF!
THAT DOES IT! I'M GOING TO SMASH THOSE LITTLE...
OH, NO!!
I FORGOT THAT THE REDUCING EFFECT ONLY LASTS AN HOUR!
POP!
POP!
POP!
POP!
POP!

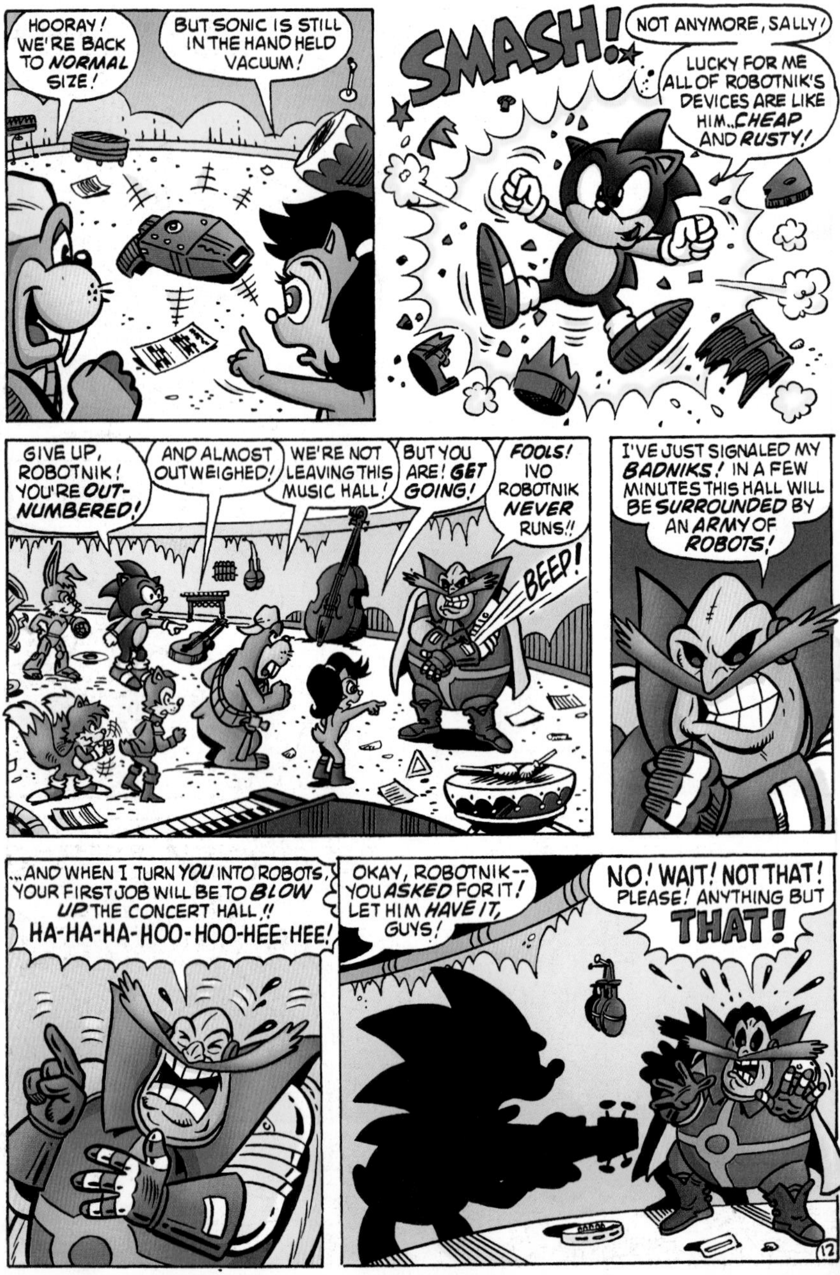
HOORAY! WE'RE BACK TO NORMAL SIZE!
BUT SONIC IS STILL IN THE HAND HELD VACUUM!
SMASH!
NOT ANYMORE, SALLY!
LUCKY FOR ME ALL OF ROBOTNIK'S DEVICES ARE LIKE HIM..CHEAP AND RUSTY!
GIVE UP, ROBOTNIK! YOU'RE OUT-NUMBERED!
AND ALMOST OUTWEIGHED!
WE'RE NOT LEAVING THIS MUSIC HALL!
BUT YOU ARE! GET GOING!
FOOLS! IVO ROBOTNIK NEVER RUNS!!
BEEP!
I'VE JUST SIGNALED MY BADNIKS! IN A FEW MINUTES THIS HALL WILL BE SURROUNDED BY AN ARMY OF ROBOTS!
...AND WHEN I TURN YOU INTO ROBOTS, YOUR FIRST JOB WILL BE TO BLOW UP THE CONCERT HALL!!
HA-HA-HA-HOO-HOO-HEE-HEE!
OKAY, ROBOTNIK-- YOU ASKED FOR IT! LET HIM HAVE IT, GUYS!
NO! WAIT! NOT THAT! PLEASE! ANYTHING BUT THAT!
12

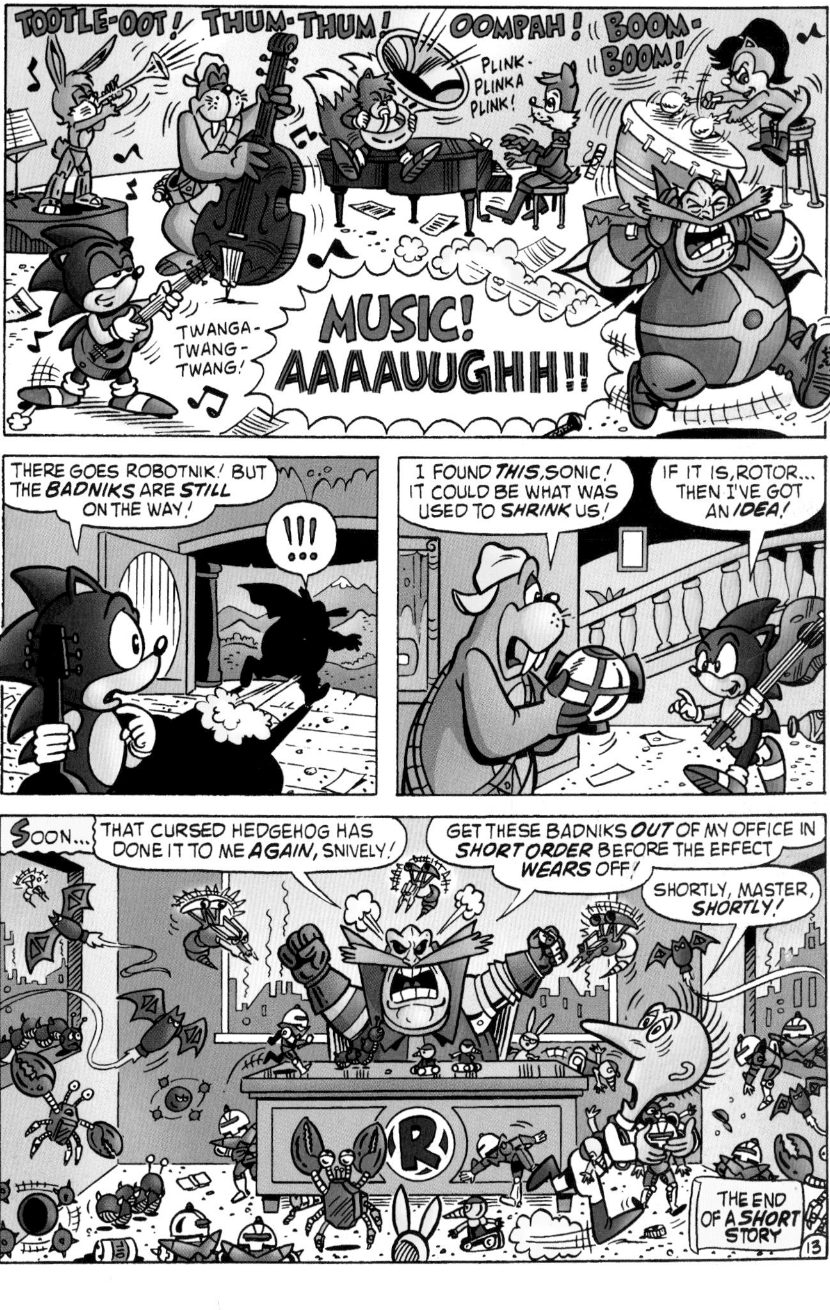
TOOTLE-OOT!
THUM-THUM!
OOMPAH!
BOOM-BOOM!
PLINK-PLINKA PLINK!
TWANGA-TWANG-TWANG!
MUSIC! AAAAUUGHH!!
THERE GOES ROBOTNIK! BUT THE BADNIKS ARE STILL ON THE WAY!
!!!...
I FOUND THIS, SONIC! IT COULD BE WHAT WAS USED TO SHRINK US!
IF IT IS, ROTOR... THEN I'VE GOT AN IDEA!
SOON...
THAT CURSED HEDGEHOG HAS DONE IT TO ME AGAIN, SNIVELY!
GET THESE BADNIKS OUT OF MY OFFICE IN SHORT ORDER BEFORE THE EFFECT WEARS OFF!
SHORTLY, MASTER, SHORTLY!
THE END OF A SHORT STORY

SONIC THE HEDGEHOG™

Welcome to a brief who's who
of the Sonic universe.
You have just read some
of the earliest
and most loved stories from the
Sonic comic. We thought
you'd like to learn a little extra
about a few of your
favorite Sonic characters.

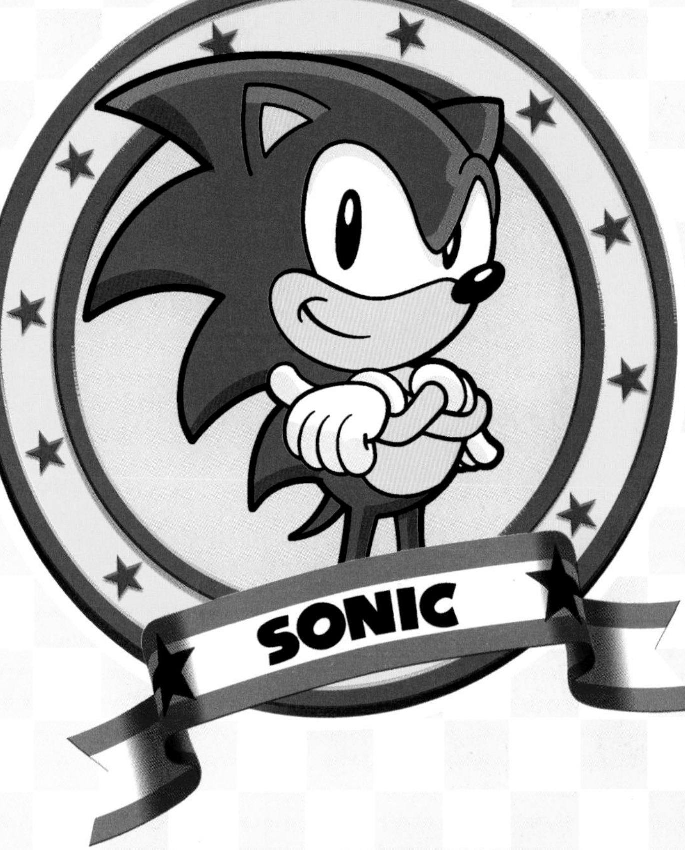
SONIC

SONIC THE HEDGEHOG

Sonic is the fastest and coolest dude in all of Mobius!
He can spin dash any 'bot to pieces
and eat more chilidogs than you can count in a blink
of an eye! Sonic has always helped
the Freedom Fighters, but now it's personal since
Dr. Robotnik kidnapped his beloved Uncle Chuck.

TAILS

MILES "TAILS" PROWER

Miles is called "Tails" by all of his friends since
he has two tails. He's such a bright little guy that
he learned how to fly by spinning his twin tails!
Tails wants to be a big hero just
like Sonic – but first he has to
be able to keep up!

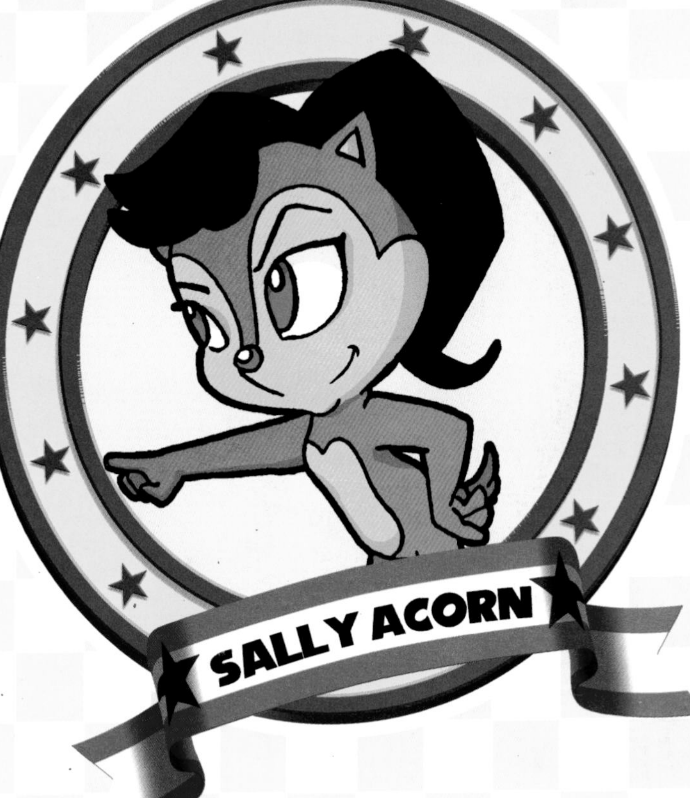
SALLY ACORN

SALLY ACORN

Sally is the smart, pretty, tomboy warrior princess
who leads the Freedom Fighters!
She hopes to get her kingdom back from Dr. Robotnik.
She also hopes to free all of her people.
And maybe – just maybe – she hopes
to win the heart of a certain hedgehog . . .?

BUNNIE RABBOT

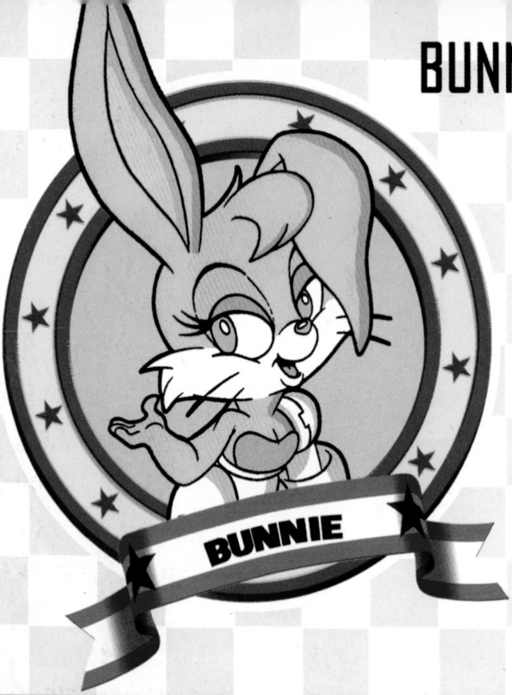
BUNNIE

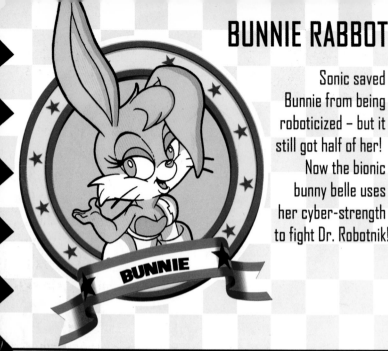

Sonic saved Bunnie from being roboticized – but it still got half of her! Now the bionic bunny belle uses her cyber-strength to fight Dr. Robotnik!

ANTOINE D'COOLETTE

Antoine is a zero who wants to be a hero! He may have a spiffy uniform, but he's a complete coward. His heart is in the right place, though.

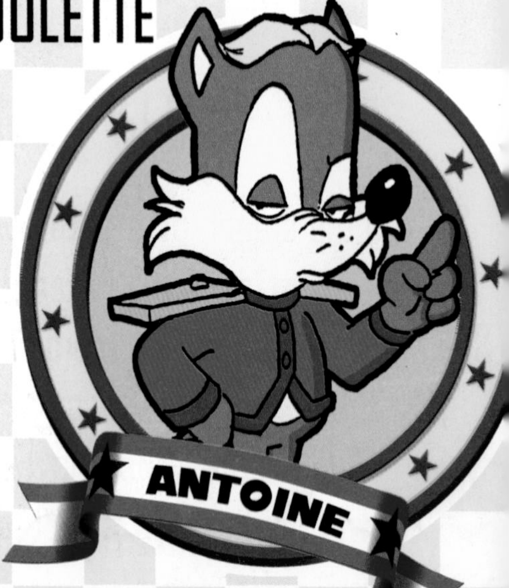
ANTOINE

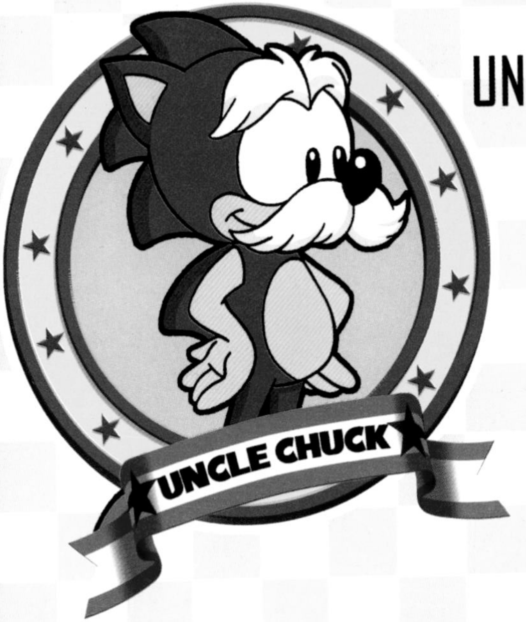
UNCLE CHUCK

UNCLE CHUCK

Sonic's uncle used to be a brilliant inventor but became the world's best chilidog vendor! Now he's one of Dr. Robotnik's roboticized slaves!

ROTOR THE WALRUS

Rotor is the handy-man of the Freedom Fighters. If his friends need a knick-nack or a doo-dad, Rotor's the guy to turn to!

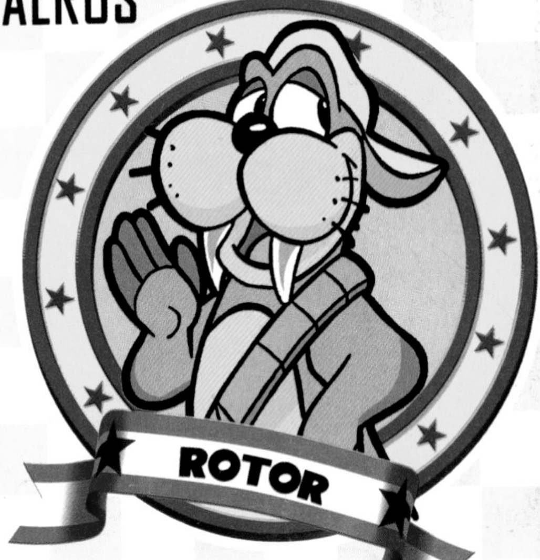
ROTOR

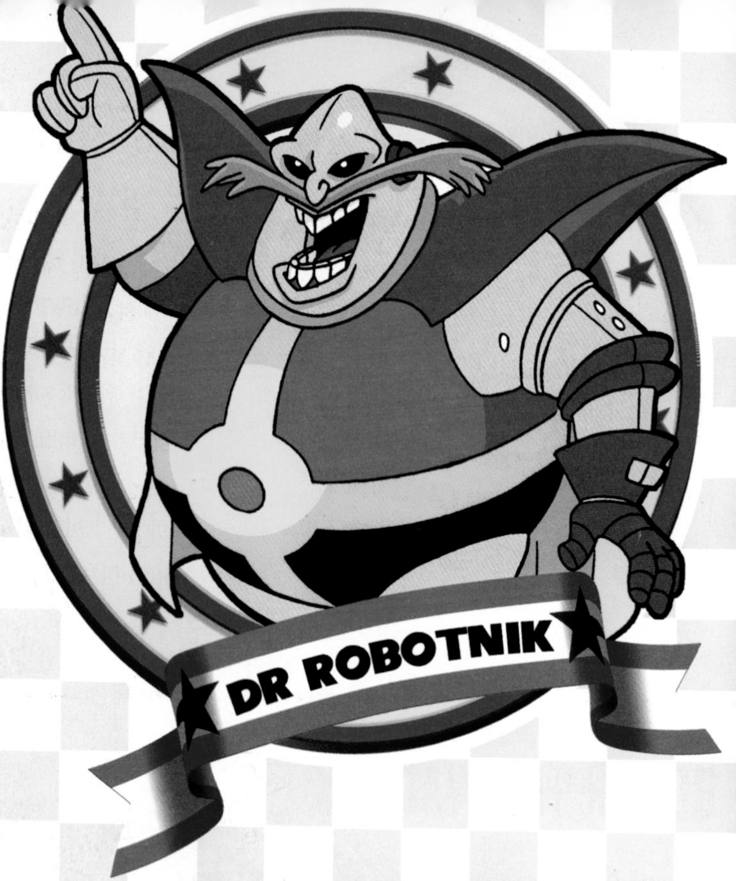
DR ROBOTNIK

DR. IVO ROBOTNIK

With a heart as black as his inhuman eyes, Dr. Robotnik is the tyrant ruler of all of Mobius! He uses his badnik robots to round up helpless folks and turn them into his slaves! The one thing he hates most of all is "that hedgehog"!

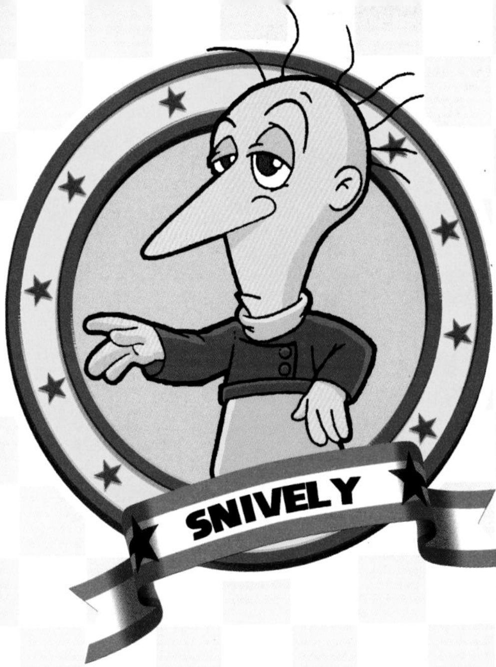
SNIVELY

SNIVELY

Dr. Robotnik's sniveling nephew and second in command. The needle-nose shares his uncle's ambition for world domination.

CRABMEAT

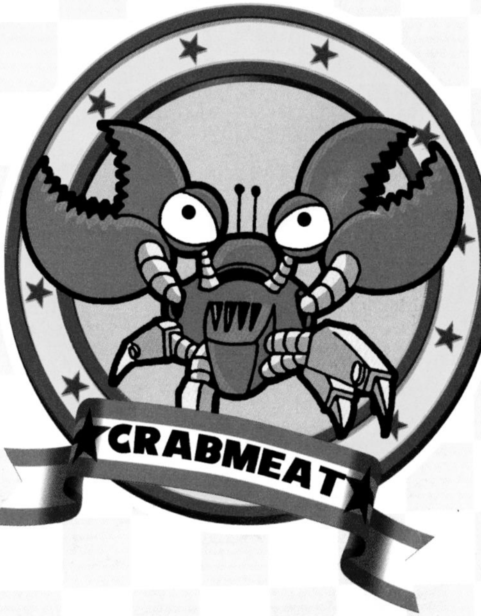
CRABMEAT

Crabmeat was Dr. Robotnik's first loyal lackey. He's small on size – and small on brains – but he works in a pinch.

SWAT BOT

The bulk of Dr. Robotnik's army is made up of the armored, laser-toting SWAT Bots. These guys don't mess around!

SWAT BOTS

MOTOBUG

With a quick little wheel and some scary-sharp arms, Motobug was meant to take down Sonic. He'll have to be faster than that to catch Sonic!

MOTOBUG

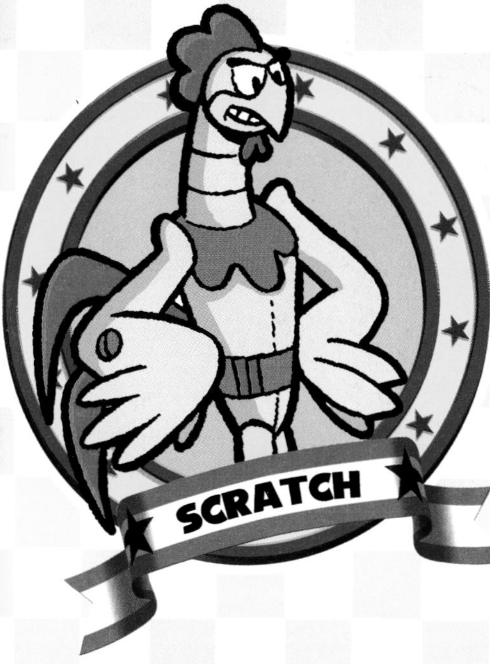
SCRATCH

SCRATCH

This loud, obnoxious chicken-bot is the smartest badnik there is! But don't worry, Sonic – all the badniks are morons.

GROUNDER

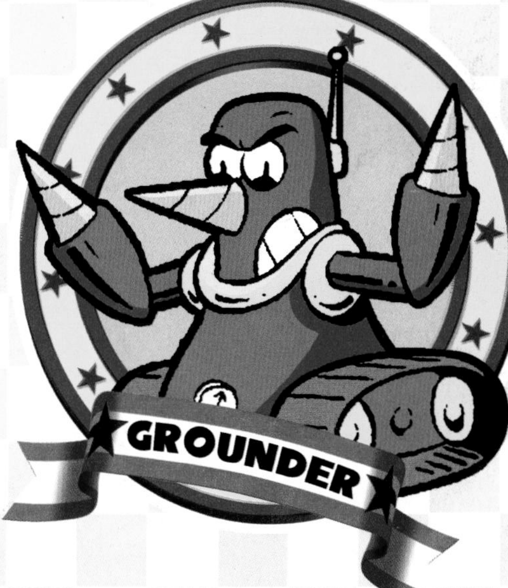
GROUNDER

Scratch's stupid "brother." This super-Burrobot has all sorts of gadgets and weapons hidden up his metal sleeve!

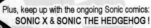